PENGUIN BOOKS

RED ROVER

Deirdre McNamer is the author of the acclaimed novels *Rima in the Weeds, One Sweet Quarrel,* and *My Russian.* She lives in Missoula, Montana.

Praise for *Red Rover* by Deirdre McNamer

**Chosen as a Best Book of the year by *The Washington Post*,
the *Los Angeles Times*, *Artforum*, and the *Rocky Mountain News***

"The account that emerges as McNamer moves from one narrative
vantage and time to another is tension-inducing in the way of the best
psychological mysteries. . . . Ultimately, *Red Rover* is no fashionable,
effect-driven assemblage but a deeply sourced imagining of circumstance
that replicates the complicated process of psychological discovery."
—Sven Birkerts, *The New York Times Book Review*

"An engaging and propulsive read that stirs profound emotions."
—Alice Munro

"Haunting . . . while the narrative hums along, steadily accumulating
tension, you may be struck dumb by McNamer's acute observations of
place. One to savor." —Karen Valby, *Entertainment Weekly*

"Ms. McNamer's novel is vividly observed and original (actually entirely
engrossing) in its conception. She's a wonderfully smart and surprising
sentence-writer, and the burnish on this work has left not a word out of
place. This is 'the novel as storytelling.' And it is of a very high order."
—Richard Ford

"McNamer can sum up a character in a few words. . . . Her writing has
a unique, aboriginal rhythm. . . . It's thrilling to find a writer you can
hang your hat on." —Susan Salter Reynolds, *Los Angeles Times*

"Such is the richness of the writing that one is constantly engaged with
it on the levels of language, imagery, and wit, even as one is responding
to the appeal of the story itself." —Lydia Davis, *Artforum*

"*Red Rover* possesses such range and immediacy that I wondered how
in a novel this length McNamer managed to have them both without
sacrificing the very moving and humane story she tells. Amazingly, not
a stitch is dropped in this remarkable book." —Thomas McGuane

"Moving . . . the fictive counterpart of an intricate navigational maneuver, a magpie's flight through a thicket of Montana cottonwoods . . .
McNamer has no formula, only a deep sense of human character . . .
and a long sense of time." —Alan Cheuse, *San Francisco Chronicle*

"McNamer's frightening but beautifully evoked fourth novel examines the pain, disappointments, and betrayals of wartime. . . . *Red Rover* is reminiscent of *In Our Time*, Hemingway's book of connected stories about World War I. It has the same seriousness, hard, beautiful language and a tireless stare at death and desolation."
— Tricia Snell, *The Oregonian* (Portland)

"*Red Rover* is wonderful for the tenderness and clear-eyed emotional intelligence with which it renders the heartbreak of beautiful young lives wrecked by the great grinding machinery of governments going about their business. And it's equally moving on the quite heroism of the ongoing repair work that must follow. This is a book filled with the most perceptive kind of love for its characters, and sorrow for what they have to endure."
— Jim Shepard

"Haunting. . . Opens with a scene of almost heartbreaking beauty and innocence. . . [It is] part character study, part meditation on aging and destiny, and part mystery. . . . Lyrical, insightful, and woven with vivid characterization and sense of place."
— Mary Ann Gwinn, *The Seattle Times*

"One of the west's finest contemporary novelists. . . McNamer's genius for capturing the unromantic realism of Montana really shines. . . . The book's true kin are quiet classics like Kent Haruf's *Plainsong* and Leif Enger's *Peace Like a River*."
— Bruce Barcott, *High Country News*

"A rare and considerable achievement, stunning actually. . . McNamer is a master weaver of prose."
— Jim Harrison

"The gripping intrigue of McNamer's plot is matched by the flinty beauty of her prose."
— Jenny Shank, *New West Book Review*

"Coincidence, valor, betrayal, fate and some dark fuel that burns beyond acceptance or forgiveness are the generative forces of *Red Rover*. . . . A harshly lovely lonely story played out against Montana's harshly lovely lonely land."
— Joy Williams

"It has been eight years since Deirdre McNamer's evocative novel *My Russian*, about a woman's search for herself. She brings the same clear, rich vision to *Red Rover*, a tapestry of lives on the Montana plains. . . . *Red Rover* was worth the wait."
— Susan Kelly, *USA Today*

RED ROVER

DEIRDRE MCNAMER

PENGUIN BOOKS

For my father, Hugh F. McNamer

PENGUIN BOOKS
Published by the Penguin Group
Penguin Group (USA) Inc., 375 Hudson Street, New York, New York 10014, U.S.A.
Penguin Group (Canada), 90 Eglinton Avenue East, Suite 700, Toronto,
Ontario, Canada M4P 2Y3 (a division of Pearson Penguin Canada Inc.)
Penguin Books Ltd, 80 Strand, London WC2R 0RL, England
Penguin Ireland, 25 St Stephen's Green, Dublin 2, Ireland
(a division of Penguin Books Ltd)
Penguin Group (Australia), 250 Camberwell Road, Camberwell,
Victoria 3124, Australia (a division of Pearson Australia Group Pty Ltd)
Penguin Books India Pvt Ltd, 11 Community Centre,
Panchsheel Park, New Delhi – 110 017, India
Penguin Group (NZ), 67 Apollo Drive, Rosedale, North Shore 0632,
New Zealand (a division of Pearson New Zealand Ltd)
Penguin Books (South Africa) (Pty) Ltd, 24 Sturdee Avenue,
Rosebank, Johannesburg 2196, South Africa

Penguin Books Ltd, Registered Offices:
80 Strand, London WC2R 0RL, England

First published in the United States of America by Viking Penguin,
a member of Penguin Group (USA) Inc. 2007
Published in Penguin Books 2008

1 3 5 7 9 10 8 6 4 2

Copyright © Deirdre McNamer, 2007
All rights reserved

THE LIBRARY OF CONGRESS HAS CATALOGED THE HARDCOVER EDITION AS FOLLOWS:
McNamer, Deirdre.
Red rover : a novel / Deirdre McNamer.
p. cm.
ISBN 978-0-670-06350-5 (hc.)
ISBN 978-0-14-311354-6 (pbk.)
1. Montana—History—Fiction. 2. World War, 1939–1945—Fiction. I. Title.
PS3563.C38838R43 2007
813'.54—dc22   2006036075

Printed in the United States of America
Designed by Spring Hoteling

PART 1

ONE

1927
North of Neva, Montana

THEY WERE GAUCHOS OF THE ARGENTINE, *horsemen to their bones.*
Wanderers, survivors, riders, and lovers, their life the life of cattle and
horses and stars. Broad grasslands, hum of the stars, meat on a spit. The
boleadoras, *ahiss through the air. Long rawhide, three stones, the*
horseman's long snare. Child of God, child of the pampas, child of
himself. Lover of the long ride.

    Straight and steady lover of the long ride. Hard luck and death itself?
The gaucho shrugs. ¡Qué lástima! *Fear cannot touch him. Governments*
fester and connive and cannot touch him, this child of himself. Judges,
merchants, officers, priests, the ruthless leather merchants, they cannot
touch him. Lover of the long ride. His soul before him like the bell mare.

It was an easy dream and they fell into it together. Don Fiero and
Don Sombra. Sir Fierce and Sir Shadow. Neil and Aidan Tierney.
And their faithful mounts, Mancha and Gato. A man in the news
was riding from Buenos Aires to the Washington White House on
horses with those names, and so they renamed their own fresh-
broke sorrels to send luck to the man and his ten thousand miles.
A year and a half out, the newspapers had the rider in Mexico.

Don Fiero, Neil, was nine; Don Sombra, Aidan, thirteen. And if the older boy was beginning to see girls and his friends in place of the gaucho life, he didn't tell that to his brother because there was no point. Riding north on the plains to the Sweet Grass Hills, they never encountered a fence. Hunting knives on their belts. Coiled lariats. Big lunches from their mother in their saddlebags. Shotguns to hunt birds to roast on a spit. Saddles their only beds, beneath the starry vault.

They were a pair. Neil, wiry and gap-toothed and quick. Aidan, darker and solid, well into his growth.

Yes, it was September and, yes, there was school. But his Spanish teacher had so praised Sombra's paper on the Argentine and its dazzling, incorruptible gauchos that the writer's parents had set him loose on a long ride with the other horse lover in the family. They'd done it before, on their own, the hundred-mile circle. See you in a few days, the parents had said. Adios. Keep your powder dry.

And there was another reason to make the ride now. Lindbergh's triumphant tour would carry him, the next day, from the mountains of Glacier Park onto the Montana plains, straight over their heads, before he dipped southward to the mining city, Butte. They would see the plane up close. They might see the man himself, squinting into the blue. He might wave down at them and tip his wings.

All quiet but for the barking of a dog and the grass-rustle of the low wind. All dark but for the light of the depot, the light of a mother up with a sick child. Their horses, picketed in the field behind the Tierney house, were warm and grassy breathed, and they snorted and stamped a little when the stiff saddles went on. A last gear check, a piss in the weeds, and they were mounted and off, the hooves tocking on the hardpan street, the leather squeaking, their breath and the breath of the animals visible, but barely, in the near dark.

And as the sky began to lighten into the lilacs and the pinks, they snapped into a dreamy, valorous state, and the bony prairie, dotted here and there with an oil well, scraped and frank, became something undulating and out of time.

"The stars fell toward the other end of the world," Aidan said. It was one of the dozens of lines he'd marked in *Don Segundo Sombra*, the novel he'd used for his translation project. Sombra, gaucho extraordinaire. This, said the teacher, holding up the book, is *Huckleberry Finn* with horses. With grasslands like Montana's. And with a comrade for the poor orphan who is the embodiment of competence, style, fortitude, and calmness in the face of any fate. The utterly unflappable Don Sombra.

Sombra kicked his horse into a single-foot and reeled off more. "The immense night frightened me as if it were full of my secret."

"The stars," he repeated, "fell toward the other end of the world."

He said it again in Spanish. *"Las estrellas se cayeron hacia el otro lado del mundo."*

The younger boy, Neil, laughed at the oddness of the sounds, and made up his own Spanish on the spot. "Dee *ah* dee dah, *kee* air lee *ho* vo, *pecker* dee *lah* dah!" And laughed so boisterously at his fine, brash ear that his horse, the just-broke three-year-old, did a little crow hop and a fast dance sideways, as if a newspaper sheet had blown up from the ditch in all its rustling horror, which made both horsemen laugh, and they turned onto the grass then, gave the animals their heads, and took off in the new light at a lope.

It was good to leave the road, graveled and straight as it was, because it would, when full light came, interrupt the feel of the pampas. There would be farmers on it in their wagons and the occasional flivvers, and the oil boys too, heading for the fields. Not many, but some. Enough to matter. Enough to break the spell.

All those miles ahead, the three low mountains stood above the grass, full of birds and waiting. The brothers would camp there, roasting their kill on a spit. But first, miles and miles of prairie. Where you squinted against the wind and the sheeting, unmediated light, the gaze stretching long before it met something that stopped it. There was the sense of being seen. Of yourself through a high hawk's eye, one that noticed you but didn't care. Still, it produced a small quiver of self-consciousness. As you moved, two flies across a table, you were watched.

From a distance, the Hills floated above the plains like an idea that was easy to understand. Up close—among them and on them and up them—they would be different. The light there became dappled, variegated. The summer's last leaves, very thin leaves, maroon and apricot, flickered on the chokecherries. There was shelter: hollows and coulees and lees. So the wind became an unsteady thing, stopping and starting, dying and rising. In the suspensions, there was the sound of birds at rest, adjusting, talking. You gained cover. You became unwatched. You moved into and out of the dappling and the pinewater smell of leaves. Sweetgrass. Kinnikinnick, snowberry, Oregon grape, cinquefoil, creeping juniper, lodgepole pine. And if you climbed high enough to survey the scraped plains, you became the hawk.

They would camp at the base of the Tower, the perfect cone. The one that seemed always very still.

To the Tower, they said to themselves. Childe Roland to the dark tower came, thought Neil, who was, like Aidan, a memorizer.

At its base, he, Neil, wanted to separate for hunting advantage and meet in a couple of hours at the camp spot they knew. It was midafternoon and they had hours of light and he wanted very badly to do this, though it was against the single rule from home. Stick together.

He made his case in his fake Spanish, lifting the palms of his hands to the still-summery sky. Aidan had to laugh. He was charmed. What, really, was the harm? The kid, Neil, sat his horse like a burr. He knew what he was doing. They both knew where they were, and where they would meet later, when the sun was three inches above the far-off line that separated the light blue from the tawny. The crease that opened upon the other end of the world.

The boy could handle himself, and he needed this. He needed this knowledge that he could handle himself on his own. And the horse, Mancha, was all right. Quite the self-spooker, quite the dramatist, but surefooted and strong.

"*Sí, sí, hermano,*" Aidan said.

"I will *sí, sí* you at the camp," Neil said, and he was off with a clatter.

He had his shotgun in a scabbard on his saddle. He had his hat pulled low over his eyes. He followed a game trail through the creeping juniper and the kinnikinnick, across an expanse of yellow grass, through more brush. He got to a copse of quaking aspen— animal tracks here—and he had a drink of water and the last of the sandwich his mother had wrapped in waxed paper. He thought about birds. Pheasants and grouse. Where they were hiding. He'd have to picket Mancha and set off on foot, to sneak up on a pheasant. He thought of a low place with cattails, maybe a mile ahead. He remembered it now. He seemed to see the very tree where he'd tie his horse, and he seemed to see many bird wings fluttering in the late-afternoon light. The wizard green of the pheasant's neck.

He knew exactly where he was going. He urged Mancha into a trot, then a lope. He ducked when the trail took them through a thicket of chokecherries and was glad he wore his chaps. Mancha seemed to know where they were headed. He stepped up the pace. Neil gathered himself low on the big red back.

He heard a gunshot, somewhere off to his right. He stood a little and turned in his stirrups to see.

And then he fell out of time.

And when he returned, he was on his back and felt that he had perhaps been on his back for many hours, many days. His hand covered an eye and his head felt axed in two. A fly crawled along the top of his hand, and his hand didn't seem to listen to the signal he was sending it to move. Finally, the fingers curled. Finally, he could lift them off his face. He felt hated by some large force, some borderless fist that had knocked him to the earth to be broken. He brought his fingers back to his head and felt the sticky blood and the shocking lump. His face felt bathed in blood.

There was a red horse standing in willowlight. Its head was lowered, but it didn't eat. It seemed simply to think. One stirrup had flung itself over the saddle. Reins fell to the ground. *Horse. Come here horse. Tell me your name if you have a name.*

The red horse walked toward him out of the green. It had a long scratch on its wither. It walked with a slight limp. It huffed, disgusted at something that had happened, something the boy had missed.

Horse, he said. Come here. And he thought about the process of getting to his feet. He sat up. His head lolled to the side and he puked a little. Horse. Come here. To me. He couldn't recall his name. He knew that he had a name, but he couldn't, at the moment, know what it might be.

He stood still until he felt his weight become evenly distributed between his wobbly legs, and he gathered the reins of the red horse and led him under the big branch that must have knocked him off. What the horse had experienced, he couldn't know. Had the animal's head been pulled around so fast and hard that he'd fallen? Who could tell? What was the horse's name? What was the name of the person trying to retrieve the horse's name? It made him want to cry, the effort of it and the fact of the big hand that had thrown him onto the ground, so unfairly, so without warning.

He led the horse and watched its careful steps, then hauled himself into the saddle. He would go home. He looked at the sun and started to remember something about it, where it appeared and disappeared. He looked at the conical mountain, got his bearings, and turned in the opposite direction. *This way is home and I will now go home.* And so he rode, his horse's long shadow stretching to the east and the meadowlarks curling and piercing the air. As he left the mountain behind, a stiff little wind picked up. An owl, somewhere, began to hoot him onto the huge landmarkless plain.

If he had possessed his faculties entire he would have remembered that he had ridden away from town with his older brother, Aidan. And he might have remembered, too, that Aidan had, on their long rides, told him not to worry if he became unsure about where exactly they were. *The horse will know the way back.* Neil said it out loud, trying to impose an interior calm, and brushed his fingertips across his face and tasted them. Blood, dirt, the tears he couldn't seem to stop. His mother was waiting for him in a bright kitchen, pouring their little brother, Mike, a glass of milk.

The sun drifted off the far edge of the prairie, leaving a red line, then a deep blue one. Stars began to sharpen themselves, a few and then more, and a moon came up that looked like a dead eye. Clouds floated across it from time to time.

Neil moved over the silver-tipped prairie utterly alone with his softly breathing horse. There were no lights to aim for, but there was the feel beneath him of an animal that had an idea about where it was going. There was the feel behind him of the mountain. There was also the growing sense of himself in some afterlife. He wondered if he had perhaps died.

The tumbleweeds began to look skeletal and phosphorescent. Coyotes yipped and chattered behind him and were answered by something low and harrowing a long, long way away. A wolf.

They traveled carefully, he and the horse whose name he didn't know.

Something large flew by him, by his face. He saw nothing, but he heard it. He felt its slipstream, felt its tug. He could have reached out and touched it with his hand. The horse felt it too. It skittered sideways, and Neil had to grab the horn to stay on; and when he did, all the ribs on his left side cried out. He kicked the horse forward and yelled at it—go!—because they were traveling too slowly and his mother wasn't going to wait for him in the kitchen forever. They loped now in the dark. He had tied the reins together and let them flop on the horse's neck and held with both hands to the horn. The sage grass, the tumbleweeds, had taken on an evil light. Bones of the dead trying to lure him to a buffalo jump, where he and the horse would sail into the air like the hundreds of buffalo roaring down to their deaths.

He wouldn't let that happen. He would keep his head. He would stop running and start to wait, as Aidan would have waited, for daybreak.

There it was, his brother's name. He remembered it before he could remember his own.

Clouds moved off the moon and he noticed a curving line on the grass, which turned out to be a dry creek bed. A shallow indentation. The suggestion of a cut bank. He could huddle against it and think about what to do next. There was nothing he could build a fire with, but there was his saddle for a bed, his saddle blankets for cover. He made his bed. He had his rope, but there was nothing to tie it to, so he worked off one of the saddle cinches and fashioned crude hobbles for his horse, who stood quiet while he knotted them, then crow hopped gently to a better patch of grass and began to eat. The boy remembered water and gave the horse half of what was in his canteen, pouring it into the tin pie plate he'd brought along for a reason he couldn't remember now.

The idea of his brother came to him. Aidan. A chance taker, an adventurer, but also reassuring, solid, wry. Keep your head, Aidan said in his new, deepening voice. Hang on. Keep your head.

So Neil did. He lay down and closed his eyes. He could feel the ground move gently beneath him, a low, syncopated sway beneath the tiny clatter of the stars. He listened to his calmly breathing, calmly chewing horse.

Mancha. There it was, the name.

Mancha! he called. His voice, because he was only nine, sounded very high and thin. The tearing sound of grass stopped for a few moments, then started again. It occurred to him, once more, that he might be dead, that this was the aftermath. And for that reason, he didn't fire back when the wind switched direction and brought him the sound of gunshots, up near the Hills. His gaze fell on his own gun, but he did nothing, because what he heard seemed to come from someplace that was not, in this new life, a possibility for him.

Sometimes, on their trips, they were Meriwether Lewis and his horsemen, riding this very prairie, just twenty, thirty miles to the west. They liked the ominous and fateful nature of the side trip Lewis took with his three best men on the way home, a loop straight into the heart of Blackfeet country. They passed twelve unbroken miles of buffalo, a river of them, the wolves haunting the borders of the animals, lolling and howling. They camped with some nervous Blackfeet teenagers they'd met, and then bad things happened. One of the boys tried to take guns and horses in the night, and there was a melee and the white men shot the boy dead. Another too. And then the explorers ran from the specter of avengers, of howling and brilliant warriors bearing down on them. But not before Lewis put a peace-and-friendship medal with George Washington's profile around the neck of the first teenager who had been shot and left him there for the crows or his comrades. Neil and Aidan didn't like that part of the story much. There was bluster and unease in it, a preening they didn't care for.

The Lewis party ran all day and night across the prairie, this prairie, to arrive stupefied and sore and panting at the Missouri at the very moment that their comrades fired a gun to announce that they were there in their boats. Aidan and Neil liked that, the idea of high adventure culminating in such a neat and fateful way.

Neil sometimes got the moonlit ride away from the young dead Indians conflated with a story he'd heard from an old cowboy in town, a rummy who'd wrecked his leg in a horseback accident years earlier and gimped around the horse sales, ready to tell stories to the kids. He'd been riding one night, drunk, yelping and howling, heading in a direction he thought was the ranch where he worked. Alone and on fire with the booze and riding across the world, breakneck, barely able to stay in the saddle. His horse, out of sheer disgust with him, he said, threw him off and thrummed away into the night. When he woke in the pink and frosty dawn, his entire body an ache, he found himself . . .

At this point, for the benefit of his young listeners, who couldn't hear it enough, he slowed the story way down.

The cowboy felt his moving fingers scout the terrain, any question of opening his eyes still ludicrous. His fingertips felt his face, his head, and moved down his neck. There. There. Everything in its place, it seemed. He felt, then, a twig, a stick, on his chest. An arrangement of sticks. Sticks with nodules. With knuckles. He flattened his hand and lowered it very slowly onto the sticks. He lifted his unbroken neck, sweat bursting from every pore, and opened his eyes upon his hand atop a hand of bones. He lay in a shallow, open grave. His own ear, the cowboy's whirled and gristled ear, rested a scant inch from the hole in the skull that had once held the ear of his new friend.

Details of that story came to the boy now. He had the terrible sense that if he moved his hand in any direction, he would feel bones. Neck bones hung with a government medal. He heard what might have been another shot, fired from a distance impossible to calculate. They shot me, he heard someone say. I lie here shot.

Hang on, Neil.

Neil! The name came to him in a burst of insight. And now he knew he might be able to lie down and sleep, because he finally knew the name of the person who was going to go unconscious.

He woke to two short whistles and a long swooping one. His horse's ears flew forward. And out of the dawn there grew a horse and a rider, small and then not small, and a call.

Aidan had his hat pulled low over his eyes. He rode his horse at a single-foot, that go-forever step between walk and trot, and he posted easily. He looked as if he could have ridden a day like that, or two.

He dismounted in no hurry and pushed back his hat. He looked pale, exhilarated, and exhausted. He blinked rapidly and touched Neil lightly on the shoulder.

"Hey, Neil," he said. "How're you doing out here?"

Neil drank in his brother's face. "Fine," he said, hating the crack of grief in his voice. Aidan touched his fingertips to the head bump and Neil's ribs, both sides. He looked as if he was listening. Neil sneezed hard, and said, yes, it made his ribs hurt but not a lot. Aidan grinned and rumpled the boy's dirty hair. He examined Mancha's hobbles approvingly and removed them and reattached them to the saddle.

They'd head for Portugal, he told his brother. It was a little rail stop, and not far. Their mother's brother, a doctor, had a little egg-colored hospital there, and he could check Neil over and they could stay the night to break up the trip back home.

"What about Lindbergh?" Neil said, everything coming back to him now.

"We'll see him," Aidan said. "He'll pass over. And you know what? You've been riding this nag long enough. Sorry, Mancha. Your rider is done for a while." The horse whickered contentedly, as if it were going along with a bad joke. "You lost your hat when you got knocked off by that big branch," Aidan said. "I found it just when it was getting really dark. You were nowhere. I fired some shots."

He touched the boy's forehead, where the big egg was. Tears started, but the boy stopped them by thinking about Lindbergh. Lindbergh all by himself in the night over the endless water. Feeling lucky.

Aidan saddled Neil's horse and mounted his own, offering an arm to his brother to pull him up. Neil put his arms around his brother's hard waist. They moved off, Aidan leading Mancha. Neil rested the side of his head against his brother's warm back. He could feel the muscles moving neatly. They traveled quietly for a few hours, saying nothing. Once, Aidan sighed deeply. Sometimes Neil slept a little. Waking, he breathed in the smell of the strong back, then dozed again.

Finally, there was a scrabble of a town ahead. It glinted in the morning light. When they moved into it, down the dirt street, people milled around them excitedly, as if they'd been eager for the boys' return. But they were watching the sky. Dogs and children ducked among the taller watching ones. A murmur grew. The sky returned a high, thrilling drone. And out of the west, lit by the climbing sun, came a bright little monoplane. Neil couldn't sit still. Hands on Aidan's shoulder, he pulled himself to his feet atop the steady horse. He watched the growing plane, the high metal bird in the morning light, hands on his brother's hat.

He cheered with the rest, with Aidan, and waved an arm to make Lindy tip his wings. On the sidewalk, a sour-faced woman in a nurse's cap called to him and shook her finger at him. The horse was stepping in place, nervous now, so Neil sat back down. The little plane inclined a wing and the crowd cheered. Neil yipped like a coyote, and then he turned to the woman in the nurse's hat and shouted a string of fake and bawdy Spanish at her, laughing as he yelled, laughing so hard he could scarcely make the words.

TWO

1944–45
Saipan

TWO NIGHTS BEFORE HIS FIRST TIME out, Neil Tierney had the dream that had scared him so badly when he'd had it as a child, a recurring one in which a series of faces passed slowly down a mirror, silent as snow, none of them anyone he knew or could remember. Just that, but there was terror in it. He woke to an air raid, everyone grabbing clothes and running for the door, then falling facedown as a plane roared over, guns rattling.

Some broke for the ditches and shelters. Neil rolled himself under the metal table where they played poker at night. Another whine, becoming a deadly roar, and the rain of bullets again, and then a few seconds later a deep explosion up on the plateau where the big bombers were. That was a fuel tank going. A long pause, and then another, different, boom. That was probably the Zeke.

He closed his eyes and watched himself fall asleep for a minute or two, his good trick.

When it was quiet, a column of smoke climbed a thousand or more feet from a B-29 burning on its hardstand. The others, a hundred of them up there, stood silhouetted in the moonlight. They were beautiful huge things with their long tapered wings and sleek bodies, silver thoroughbreds that made other bombers seem like burros.

They waited up there in their long rows like patient animals as the men down on the flat milled around in skivvies and bare feet, smoking, swearing, shaking their heads, watching the long white pincers of the searchlights. A wire of siren reached them from somewhere up on the far bluff, where the colored gunners lived.

Neil's bombardier, a thin, dark-haired kid they called Dante for his poetic ways, ran up to tell him about the Zeke that the gunners on the bluff had shot down. There were parts of the pilot all over the runway, he said, white-faced. They looked like seared roasts. They were, those parts, the first dead person he'd ever seen.

All the B-29 crews had arrived on the island during the previous couple of weeks, ready to commence long-distance air war against the empire. Already, Neil had learned to stay away from Dante as much as he could, because the man thought too hard about everything and seemed compelled to register his reactions to each and all. He was the one who'd told the rest of the crew every detail he knew about the suicides of the island's Japanese civilians, thousands of them leaping from Marpi Point after the invasion. And he was the one who knew about the marine who'd been swimming in the lagoon and come face-to-face with a dead woman in a polka-dot blouse, her lampblack hair snaking behind.

The rest of them had to shut him up on a regular basis, and then he'd grab his notebook and start writing, or fall silent with his feelings all over his face. He made you nervous because he seemed so alert that he lit up like an electric bulb, a beacon for trouble to find.

Neil told him he didn't want to hear the details of the dead Jap. He said he was glad the bastard got it, sounding more curt than he'd intended. Dante went inside to his cot, where he sat tailor style, a shock of black hair falling over his beaky nose, and scribbled in his notebook. Then he left the Quonset, ambling into the full-moon night, while Neil pretended to write a letter and watched him go.

The next day, retrieving cigarettes from his trunk, Neil found the Quonset empty. A corner of Dante's notebook edged from his pillow. Surprising himself, he pulled it out and read the last entry.

> *After the racket and roar, waterfalling moonlight upon Milton's "smoke and stir of this dim spot which men call Earth."*
> *The silent stars go by.*
> *"When it came night, the white waves paced to and fro in the moonlight, and the wind brought the sound of the great sea's voice to the men on shore, and they felt that they could then be interpreters." (Thank you, Wide-Winged Crane.)*
> *But . . . Interpreters? How, please, do I interpret this?*

The question gave Neil a small, cold feeling, and he quickly replaced the notebook.

The next morning they were rousted early to dress, eat, and board the trucks that took them to the line. Time to fly. Neil carried in a slim wallet in his jacket a photo of his older brother. It was taken about the time that Aidan requested hazardous duty with the FBI, and got sent undercover to Argentina. Red Rover, Red Rover, send Aidan right over, Neil sometimes thought as he studied the photograph. Aidan wore an expression that was both somber and wry, and that Neil recognized as well as he did his own face. There was a certain gravitas in it—reinforced by Aidan's intelligent eyes, his unperturbable good looks—but also something buoyantly alive, connected and curious. An intense alertness. Like Dante's, Neil sometimes thought, but without the wavery emotional edge.

Aidan had signed the photo in his distinct, up-and-down hand. *Ten-tenths to you, hermano.*

One by one, the engines roared thunderously to life. Ten-tenths, Neil thought, as he taxied Z Square 7 into the lineup. He pulled into position for takeoff, stopped and pushed hard on the brake pedals. The starter signaled them to increase the rpms. Lewis, his copilot, set the wing flaps. Bond, the engineer, increased the fuel-to-air mix ratio to auto-rich and placed the engine's cowl flaps at trail. Neil and Lewis both pushed the throttles forward slowly, and as the rpms and manifold pressures reached military power, the plane began to vibrate and shake. Neil watched the starter and the tower. Lewis monitored the instruments. The starter gave the forward wave and the tower flashed the green light. He released the brakes and began the heavy roll. Ninety-nine feet of plane, eleven men, seventy tons. Fuel enough for the trip, but just, and the bombload adding ten tons to the plane's theoretical capacity.

Lewis called out air speeds. Neil gently fed in enough left rudder to compensate for the torque in that direction. There was something in it of the headstrong racehorse wanting to turn a circle before moving into the gate, and you had to pull her to the right to line her out, to really run.

Now they were pulling takeoff power, and the plane thirty seconds ahead of them was staggering into the air. The tower flashed by. Lewis called out numbers. 135. *Go!* Neil whispered, full throttle, and *Go!* he whispered again as Lewis called 145 and the edge of the island charged toward them. He eased back on the stick, but not before they knocked out a couple of lights at the end of the concrete.

The last figure on land was the priest in the flapping cassock who made a big cross in the air as each plane roared and wobbled into the sky.

Gear up, flaps up, five-hundred-feet-per-minute rate of climb and they had begun the fifteen-hundred-mile trip to Tokyo.

The water became a metal, white-flecked floor far below. Talc on steel. They pressurized the cabin to climb into the icy skies, and then the crew played cards and ate canned turkey sandwiches in shirtsleeves in their luxury liner. The formation was loose. They could see Z Square 8 off in the distance, and the glints of several others below. Neil checked the bearings, and Lewis took over while he unwrapped his sandwich. He chewed slowly, studying the sky through the latticed cockpit. He could see in every direction. And be so seen. They were so large and available to the enemy. So silver and long and heavy, with their little heads up in the glass, the brains of the thing.

He closed his eyes, trying to rest them before whatever awaited them. He adamantly did not consider in detail what might lie ahead. They churned on, five miles above the water now.

He ate, he flew, he catnapped. Seven hours passed. When he opened his eyes, there ahead on the horizon was the snow-topped cone of Mount Fuji.

He blinked. It was perfectly symmetrical, perfectly beautiful with its cape of white. The clouds around its base unlinked it from the earth and it floated like some vision of ultimate order and light. Neil felt a twang of dissonance. How could something that looked like that—so ancient and serene—be the initial point of a bombing run? The mountain was out of time and unto its blue and snowy self. They were boys playing war in her sky.

Lewis swore at it. There it was, the signal to go in together, and they were straggling way behind the formation, not ready at all. They all scrambled into their flak vests, and Neil pulled takeoff power to try to catch the big birds that were moving in a slow dream, a glide, around the west side of Fuji. He cut to the right of the mountain to catch them. And now there were bursts of flak— black flowers blooming in the air—as they moved in with the other planes, in formation now and halfway from Fuji to the target.

Through a bank of thick clouds they flew, so tightly that Neil could feel the slipstream from his wing plane, that little tug. And then—as if the enemy had simply been waiting for them to arrange themselves as targets—the clouds evaporated and screaming Zekes flew out of the sun through the long silver ships, guns blazing. Sixty, seventy of them, all over the sky, flying at every angle but right side up. One of them barreled past in a vertical bank, two wing lengths away.

Everyone was on the interphone at once, shouting positions and hits and incoming. Lewis pushed the toggle switch to drop the bombs. When the bombs didn't drop, Dante hit the salvo. Nothing.

The tail gunner's squeaky yell came over the phone then, sounding panicky. "Tail's out! Tail's out!" and then the steady clank of the landing gear going down and the sound of hard rocks thrown at them, the wild clatter of them.

Neil yelled at Lewis to flip the up switch. Ahead of them, the lead ship with two colonels aboard streamed smoke from both engines on its right side. Fighters fell upon it and it hesitated, then dropped like a toy from a sleepy child's hand.

A Betty flew straight at them. The gunner hit him and the plane exploded in front of their left wing. Its engine flew under the wing. The fuselage with its goggled pilot flew over, so close they could have touched the boy's face.

And it was over.

The fighters went away, as suddenly as they'd come, and Z Square 7 headed out to sea, the cone of Fuji on the horizon behind it, into the quick, amazing silence. The huge sun was beginning to drift down. They flew alone as the sky dimmed. They took stock. Tail turret out, trim tab cables gone, C-1 partially out, gear nacelle doors down. They managed to release the bombs, dropped them in the drink, and tried to take up a course for home.

The plane was full of holes. Radar was picking up nothing. One engine's rpms were stuck at a screaming 2300. The jammed bomb doors produced drag. But they were out over the long water. Seaver, the navigator, reported that the best-guess ETA and the end of the fuel were the same. Too close to call.

They flew on an assumed course. They talked about how they'd ditch. They flew.

After a few hours, the radio operator got a faint signal that told him they were on course for Saipan. It disappeared. An hour later, he got another.

Lining up star shots with his sextant, Seaver looked like a mythical sailor, though his face was a baby's. A baby-faced nineteen-year-old, but he had a crisp, assured way of reporting the data. The shots didn't line up. Then they did.

Saipan began to come in very faintly on command radio. The fuel gauges hovered near empty. Neil set 2130, a half hour away, as the time to prepare to ditch.

They flew in the noisy darkness, all attention on the fuel and the clock and the frantic calculations.

Time and fuel. A huge damaged plane, alone and star dazzled, its half-wrecked instruments aglow. The shrieking, stuck engine. The thump of blood in the ears.

At 2130 he had the crew throw all the loose equipment into the bomb bay and reminded himself of the rules: Approach upwind across the waves if the winds are strong, along the top of the swell if they aren't. Don't glide in. Stall in, to reduce the impact. He'd need to control the descent, if it happened, and he needed the last fuel for that, or they would just fall out of the sky, to be broken on the water.

The Saipan signal got louder.

Seaver estimated on the basis of his star fixes that they'd reach land in forty minutes.

Bond, the engineer, estimated that they'd run out of fuel in twenty minutes.

Neil thought about the gauges, which were not absolutely reliable at low readings. He thought about ditching and how he'd once helped search for a ditched plane, how the Pacific grew immeasurably large when you were looking for something on its surface. It flashed its millions of mirrors and stretched itself out with a glittery malevolence.

Keep your head. Adrenaline skittered down the surface of his arms. He felt for the wallet inside his flak vest; touched it to feel his brother Aidan's face.

You didn't just set her down the best you could and wait for a friendly sub to come bubbling up. You might crack up on impact, and sink, and die. Or be out there in rafts, flashing pathetic signal mirrors, their light lost among the ocean's own light. You might set off flares and try to get a weak balloon to lift two hundred feet of transmitter antenna into the air. You might have lost the handle of your generator in the crash. You might be listening to the searchers, droning through the blue, peering down at you with blind eyes.

A twenty-minute gap. More fuel or fewer miles and the gap would shut. But how would they know it was happening?

Split the difference. The distress signal would go out in ten minutes, at 2200. They'd get as close to the island as they could before they went down.

And then, at 2150, the miracle of lights. A prickle of ground lights and poking up through them the skinny fingers of the searchlights.

There she is! they all shouted, and Dante pressed forward in his bombardier's bubble, as if he were pulling the big ship himself.

Down, down, down. Neil pushed the right rudder and dropped the left wing, so they side-slipped down the long sky, fast, to the tiny island below. They roared over the field and called the tower. The operator told them to land on the emergency runway. Neil threw down the gear and felt a lurch run through him as the board showed only the right wheel green-lighted and locked. The left wheel and nose showed red lights. That meant they were either not down or not locked. But the wiring was half shot up, so who knew if the lights were right?

He shouted through the interphone at the gunners, and they said the left wheel seemed to be in place. He yelled at them all to prepare for a crash landing and he took one more circle of the field, the huge plane light and wieldy without gas or bombs, and he landed it on the right wheel. They ran like that, a one-legged skate, and he slowly tipped down on the left. Which held. As they lost speed, the nose gradually descended.

"Come on, baby," Dante murmured. He was sitting now behind the pilots with the radio operator. The wheel hit and collapsed, pulling the nose down to the ground. Dante shrieked as the gun turret starting pushing up through the floor where he sat. He scrambled toward the nose, but the cone started to collapse so he scrambled back, shoving himself into a niche behind Lewis with the radio man. The plane had stopped. The tail was high in the air, the nose crushed.

"Out!" Neil shouted. "Out, out, out." And they scrambled. They watched the tail gunner perch for a moment before the thirty-foot jump, and roll when he hit. Two of them lifted him up and hopped him away from the plane, and it was done.

The next night the whole crew sat on damp sandbags watching *Laura,* the new movie, on the outdoor screen. They smoked, and the smoke mingled with light island rain, a mist, that softened everything, including the young stripped faces of the men as they let the movie take them away from their patch of coral with its wild bright birds deep in the leaves, its encircling lagoon, and all its fresh ghosts.

And so you go back to your cot after a movie with carpets and martinis and Gene Tierney; you go back under a huge moon, walking the patch of coral; and outside the Quonset is a big Thor washing machine and a clothesline with socks and shorts and shirts floating in the moonlight, a clothesline like your mom's, and near it the scratchings of a little garden put in by Dante, who tends it daily, and there is his half-finished attempt, also, to make a chair out of a packing crate.

That was the first part of the air war, when they flew in at five miles of altitude, aimed for a military target, and hoped they didn't encounter the huge terrifying winds up there that could skate a ninety-nine-foot plane sideways like a skipped stone. Hoped, too, that the fighters that came after them like harpies were at the limit of their altitude, that they wouldn't find a way to come at them from above.

That was the first phase, and not so successful in military terms. There were bugs in the big sleek planes, a lot of missed targets, trouble with formations. No one had ever done this before: made three-thousand-mile day trips to run through hell for a half hour or an hour, and if you were very lucky, crawl into your own cot that night, an ocean away from the trouble. Away from the Black Corridor, as Dante called it.

By Christmas, one plane out of four was gone—shot down, mechanical trouble, ditched. Gone. The number men had the odds: six or seven missions and you could expect not to make the next. And the allowable maximum per man was thirty-five.

As the losses mounted, the men felt their individual visions of a future apart from war grow vague and naive, all their attention now on the next mission and how they might endure the days and hours before it. Dante stopped tending his little garden. He wrote less and less. He played as much baseball as he could, standing out there in the sun for three and four hours at a stretch to bat, run, and throw until he could feel himself to be exhausted.

They stopped building chairs out of crates. They stopped reading books, most of them, preferring magazines, which don't await your return. Some of them wrote letters to everyone they could think of, and some wrote none at all.

And then the new general came in and lowered their bombing altitude by a mile, and it felt as if the last margin of safety had been taken from them on the bet that they would hit targets more accurately, though even more of them wouldn't live to tell about it.

Two weeks later he ordered everyone way down, to five thousand feet, and the B-29s were going in without gunners to firebomb the country to cinders. Now it was napalm. Rivers of fire. A program of annihilation, soldiers and civilians alike. The roar of burning paper houses, sending updrafts so powerful they shot the bombers hundreds of feet straight up. A war that did not bear thinking about.

Dante abandoned his journal and began to write a letter he never tried to finish. For his mother, he said. But he never signed off or mailed it.

"I'm not afraid now," he told Seaver one night in the officers' club. "It's just that it's so hellishly stupid. All of it. Wouldn't you say?"

A week or so later, the skin on Neil's face erupted in an infection, a nasty one, probably from the oxygen mask. He was hospitalized and his crew was broken up.

Dante went to Z Square 19 and flew three missions. On one, the copilot was shot and bled to death halfway back to Saipan.

Neil's old engineer, Bond, came to his hospital room one day to give him the next news. He stood at the foot of the iron bed, and the island light through the moving window shades made his face seem to fold and unfold.

Bond's new plane and crew were flying wing with Dante's, so close he could see the poet's young hawky face in the bubble. Suddenly the right wing of Dante's plane was on fire, the engines belching smoke, and it began to drop. Bond's plane tried to stay with them, shielding. But the other fell faster.

Dante looked at him, he said. Straight at him. And he raised his hand in a wave and held it there. An almost jaunty wave, Bond said. And then Dante was down and gone.

THREE

1946
To Missoula, Montana

THE AUTOMOBILE, A HUMPED STUDEBAKER, CRAWLED out of Neva onto the highway, going south. It was morning, bright winter, and the plains stretched frozen and shining around them. The moving air, the ever-moving air, pushed dry snow across the concrete so that the road seemed to smoke.

The travelers appeared, each of them, as if they had been hit in the face by a stranger. They were four: a middle-aged couple and their grown sons.

It was two days before Christmas. There was still in the car something from a holiday party the night before: a length of curly ribbon that Neil Tierney had tied to the gearshift. A pretty girl had put it around her neck so he would want to take it off, and there it hung, silver and insouciant, a meadowlark on the moon. It caught Neil's eye now and he stared at it, amazed at the way it had slipped the border of the old life.

He closed his eyes against the ribbon. He grabbed his knees with his hands. He and his younger brother, Mike, in their big military overcoats, were crammed into the backseat. Their father piloted the car. He wore large leather mittens, a woolen overcoat, a

Scotch-plaid driving cap with ear flaps. His face had a kind of stiff, unblinking awareness, something alive behind the stone. Next to him, their mother sat with her arms around herself, rocking almost imperceptibly.

They were virtually alone on the road. It was well below zero. The car cut a clean line across the plains, then turned west toward the mountains, the ancient faces. And as the faces grew, the sky thickened and pulled in close. Snow began to fall. A big gust shook the falling snow and the snow on the ground like flour in a paper bag, and they were blindered for a few moments.

The ground tipped up and arranged itself in layers. The Studebaker chugged upward, pushing through the places where the wind had created shallow drifts across the pavement. No traffic at all now. The sky fell below the tops of the pines and stayed there. The wind rattled the car. They had been traveling for five hours, stopping once only, for gas.

Neil and Mike sat unmoving in the backseat in their big coats. Mike caught Neil's eye and cut to their father, the driver, and to the thickening white outside the windows. Neil shrugged curtly. Their father wanted to drive. Let the man drive.

Rebuffed, Mike hated for a moment the pilot next to him, the curt hero. He hated, too, what waited for them all at the other end of this interminable journey. The undiluted travesty of it. I will never leave home now, he thought. It will become an impossible thing.

His feet were frigid from his damp shoes inside galoshes, damp because he'd left them outside the door when he returned from the Christmas party, so he wouldn't wake the baby and the wife that he hadn't taken to the party because she was screaming at him.

That curt shrug from Neil, and here came the high, familiar whistling in Mike's ears. The eyes of everyone in the family were always somewhere else, the voice of pride always attached to someone else. He, the youngest, was the burr, the irritation always, no matter that he had his own respectable service record and was the planted one now. The child, the ring, the job, the wife.

He tried to think of something to say. In ordinary circumstances he had a canny impetuosity, a litheness, physical quickness certainly—track star and jitterbug king that he was—but also the ability to see swiftly what a complicated situation might contain at its core. What its real nature might be. And fearlessness about saying what it was, even a degree of perversity and impatience in the saying. He could trick the truth out of its corner sometimes, simply by naming it. He badly wanted that quality available to him now.

What came to him to say was a surprise to him. *While we were at the party.* While most of Neva, our little town, was at the party and we danced and sang and toasted and flirted, a disaster had happened and we didn't know it. While a tipsy neighbor pranced about with a sprig of mistletoe brandished like a sword. While someone else lifted a glass to the Tierney brothers—Neil the pilot, Mike the dancer, Aidan the agent, the spy—all of them home in one piece, these sons of a well-liked family, a family you could count on during the worst of things and the best.

But only briefly did the glasses go up, because there were those in the room who hadn't been so lucky. There were the O'Briens, whose son survived twenty-one bombing runs over Germany, only to die later in the crash of the commercial airliner he was piloting. There was a specter named Buck Blankenship, high school valedictorian, who had spent eleven months of the war crouched in a cage. Everyone, spared and unspared, felt the danger of indulging a sense of reprieve. That's when you got zapped. That was the noiseless count before the buzz bomb's exploding light.

Small groups left on a regular basis to stand outside in the icy night and pass a flask. It was uncustomarily still—not even much of a breeze—so you heard the thin wail of the train when it was miles and miles away, and something in the upward sound of it made you notice how the stars had arranged themselves perpendicularly, in vaults, as they sometimes do.

A very small town, out there on the night plain, is its own campfire. And the conversations at winter gatherings are campfires too, each group warming its hands on a single story. The time Blankenship sank the last-second basket that won the tournament. The day a gale blew the littlest Williamson girl down the hill. The summer Aidan Tierney—gallant, civil Aidan, all of seventeen years old—calmly punched out a two-hundred-pound truck driver. Summer of '31, up in the oil fields. Both of them hauling gravel. The big guy a Bohunk bully who slowed way down on the narrow washboard road and kicked up dust and rocks at Aidan for twenty miles.

" 'Say, you,' " says the man who saw it happen. " 'Could I have a word with you?' " The others in the circle shake their heads.

"Boom," says another, "and Aidan's knocked him to the ground." He passes his gaze around the circle and they take the cue. Three men in one voice: " 'I'd ask you not to do that again.'

" 'I'd *ask* you!' " says the man who saw it. They're laughing now, the way they did the first time, but harder. Because the years have been fierce and they need the story more.

Aidan Tierney was not at the party, because he lived over on the western side of the state where the mountains and the trees were, lived in Missoula, the university town, and practiced law there and tried to recover from whatever illness he had caught, whatever had caught him, down there in Argentina on his secret work. He was tired. He'd lost a lot of weight. Thin Man, he called himself.

He had telephoned his brother Mike a few weeks ago to congratulate him on the birth of his child, his son. A special thing, a phone call instead of a letter, because this oldest son, over in the mountains, had a certain flare, a sense of the right thing to do when it counted. He had called to offer his congratulations, but what he was really doing, and they both knew it, was consoling Mike for the end of his fast-footed days. Yes, it had to be done. Yes, the girl, his high school girlfriend, had wanted the pregnancy so a marriage would happen. And it would all work out, most likely, and there was nothing like a tragedy involved. But he knew, Aidan did, that there was grief in it, in all of it, for Mike. A sense of stoppage, of heaviness, for this one who was so fleet. Who was also the loose cannon, the troublemaker, the jitterbugger, the flirt. That one is out of here fast, the people in Neva had said when he was a teenager. He is too impatient. He will want the cities, the lights, the electric life. He was born to it.

So the message from Aidan, over in the mountains, was this: I know how you feel, but you are not stopped. This is a development, a turn. Have faith, young Mike, he'd said. In those very words.

And don't you have to have your own faith if you're to urge it on another?

He was generous and grave, Aidan was, and equipped with such frank curiosity about himself and how his life might unfold that he heartened those who knew him, made their own lives seem capable of extravagant fanning trajectories. He helped his parents and their friends remember their curious selves in the first decade of the century, flinging themselves west to begin their new lives, guessing never in their wildest dreams how knocked down they'd be, most of them, when the drought years came around and that big table of land turned to dust and grasshoppers, and the adventurers themselves turned, chastened, into citizens.

He was the firstborn. The dear first boy. Born just before the drought years, when life felt lucky. Born the spring of what would turn out to be the first dry year, to be precise. But trouble isn't trouble until it won't leave. Life that year still felt lucky, and so this dark-eyed, handsome, helpful, serious, hoping boy was the emblem always of the parents' highest imaginings. How could he not be?

The brothers in the backseat strained forward now, as if to pull the car. They were intent and pale, lanky, thick haired. Neil put a hand on his mother's minutely rocking shoulder. He studied his hand and thought about how he had sometimes noticed it during a bombing mission and had wondered, trying not to, whether it would soon be forever still. And here he was, odds beaten, the one alive.

The car pulled slowly up the highway into swirling snow beneath pointed black pines. The side of the road began to drop off steeply, and before long it seemed they crept along a sidewalk, a runway, that hugged the mountain on one side and ended in air on the other. A huge gust and the mountain vanished. Now they were utterly lost in snow so directionless and whimsical and blinding that they could have been traveling sideways through it, upside down. They could have been lifted off the earth.

Neil raked his eyes unthinkingly across the seatback, searching for the tipped horizon, the altimeter.

The father nervously tapped the brakes—there had been smears of ice on the concrete—and the car seemed to stop, though the snow tornadoed around them in a way that destroyed all relationships between moving and unmoving, and so he held the brake down hard and steady to try to be sure. They were stopped. Engulfed and stopped on a high mountain road with more than a hundred miles to go. They took shallow breaths. The mother closed her eyes and kept them closed.

Mike thought of a thing to say. "We'll walk it over," he said to Neil.

They pulled up their collars, pulled down their hats, stepped out into the howling cold. One on each side, they rested their gloved hands on the car and they walked. They could see their feet and short distances beyond and beside their feet, which was enough. They motioned sometimes to the driver, who kept the car moving at the pace of a walk. For a quarter of an hour, arms out for ballast, the brothers made their way through the stinging white, their parents in a litter, carried by their sons to the very top of the mountain pass. Slowly they descended then, until the sons walked fast, broke into slow runs. The wind, blocked by the mountain behind them, died away. The road cleared and what was beyond the road. The car stopped and the sons got in. Their gloved fingers, their faces, were numb, their eyelashes crystallized.

Here the world was textured, vertical and full of the feel of rooms. The silvery sheet of the plains had receded in space and time to become a fantasy of clarity. Here the trees were swaddled in the kind of snow that sticks. Clotted snow, corners and walls, a sky of steel. They'd entered the land of no wind. A little city sat on a valley floor, ahead of them, waiting.

Emboldened by the way he and Neil had almost carried the car across the mountains, or so it felt to him, Mike remembered his own incisiveness. The quickness that could come to him. The freedom from cant.

"We'll never know," he said. "There will be this story and that story. But all we will ever know is that there was a freak moment. A moment when everything that could go wrong did." His frozen mouth was slow with the words.

The car seemed to drift to the side of the road. Their father pulled on the parking brake, left it rumbling. He got out, stepped away, and bent toward a snow bank, back heaving. They waited for him. When he returned, he didn't so much as glance at his wife or sons. Then they drove again, through the still trees. It was three o'clock and almost dusk.

She waited for them. Opal Mix waited in her office. She had just finished speaking to a desk man at the newspaper who was filling in for Wendell Whitcomb, the police reporter whose mother had just died. She had also spoken briefly to Agent Roland Taliaferro, the FBI man from Butte. Now there was just the family, the Tierneys. She turned on a second light.

A hard knock on her door and when she opened it, they stood there in their winter overcoats and their boots and mufflers, red-eyed, sucker punched.

She invited them in and asked about their coats, which they kept on. They took chairs and moved them forward. The men lit cigarettes and leaned toward her, and the older son, Neil, asked her the facts.

She sat in a pool of yellow light and straightened the skirt of her woolen dress. She touched her fingertips to her white hair and leaned over the file that was the only item on her shiny desk. She had a jowled, adamant face and scribbled eyes behind rimless glasses.

She had, she said, been about to complete the paperwork. She would work from her notes, she said, as she opened the file.

No, she said, it would not be wise to view the body. The body was in no state to be viewed. It was at her mortuary, the coroner's mortuary, the mortuary she had run with her husband until his untimely death in '39. She looked up. Septicemia, she volunteered. A ruptured appendix. A terrible shock.

Neil Tierney made an odd sound in his throat, and she bent back to the file.

A week, she said. Or thereabouts.

In a chair, she said. In a chair before the grate.

Beside the chair. On the floor.

One.

In the mouth, she said, touching her long white fingers to her lower lip. She leaned back from the new sounds in the room.

Oh yes, no question. In the mouth.

So you see, she said. The reason. The mess. The time. The mouth. She felt the need, she said, to be perfectly clear.

Neil grabbed the coroner's file and flung it at the wall. They left, then, in a clatter, arms around the mother and her terrible low moan. Papers flew through the yellow light. Opal Mix folded her hands and stood, and studied the papers falling to the floor.

There were a number of them. Her coroner's report. The official death certificate for the courthouse vaults. Notes to herself after viewing the body. She always made many notes. Many notes she made, these days.

The death certificate, the document she'd just typed, lay at her feet. The steps of the family receded and a door slammed heavily.

She picked up the certificate and read the key lines again, for typographical errors. Full name: Aidan Franklin Tierney. Age: 32 years, 8 months, 15 days. Usual occupation: Attorney. Date of death: About Dec. 16, 1946. Due to: Shotgun Wound in Chest. Probable accident.

It was all in order. She signed her name in India ink, and blotted it, and blew on it carefully until it was dry.

FOUR

1946
Neva

THE SKY WAS GUNMETAL AND VERY low. When Agent Roland Taliaferro stepped out of the car, he felt clamped between it and the
ground, and bent his head beneath the weight. One of the straggly
pines in front of the stucco church had ropes of tinsel flying from
it sideways and a one-eared sheep dog sitting near its trunk, alert to
the mourners filing in, as if waiting only for the sharp whistle to
round them up. Roland felt conspicuous and wished Travers, the
special agent in charge, was with him as planned. But Travers had
eaten some bad fish and was home in bed, dog sick. Or so he said.
Maybe he just smelled the stink of all this and wanted no part. He
had a superstitious streak, Travers did.

Roland looked around for the brother, Neil Tierney, the one
he'd met once or twice in college. He'd had a contained swagger, an
easy laugh. He'd been able to make Aidan laugh too. The brothers
sometimes spoke a little Spanish to each other, some kind of bas-
tardized version that sounded like a language they'd made up, their
own code.

What did he look like, this Neil? Roland couldn't put a picture together that went beyond a head of tight, dark wavy hair; long limbs; that delighted, head-back laugh.

The little church, inside, out of the gunning wind, was still decorated for Christmas. Pine boughs filled the window wells. Three spruce trees to the right of the altar were hung with children's paper snowflakes that twirled dreamily in the rustlings and exhalations of the packed room. The wooden pews had thin, hard kneelers and clips for the men's hats.

A life-sized crèche filled the corner to the left of the altar. Joseph, staff in hand, scanned the horizon. Mary, folded and blue, studied her stiff baby in the straw.

More and more people filed in. The aisles were now filling with the standing. In the back, where Roland sat, two young women in the pew ahead wept quietly, the squared shoulders of their woolen coats lifting and falling in tidy rhythms. To his side, on the outside aisle, a white-haired, white-mustachioed man in a formidable black coat consulted a watch he had pulled from somewhere within his deep clothes.

"What utter nonsense," the old man murmured. He turned to glare at Roland. His hair fell over the top of his stiff collar. Roland tried to convey with a curt nod his own acquaintance with the absurd.

"The coroner says suicide. Then the Mick sheriff says maybe an accident, so the boy can get properly buried in the church," the old man said. He had a ruined, hawklike face and eyes so pale they sent a chill into Roland. "What sheer nonsense." One of the young women turned around and asked him in a whisper if he could do his talking after the service. She had red eyes and a spot of red lipstick on a front tooth.

"Dropped his shotgun," the man said, leaning over to speak in Roland's ear. "Someone said the sheriff said Aidan was examining the gun and must have dropped it, and the thing went off." He smelled like smoked leather. "That boy's been firing shotguns since he was nine years old. You think he's going to handle one so stupidly that it slams him dead?"

"I ran against that boy for public office," he whispered again. "He was right out of law school and arrogant. Had a certain what I'd call conceit. But he wasn't stupid. He was far from stupid." He examined Roland's face, and Roland willed it to stay impassive. "As you would know yourself, young fellow, being that you were, I assume, a school pal of our boy. Down there at the law school, before he joined up with the FBI." Roland nodded. The man closed his eyes, satisfied.

There was the sound of the big door closing hard and the sound of shuffling adjustments at the back of the church, and then the altar boys and the incense and the robed priest. From the choir loft, then, a surprise. Not the choir with a hymn, but a single boy, a soprano, singing the Dies Irae. An angel's cry. Oh no, Roland thought, and he locked down his heart.

Eight young men followed the priest, carrying the draped casket. One had a deep, lurching limp, but he kept his arm steady and didn't throw off the slow march. Another had a shiny burn mark across one side of his face, and the eye on that side was sealed closed.

Roland waited for the casket to reach the front and stop. He turned to the old man and inclined his head. "The stupidest things can happen, even when you think you know what you're doing," he whispered. The man calmly shook his head and Roland was furious with himself for having said anything at all.

The Mass had started and the boy singer was joined by a small choir that sent back responses to the priest. The old man murmured something and it moved beneath the priest's voice and the choir's voices like something dangerous and unobserved. He leaned into Roland and hissed. "A person can have enough. Can be worn out. Where's the shame in that? Can you tell me where the shame is in that?" Someone's hand fell on the old man's shoulder and gave it a curt shake. Roland felt necks stiffen around them.

"A person can have enough," the man murmured, closing his frosty eyes.

It was perhaps the crucial quality in this line of work, Roland knew, the ability to watch yourself be yourself. Be *a* self, at any rate. You split, and then watch the performing self do whatever the occasion and the people and the agenda require.

After the service, the old man didn't linger with the others outside the church door but set off at a brisk walk, swinging a silver-knobbed cane, and Roland felt both of his selves—the anguished one and the cool professional—watch him go. They wanted to go with him.

"Our county attorney," someone snorted quietly, "could use a manner or two." Roland's cool performer nodded sympathetically, then retrieved a cigarette and passed the pack around. The mourners stood in groups, huddled against the wind and the charcoal sky. They looked, some of them, as though they'd been snuffed out, as if the real people had been erased and it was their facsimiles that walked around and nodded softly to friends and touched elbows with gloved hands. They looked like remnants of themselves. Others had gone to their cars to wait for the procession to the cemetery to begin.

The hearse, someone breathlessly reported to those back on the steps, had a flat tire.

"Christ!" barked a tall young man as he stalked over to it. There he was. The brother, Neil Tierney. "Unbelievable!" Neil shouted, too loudly. Several others threw their cigarettes to the ground and huddled with him around the back of the big Buick.

Here was something Roland could be a part of. He made his way through the people who were going back inside the church, out of the weather, to wait. The casket was placed on the narrow sidewalk. Several people stood near it, their gloved hands on its top.

This was precisely the sort of moment Aidan would have helped the others through, Roland thought. Calmly, efficiently, good-humoredly, he would have organized them to get the job done. But there was too much milling and advice and then sharp shouts, and several men flew back from the hearse as the jack slipped on the frozen ground and the Buick thumped to the ground.

Neil, the brother, signaled peremptorily for Roland to step in and help, then slapped his hands together and marched furiously to a little group that stood together at the foot of the church steps, at a loss, it seemed. The rest of the family.

Neil spread his arms behind mother and father and herded them gently to a humped Studebaker parked down the street from the hearse. He got them inside the car and was joined then by a slimmer, lighter-haired version of himself. The other brother, the one Roland had never met. They bent their heads together and conferred, and then the younger one got into the car behind the wheel. Neil rejoined the men at the hearse, who reset the jack and got the thing in the air and the spare tire on.

The big car was ratcheted down, and the men wiped their hands on their handkerchiefs and kicked the creases into their slacks. They moved in a pack to the coffin. Roland joined them. They lifted it hip high and walked it toward the hearse. It was heavy.

Roland was directly behind Neil, the brother. A few steps along and his foot slid sideways in an icy rut and he lurched forward, smashing his face against Neil's scratchy overcoat. It was the moment that would stay clearest to him: the sharp stagger, the box slamming against his thigh, his face in cold wool, the clenched feel of the human back beneath the wool. He muttered an apology, but Neil didn't even turn around. He seemed not to notice.

The grabbing wind turned the sweat on Roland's face, on the back of his neck, into a clammy patina. What grim country this was. What a darting, biting thing the wind was, like an animal grabbing at your clothes.

His calm self, the professional, now watched it all from back on the church steps, a hand steady on the iron rail; watched the dark coffin, a nightmare keyhole in the day. Roland wanted a drink so badly he had to lower his eyes. He felt engulfed in revulsion. For the situation, for himself, for these people, for the black box pulling them all behind it.

Look at me, he wanted to shout to these stunned, weeping, milling innocents.

Look at me hard, you fools.

Travers had given him assurances. A letter would go from the Old Man himself to the family, explaining that the Bureau's investigations pointed to an accidental death. Coroner Mix's earlier statements to the family and newspaper notwithstanding. If questions were forthcoming, Travers would offer them fortifying details. The absence of a note. The obliterating nature of the shot. Aidan's strong religious beliefs. His possibly improving health—all of it adding up to the probability of an accidental death. But they didn't expect a lot of questions to be forthcoming. When you've been given the gift of an accident, you don't turn it over and poke at it with a stick.

It was also the only option that left the Bureau unculpable, and so it was the one that would be officially put forth. Suicide or murder raised questions of precipitating conditions, and precipitating conditions inevitably involved the Bureau and what it had exposed an agent, or former agent, to. Or failed to protect him from.

It was a matter of nuance. Opal Mix had been told to suggest the possibility of suicide, so that Aidan Tierney's survivors would not press to see the remains. But she had badly overstepped; had been so crazily blatant that the family, over time, wasn't likely to let her statements stand.

"We'll give them something else," Travers had offered. "If they aren't left with suicide as the only possibility, they can just go away and grieve."

"Just go away," Roland said.

"However you want to think about it," Travers said, shuffling through a stack of papers to send him on his way.

The other assurance involved Roland's professional future. Travers had told him that if he represented the Bureau at the grave, kept his counsel, conducted himself with discretion and tact—as he had so far—then he had a chance of keeping his job. Roland suspected they'd want to transfer him out of Montana, but he could live with that. He was sick to death of Montana.

Travers had said something at the end of this conversation that came back to Roland now. "Get this done," he'd said with a stiff clap on Roland's back. "Most of the problems are now behind us."

After the burial, Neil shook Roland's hand and asked if he would come to the house to speak briefly with the parents. This wasn't a surprise, but Roland found himself desperate to delay it. Neil had a kind of tensile, pale fury in his voice, his movements. The anger didn't seem directed at Roland, on the contrary, but it had force to it. It threw you off balance to be near it. Rage always did. Buttoned-up, civil rage, in particular. He told Neil he'd get some gas in his car for the long trip home, and be there in a few minutes. He drove to the station, studied the flying red horse on its wall, gassed up, and thought for a moment that he might try to fly too—down the street, onto the highway, out of here.

Instead, he turned down an alley and parked and took a few deep breaths. He retrieved a bottle and took three long slugs and leaned his head back and closed his eyes. *I will count to one hundred, and then I will go up there and say my piece, and then I'm out of here.*

Any soldier you talked to had something from the experience that didn't bear discussion or dissection, he counseled himself. The mad joker came whirling down, dancing on his strings, and something happened that was never supposed to. Why should Roland Taliaferro be exempt?

He put his forehead to the steering wheel. Dry-eyed, he rested there for a few minutes. And then he drove the few blocks to the house of the bereaved.

Where he stood with them in a small room with drawn drapes. The drapes had heavy roses on them. The gas heater in the front room ticked. There was a table with a white cloth and plates of cookies and a pot of coffee. Two silent women, the attendants who materialize in these situations, poured coffee and murmured and waited for a chance to replenish something. The family looked drained of blood, all of them. The father was narrow faced, a little hunched, with calm, protruding eyes. There was an eerie stoniness to him that Roland would remember later when he heard that the man, catatonic with depression, was getting electricity run through his temples at the state hospital in Warm Springs.

There was the sweet-faced mother, her soft hair prematurely white, haggard, red-eyed, seemingly willing to speak with him but unable to come up with a voice that he could hear. There was the fair-haired brother, Mike, the younger one, talking in low impatient tones to a girl with a baby in the kitchen. There was Neil, the brother he'd first met in happier days.

He must have said the expected things. He had the strange sense that he was expected to furnish information but not to speak it aloud, not to talk to the group in any explicit way. After a decent interval—in which he must have said what a fine man their son had been and how he would miss him and knew many others who would miss him, and offered his deepest condolences on the part, especially, of the Bureau—the mother brought him his coat. He kissed her on the cheek and, for the first time, felt utterly unable to say anything at all. He walked outside with Neil for what he knew would be the real conversation.

The snow had started. It flew down, fine and dry, and was shoved by the wind into smoke and swirls.

"You know," Neil said, as they lit cigarettes on the porch. "Aidan drove a truck for a gravel outfit during summers when he was in high school. They hauled gravel up north, to lay on the roads to the oil wells. Took him half a day to get to some of the work sites."

Grief was a strange thing, Roland thought, as he listened to the flat voice. It produced such desperation for the mundane.

"So this other driver is headed in the same direction, and he passes Aid—the road is rough and rutted—then falls back to a crawl, staying smack in the middle so Aidan can't pass and he's taking gravel hits and honking and the guy won't pull ahead and he won't pull over. Well, what the hell?

"He couldn't pull back, go slower, because the site was a long way and he had to get the load there by noon. But any damage to the vehicle came out of his pitiful salary and he saw that happening too.

"They drove toward Canada. A stifling summer day. The road a washboard with a slippery gravel surface, and it turns out—Aidan recognizes him now—that the driver giving him grief is the boss's nephew, new guy, dumb as dirt and a mean streak a mile wide.

"They get to the site, finally. Aidan has chips in his windshield and little bloody nicks on his window arm and on the side of his neck. The guys at the site watch them both pull to a stop. They direct Aidan to the turnout where they want him to dump the gravel. The big jerk, the nephew, is taking a leak in the ditch.

"Aid, very mild, very calm, waits for the guy then asks him to come over and look at his wrecked windshield. Very nice. Very polite. Guy walks over. 'Pretty sorry windshield you got here!' Big joker. Turns around with his big grin plastered across his face and Aid knocks him cold. Just winds up and lets him have it—this guy twice his size."

Roland smiled politely. Shook his head disbelievingly. "He wouldn't take grief from anyone," he agreed.

"He wouldn't play the fool," Neil said. "It wasn't in him to just take it, you know. Even if it cost him not to. Even if it cost him a lot." Now he was looking hard at Roland. What did he know? Roland wondered. What griefs, precisely, had Aidan shared with his brother?

Roland lifted his cigarette and the wind blew the ash off the end, into a corner of his eye. He swore. Rubbed at it, eyes watering. Neil didn't seem to notice. He studied the weather vane on the roof of the neighbor's house, spinning in the wind.

He turned to Roland. "That coroner," he said. "She just about killed my mother. Blow by blow by blow. She couldn't get enough of it. The shot, the decomposition, the angle, the mouth. The mouth! Where did they find that woman? She's a monster."

He peered at Roland, cocking his head to the side. "Then the sheriff says maybe an accident. So what's the story here?"

"The cops tell us the coroner, Mrs. Mix, has been a bit of a problem lately," Roland said carefully. "They say she is prone to a certain overstatement, a certain adamancy that sometimes isn't warranted." He sounded like a fool. Neil suffered him, for the moment. But he looked as if he wouldn't for long.

"Okay," Roland said. "She's incompetent. And it's possible she's crazy in a quiet sort of way. In one of those churchgoing, gray-haired ladies' club sort of ways. Not so long ago she said that a loner who'd been found dead in the woods was the victim of a bear attack. The guy had more than a little buckshot in him. Pellets were falling from him, as a matter of fact. Turned him on the table and they rattled off across the floor, so the story goes." He looked up at Neil. "Sorry," he said.

"I could kill her," Neil said quietly. "I really could. My mother is the original Catholic, you know. Daily Mass, the whole works. Do you know what happens to you when your son—your first, your highest hope—elects to effect his own exit, so to speak? Do you know what we're talking about here, in a theological sense?" The dry, professorial cadences sounded so ghoulish to Roland that he needed to make them stop.

"I was raised a Catholic," he said shortly. "I'm married to a Catholic."

"Well then, you know what they say: Suicide is the enactment of despair, and the enactment of despair is spiritual suicide," Neil said. "They get you coming and going."

"It's not certain at all that he killed himself," Roland said flatly.

Neil's face opened up then. For just a moment. It dilated with hope. Then it closed down, as if to protect himself from that hope. "There's no need to offer reassurances that make it sound better," Neil said. "Don't do that. There's no need. Not with me."

"You'll be getting the details from the director," Roland said. "Opal Mix and the sheriff weren't the only ones to investigate this death. The Bureau has been investigating too. Any agent or former agent's violent death gets a hard look. You'll be getting a full report."

Neil was clearly not going to accept Opal Mix's version of events, Roland saw. He'd go after it. He'd get the body dug up. He'd get himself a forensic specialist from a city, and then there it would be, the sort of wound that could not reasonably have come from any action by the deceased.

Roland would write to the director himself and tell him the family was expecting a report. Not that he had to. He was sure the Old Man intended to send one. But he'd remind him. He'd relay what he had already decided was Neil's demand. In the end, there would be enough accident to appease the family, enough suicide to keep them from investigating.

Enough accident.

"Three of our best guys are going through it step by step. It hangs together. One of those weird, tragic things, we think. To all appearances."

Neil looked at him hard.

"And what about foul play, as you boys like to phrase it? What about pure and simple murder?"

"No indication of it," Roland said. "No known enemies. No forced entry. Nothing pointing to it."

Neil had come outside in his shirtsleeves. He seemed oblivious to the cold. Roland felt himself shivering very slightly from the top of his head to the soles of his feet. He was thinking about Melvin Purvis. He couldn't stop it. Out in the cold. That's where the Old Man had decided to put Melvin Purvis, legendary agent, the man who had caught and shot Dillinger. Because Melvin Purvis had subsequently stolen the limelight, had forgotten his place, the Old Man had frozen him out.

"One for the road?" Neil said politely. Without waiting for an answer, he went to the Studebaker and opened the trunk.

"Come here," he said. There were three boxes in the trunk filled with clothes, with books, with the specific remains of Aidan Tierney, Roland realized with a small shock. There was so little, really. Three boxes. On top of one he saw a Spanish breviary, a *maté* gourd, and a framed law school diploma.

"I don't know what to do with these things," Neil said. "I don't want to bring them into the house yet. No one is ready for it."

He retrieved a bottle from one of the boxes, half full of Johnny Walker Red. He retrieved two cups.

"A toast to Aidan," Neil said gruffly. He poured into the cups. His hand was clenched so tightly the knuckles were white. He looked into his cup and screwed his eyes shut as though he waited for a blow. He opened them. He was a shade paler. He lifted the cup, shoulder height. Snow fell into it. They clinked.

"He will be so very missed," Neil said in strangled low tones.

Roland drank his in two long swallows. They stood. Snow began to freeze on his eyelashes. "Well," he said. He was beginning to feel he might have new things to tell this brother: subtle variations on

what he had already said, variations that would offer further consolation, the way elaborations of anything—a truth, a lie—always
have a fortifying effect.

He held his glass forward, discreetly, for another belt.

Neil looked at him. His face was cold and his movements were
cold. He replaced the cap, deliberately, and put the bottle back in
the box.

"I think a single toast will do," he said. He held out his hand
for the cup. "I think this is an occasion that doesn't warrant much
more. You tip your hat to the deceased. You don't pump his dead
hand."

Roland felt a jolt of caution. He wrapped his muffler deliberately, adjusted his hat, and offered Neil his hand. He said he would
be in touch. He said there would be an official communication.
Whatever he could do, et cetera.

Neil turned and walked away. No good-bye, no thanks for
coming, no nothing. He was outside in the snow in his shirtsleeves,
and then he was a shadow in the window of the door.

Roland drove slowly through the thickening snow. The last light of
the day was seeping away and the countryside—the fence posts, a
barn, a farmhouse, a few cattle—came to him blurred and without
color. One of the farmhouses had a yard light that made a lonely
circle in the dusk. Inside, they would be sitting down to an early
dinner, everything prompt, the way they did it on farms—all that
rising and feeding and watering and tilling and herding. There
wasn't time or energy for deciding when something necessary had
to be done. You just did it, every day, and you did it in its exact order; and if you deviated from that order, a domino effect occurred
and that single lapse, that single oversight, produced many more.
The wife falls ill, breakfast goes uncooked, the hungry and cranky
son takes a shortcut fixing the baler, the thing breaks down, the
meadow goes unbaled, a freak hailstorm ruins the loose hay, and so
on. He'd read this somewhere. Or someone had told him about it.

The car heater was cranked on high and his feet were frozen.
He was probably ten miles out of town, no more. There was not a

chance he'd make Butte tonight. In fact, the prudent move, he now knew, was to get fifteen more miles down the road and put up in Conrad for the night. Get a dry, warm room in the hotel and have a couple of drinks and treat himself to a steak. If there had ever been a day he deserved it, this was it.

His windshield was icing and he slumped low in his seat to squint through the clear hemisphere at the bottom. A car passed and its lights made the ice patterns on his windshield into brief, frantic hieroglyphs and sketches of faces. Just for a moment. He thought of the eyes of the silvery man next to him in the church, and he wondered if they had always been so wintry or if his life had bled them pale. Even his whispering had sounded frozen, like a scraper on ice.

I should have taken him aside afterward, Roland thought. I should have told him that an investigation had been conducted and very competent investigators had concluded that Aidan Tierney had died in a fluky gun accident. He realized he was talking aloud to himself. He was going to have to stop the car in a minute and get the windshield clear. The snow was blowing sideways and he knew where the edge of the road was only by the fence rails beyond it. He tried to keep them at a fixed, unvarying distance.

He stopped the car. "There will be a letter to that effect to the family," he said aloud. "The director himself will send a letter to that effect." Then he saw the Old Man's adamant hound's eyes, and he knew.

No letter would be sent. He knew it, this moment, as if he'd just opened a telegram to that effect. The Old Man didn't forgive. He had fortitude and vision and a genius for organization, a genius for promotion—qualities Roland admired fiercely—but he also had a need for revenge that did not discriminate between slights and perfidies, between the undeniable and the imagined. He was, in that sense, small. Small of soul.

How long have I known this? Roland thought. For the first time all day he felt like weeping.

The Old Man found all his answers in details, and that trait, combined with an essential woundedness, made him a connoisseur of intricate and protracted revenge. Aidan had taken him on. Aidan had dared to criticize. And Aidan's survivors would pay the price. In this case, the price would be a withholding of consolation. Just that. A lifetime of that.

The lights of Conrad finally appeared in the dark, so scattered and few that Roland thought at first they couldn't be a town. He felt numb with cold now and full of the old stories about motorists who'd made the mistake of stopping in blizzards to walk what they thought would be a short distance to find help. He'd never do anything like that. But his heart had jumped a time or two when the car seemed to balk at crossing a low drift, or when he lost sight, for a few moments, of the fence posts.

The clerk at the hotel desk slept on his arms. Roland woke him curtly and left a few minutes later with the key and a warning that the hotel restaurant closed in a half hour and it was the only place in town he was going to get a meal.

It was chilly in the lobby. No one there but an old dog sleeping near a dusty rubber plant. He peered into the dining room. No bar. Just wooden tables and a waitress smoking over the crossword puzzle. Two couples on the far side, eating silently the way they did in these small towns.

Roland realized he was in a vile mood, the kind that wouldn't subside with a few quick drinks before he came down to eat. He went over to the waitress and ordered a club sandwich to take to the room. She said the special was the hot roast beef and gravy sandwich and maybe he wanted that. If he wanted that, Roland told her, he would have ordered that. He wanted a club sandwich and he would be back to get it in a few minutes. Something in his voice made the two couples look up from their food at him, made the waitress shrug elaborately and get up a little more slowly than she needed to.

He went back to the desk clerk and asked if there was someplace he could park his car where it wouldn't be all frozen up in the morning. The desk clerk thought about it, and reported that no place came to mind. Roland told him it didn't matter. If his car didn't start the next day, there was nothing he'd be able to do about it. If your car doesn't start, we'll get someone to jump it, the clerk assured him.

Roland went out to lock it up. The wind was moaning now, though the snow was lighter. A single car crawled down the main street, through the blinking red stoplight.

He retrieved his briefcase and the spare blanket he kept in the trunk and a fresh bottle. There, next to the bottle, was the letter Travers had handed him as he left. It was from headquarters, the Old Man, and it was, Roland knew, the director's decision about the future of Agent Taliaferro. He was surprised that Travers gave it to him before the funeral. Some kind of test, apparently. The letter was cold to the touch, as though it had been there a long time.

He knew he would do it when he'd had a few drinks, and so he decided to do it now. He held the envelope to the wan light of the hotel sign and it turned a faint pink. It was thin: one page. He saw, or imagined he could see, just a few lines of type.

He carefully placed the blanket and the bottle and the briefcase on the hotel step, and sat down next to them.

He'd fire himself before he let them fire him, or before they let him stay.

He tore the unopened envelope in two. And he tore the twos in two, and again, and one more time, and a last for good measure. As his last official act as a special agent with the Federal Bureau of Investigation, he tossed the white scraps into the air, where they fell and swirled and blew sideways, around corners, into the moving snow, and except for a last few, out of his sight.

FIVE

2003
Neva

IF HE HADN'T NOTICED THAT THE diamond was missing from Rosalind's ring, Neil Tierney wouldn't have been creeping stiff-kneed across the carpet, peering at its flecks, and his sunglasses wouldn't have slipped from his pocket to lie unnoticed by the hassock.

And if Rosalind Tierney hadn't been on the phone when the sparrow hit the picture window, she might have watched where she put her foot. The bird hit, Rosalind stepped back from the bright window, the glasses crunched. She examined the damage and shrugged an apology to her husband, then helped him to his feet while she continued to talk.

Neil deposited the wrecked glasses in a wastebasket and placed himself in his leather recliner to regroup and to imagine the diamond, which seemed to him now to be deliberately evading them. How many times had he watched Rosalind lift her coffee cup to her mouth? Each time, there must have been a glint of light off her ring because that was all it had taken, the absence of that wink, to make him lean toward her hand and see that the stone was gone. She knew it was there when she brushed her teeth, so it was in the house somewhere. They would find it in time.

Rosalind moved close to the window to scan the lawn for the bird. She lifted her palm to tell him she saw nothing. Stunned it was, then, and on its way.

"Where are you now?" she said to the phone. She massaged the side of her neck, a gesture as familiar to him as his own hands. She had been talking for a while now with their older daughter, Ariel, a pharmaceutical researcher in San Diego. Later in the day she planned to call their daughter Anne, a tax lawyer in Baltimore. It was a telephone day.

"Baggage pickup?" She listened for a few moments. "After what disturbance?" She listened again. "Why is it a disturbance if someone in a Burger King demands his money back? How does that constitute a disturbance?" The delving tone in her voice meant she might want to use the incident, whatever it was, as a springboard to a further-reaching discussion of power and its distortions. She had vehement sorrows about the state of the world and its leaders, and worried that their daughters were handing over their best energies to the sources of a lot of the trouble.

Neil put on his cap, found his keys, and waved good-bye. He had a ten o'clock Chamber meeting. She pointed inquiringly at her eye. He blew her a kiss. He had advanced cataracts in both eyes and was supposed to wear sunglasses when he went out. Bright sun had the perverse effect of making the cataracts more cloudy.

He went to the half basement to say good-bye to his brother Mike who was watching a television program about the intelligence of border collies. Mike was gaunt and white, dying of cancer that had spread to his bones, and lived for the present in the Hillsview, Neva's assisted-living facility. Neil or Rosalind brought him to the house most mornings. He visited a little, watched television, had lunch, and went back to his linoleum room to sleep most of the rest of the day away. Except for the war, he had lived in Neva all his long life.

Neil drove very slowly toward the school gym, where the meeting was. The sun had leaped out from a large cloud to irradiate and blur Neva's pale, low-to-the-ground buildings, the little scramble of them along the railroad and highway and south for a few blocks to the beginning of the grass. Light shot off all the surfaces and hit him in the face. He fixed his gaze on the concrete that arrowed ahead, un-trafficked. He thought of what the man who drove up last time in a rented Expedition had told the Chamber: There were more than a few people, out in the cities, who would pay good money to experi-ence the sort of emptiness that residents of end-stage prairie towns like Neva took for granted. It was an interesting, if outlandish, idea.

A long charcoal cloud moved into the sun, and Neil could make out the Sweet Grass Hills, three protrusions from the flatness off to the north. They took on different looks at different times. Their color changed and, so it would seem, their distance. But he knew their variations only in a theoretical sense now. He remem-bered them. With the cataracts, the mountains had become little more than intensifications of the horizon sky, though he could, he realized, distinguish the adamant symmetry of the middle one. The cone. The one Meriwether Lewis had called the Tower. The miniature Fuji. He pulled to the curb and covered an eye to test the acuity of the other. Uncovered it. Trained them both on the Tower.

The car gave a little jump and he saw that it had rolled forward to scrape a telephone pole. He backed away, put it carefully in park, and got out to inspect the damage. Hardly anything. A long faint mark, something you'd have to be looking for to see at all. Out from behind the windshield now, he tested his less-bad eye on the Hills and decided that he could make out a marginal degree of de-tail that was missing when he looked with the seriously bad one.

The Hills were time islands. Three thousand feet above the sur-round, they had escaped the scraping glaciers, then the eons of howling desert, to remain shelters for the plants and animals of an-tiquity. He knew them. Had known them for many decades. It was old up there, smelled like water, and you found odd things: animal bones that you didn't find on the prairie; maybe, up high, a buffalo skull, hauled to the top by a visioning Blackfeet boy who had pulled the big head with rawhide strips tied to skewers run deep into his young-muscled flesh. A ring of rocks and a buffalo skull you might find, up there on the top.

Neil could look at the mountains, faint as they were, and see hooves sunk in loam, high above an endless sea of ice. Or calm eyes behind damp leaves, dappled flanks, ears rimmed with hairs that quivered in the remnants of the wind that rose from the yellow desert all around. Desiccation to the far horizons, but up on the Tower a gurgle of water.

Did they sense, the animals, how long they would have to wait? That it would never be they themselves that would leave the refugium, but only their streamlined and adapted descendants? That they would never know the segue?

He and Rosalind were their own time island these days, Neil sometimes thought. They had drifted apart from the present—its excruciations and vehement concoctions, its clatterings and chants—to float in a quieter, differently lighted place. Though even at a remove they could hear the exhortations, the high-wire hum, the urgent oars of the sad-eyed, the millions of sad-eyed, pulling, so hard, for some glittering game-show shore.

At the four-way stop, it came to him that he might be an hour early for the meeting. Possibly it was at eleven, not ten. Maybe he had the wrong day too. He retrieved from a pocket the note he'd written with the correct information, slightly surprised that he'd remembered where he put the note. The day was correct, but he had an hour to kill, and he couldn't do it at home because Rosalind had worries about his memory and this would confirm them.

A horn screamed at him, flopped his heart over. How long had the pickup been behind him? More than a few moments, he guessed, as he gunned through. Without the cataracts, he would have been able to see in the mirror whose rig it was, who was driving. With them, he couldn't even guess.

Back in the sixties, his mother had had the surgery. The doctor hadn't told her not to bend over afterward, and she had ruined an eye by retrieving her granddaughter's stuffed bear from beneath a bed. She'd had a delicate, big-eyed face, and the Coke-bottle glasses worn then, after the operation, had magnified the dead eye, carried it down the decades to Neil, who feared—unreasonably, he knew, given the advances—a similar result in himself.

He had studied the flecked carpet closely, crawling around like the Tin Man, and there had been minuscule centaurs, there had been microbes and tally marks, but nothing like a diamond. It would have to glint. They would have to wait for the moment when the light was right and their attention was right, for the kind of fortuitous intersection that would echo, it occurred to him, the criss-crossings of fifty-six years ago that had produced the diamond on her finger in the first place.

After the world battle and their separate strifes, they had wandered into the same burned forest and sat on separate burned stumps breathing hard. So he sometimes pictured it later. They had heard the other's breathing before they saw each other; had heard in the other the shock of big hits taken when the danger was supposed to be over.

Her first, brief husband, Frank O'Brien, who'd survived two years of air war to take a job with an airline, went down in the Pacific off San Diego a week after their wedding day. Neil's brother and best friend, Aidan, had returned from his secret war work with a mysterious and sapping illness, and had died of a shot from a 12-gauge at the end of 1946.

He and Rosalind had survived those aftershocks, but the future then stood before them differently. It was still chancy and bright colored, but with something in it, now, of the nightmare clown. The thing to do, then, was to be home. To stay put and make a real life in a decent small place, try to be positive and upbeat, try to stop listening for the other shoe to drop. In the main, with two or three exceptions, they had succeeded.

"There's a black-footed ferret if I ever saw one." That's what he'd say to his old friend Timer Raeburn when he saw him at the Chamber meeting. The man who drove the rented Expedition, Troy Grove, was scheduled to speak again. He represented a deep-pocketed environmental group that wanted to rope off the prairie and take safaris through it, the promise being that the Nevas of the world would service the seekers of emptiness and enjoy the economic fruits thereof.

Neil didn't object to the idea of restoring a grassland environment, thick with buffalo and black-footed ferrets, but he couldn't stop thinking about a magazine article he'd read at the eye doctor's about tribal women in Thailand who stretched their necks to immense lengths with metal rings. The practice once had some logical justification—protection from tigers and from kidnapping by rival tribes that saw ugliness in a stretched neck—but continued into the present because it's what the tourists wanted to see. In the course of things, over time and in the absence of tigers and kidnappers, the necks would have been allowed to sink to normal flexible lengths. But once the women had been paid to stay strange to others, they were frozen. They were entertainment.

Neva had become so elderly and gray that youth and noise jumped from its surface like colored fish. The skateboarders were at it again. Neil parked the car to watch them and kill time. They had placed a ramp at the bottom of the sloping sidewalk along the playground and flew off it to whirl in the air before they touched down, veering sharply to stop themselves a few yards from the street. One of them was a girl who was a little less sure of herself than the others but clearly learning fast. She was possessed of the careless grace they all had, though she wobbled more than the others on her landings. Her hair was a fake color, a flamingo pink, and it flew out behind her as she leaped off the ramp and drew her long legs to her body like a water bird.

He couldn't see their faces clearly, but their daring and color and a certain seriousness of purpose—off the ramp they launched themselves, again and again—made him want to clap. They seemed to embody receptivity and alertness. One moment they would be clicking along the sidewalk like train cars, eyes ahead, their feet and the board something they had no need to notice. They looked then like formal old men, leaning back from a loud crowd. The next moment, coming up on some homely, utilitarian town thing—a flight of steps, an iron handrail—they exploded in acts of derring-do. They leaped upward—boards miraculously clinging to their feet—and rode the rail, 360-ed the steps.

Neil watched them whenever he got the chance because they

reminded him of certain rules that he had almost forgotten. That it is important to stir up your own blood. (And how resourceful these young ones were, to find their triumph or wreckage in a handrail.) That you are more likely to hurt yourself when you hold back. That it is aerodynamically possible to take your foundation with you when you jump.

Sometimes one or the other would mess up on landing, but they managed always to stay upright, even when a board went flying away and the rider careened beyond it on foot. It happened now to the pink-haired girl. She lost her board and galloped wildly into the street, arms windmilling. The others called out something that could have been an instruction or a cheer and which ended in her name. Valentine. A girl on a familiar, last-name basis with the boys.

He was the man who had run off to the Hills, thinking he had stabbed a man to death. Ronny Valentine. The details swam up. A love triangle. The bartender at the Stockman's, Rhea Valentine, and her husband, Ronny, and some new man who had purchased the place. Rhea standing there one night, back to the bar, washing the glasses, holding them up to the Budweiser clock, talking over her shoulder to the new owner. No one else there. Then Ronny, she said, came stomping in and the next thing that happened was Ronny and the new owner on the floor, and then Ronny out the door in a gust and the other one bleeding hard from a knife in the ribs.

They found his pickup, out of gas, a few miles from the base of the Tower. That was the detail no one could let go: that a man would unleash his furies with only half a cup of gas in his getaway vehicle. And that he would give his pursuers such a clear sense of where he was going. Though that was also the eerie part. For weeks, men and horses and dogs combed the Sweet Grass Hills for Ronny Valentine and didn't find so much as a cool campfire. Nothing. It was as if he had run up the middle one and launched himself from its top, into the ether.

The victim, Leon Sargent, lived; and he moved in with Rhea; and Rhea's story about the incident kept developing discrepancies and holes; and the knife turned out to belong to Sargent; and so, eventually, there were occasional parties of men who drove to the Hills in hopes of finding Valentine, a well-liked sort, to tell him he was no murderer and would never even be charged with assault. The circumstances were too slippery.

But he was gone. Probably he had just kept walking the last miles to Canada, moving across the grass and wheat at night. Perhaps he never looked back, never knew he could have come home. Or didn't care. Or never left the Hills. They held pinpricks of light some nights. He could still be up there, then, watching his life go on without him.

How, though, could he leave his child so completely? This bright skater leaping into the air. That's what you had to wonder. Had his disrupted sense of himself and his possibilities made him blind even to the ongoing girl?

The former gas station with the winged red horse on the wall was now a gallery that nobody visited very much. The owner was a local artisan who made crosses and hearts out of stalks of wheat. Neil couldn't remember her name. He stopped the car because it seemed to him that the flying horse was significantly fainter than it had been. They got worse, inevitably, cataracts did. There was no reversing them with vitamins.

He held a hand over one eye and examined the faded horse through his open car window. The wind had picked up and was pushing dust devils down the street. The sun flickered on and off behind a slow flotilla of clouds. Dust and gravel flew up and stung the back of his hand, and he waited for the devil to pass then peered with his other eye, and the horse was a notch brighter. If he had the operation, he'd start with the worst eye and see how that turned out. He'd get on the train and go to Mayo, where the hotshots were, and have them start with the really bad one so he'd have something left if they goofed. And he would quiz them about every aspect of the postoperative business and get it all down in writing. And be very careful not to bend over suddenly, or fall.

The skateboarders with their bright sweatshirts and floppy shorts clicked down the sidewalk on the other side of the street.

They moved from locale to locale—sometimes the IGA parking lot, sometimes the retaining wall behind the library, then to the Sweet Grass Cafe where they leaped up on the low iron rail that bordered the handicapped ramp and zoomed along it like neon messages. Sometimes they seemed like the only things in town that moved. Bright flickers in the corner of the eye, migrating tropical birds pausing on their way to less quiet lives.

He could just make them out now, crossing the highway to some practice spot by the stockyard. Was there pavement for them there? Neil couldn't think of any.

The highway threw off a glare, and he thought of the ice-bright day when his brother Aidan rode a runaway sled under a moving truck. He'd started four blocks away at the top of the hill that ended at the highway. Bundled up and squinting in the brightness, he'd pushed off on the ice, and was moving so fast by the time he reached the highway and the truck that had turned onto it from the stockyard, that he seemed not to have time to think or roll or do anything but duck his head and dart like a swallow beneath the front and back wheels of the truck. The driver, unnoticing, shifted into a higher gear and moved down the highway while Aidan leaped off the sled and jumped in place, arms like a prize-fighter, for the benefit of his gaping friends at the top of the hill. "Aidan Tierney! Aidan Tierney!" one of the boys called in a wild little voice, over and over.

That big feat and then, just a few weeks later, a muddy game of Red Rover and Aidan had crashed so hard through the chain of hands—older boys, most of them, who'd thought he was too light to do it—that he couldn't stop for a mongrel running across his path and broke his leg so badly he'd been laid up for months.

A mind like a sieve. That's how old people described themselves, implying that all the good stuff got washed through the netting and they were left to wrestle with infuriating fragments. Neil felt his mind to be a sieve of a sort, but what surprised him was that he was left with memories, feelings, images, moments that finally, after all these decades, had begun to arrange themselves as a constellation.

Reasoning with himself hadn't done it. Religion hadn't done it, though it had sometimes helped. But it seemed that time, the passage of time, had.

He couldn't say what the constellation evoked, what the picture was exactly, but now he knew it *was* a picture, and there was such unexpected peace in the thought that it sometimes made him unable to speak.

Aidan flinging himself down a hill and under the chassis of a truck. Aidan crashing through the linked hands of the strong boys, heedless of his own safety, eager for surprise. Neil could think of those moments now, the better part of a century later, with curiosity and affection, without the anger at their predictive nature that he had carried for so long. He could think of his brother requesting hazardous duty during the war, and not feel a fury of desperation to pull him back.

Life dished it up. You didn't get to the end unscathed. But finally, in his own case, he'd got near the end with an intimation that it all cohered.

He looked at his watch. One more slow circle around the edge of town and he would park at the gym and be only somewhat early for the meeting with Troy Grove, and maybe someone would have an urn of coffee. He did a U-turn and drove carefully into the sun, an elbow on the windowsill, a hand shading his eyes. Everything was bright and smeary. Up ahead he saw an Expedition that appeared to be Grove's. Instead of turning right at the intersection, toward the gym, Grove went straight and appeared to accelerate. To catch him, so that he could point him in the right direction, Neil speeded up. Light flashed off the roof of the Expedition, shooting everywhere. Neil accelerated again, decisively. The blood thumped in his ears. He could honk, but he didn't wish that kind of startlement on the guy. He seemed to be gaining on him, but not quickly. What could the man's hurry be? He squinted and bore down.

She came flying off the right fender, executing the maneuver she might have been working up to all this time (or so it seemed at the front end of the moment): a corkscrew leap, and then the head tipping parallel to the ground, moving straight past his poor eyes.

The skateboard clattered up the hood and battered the windshield. The brakes shrieked.

Off to his left, the horizontal girl seemed to pause. She appeared to look him in the eye. What did she want him to know? What was it she asked? He scrambled to respond, but it was too late because her head now tipped toward the concrete. It led the rest of her down. And there she lay unmoving. All but her flamingo-colored hair, which had arranged itself in a fan around her skull, the tips of it lifting calmly in the breeze.

SIX

2003

To Butte, Montana

CHARLIE TALIAFERRO DROVE SOUTH ON A mostly empty road. It was afternoon. To the east, the plains stretched weightless and blue, a scarf on a breeze. Taylor Kaye pointed to the mountains on their right and told him their rock faces were a billion years old. When they were formed, she said, the lightless earth sweltered beneath a cover of clouds.

"The geological record tells of an earth so different from ours that it might be another planet, as distant in space as in time," she read from the guidebook. She closed it with a sigh and closed her eyes.

A week ago they'd driven from Bakersfield, California, where they lived, to Missoula, Montana, bringing Charlie's old father, Roland, with them. They had installed Roland in a rehabilitation facility, tried to ease his confusion about where exactly he was, then had taken a few days for themselves to sightsee in Glacier Park. Now they were returning to Missoula via Butte.

They had been driving for hours. Taylor said Glacier Park had been a pretty place, but overall, she got an off-putting feeling from northern Montana. It didn't feel welcoming. The Rockies, she added, hadn't been as relaxing as she'd hoped they'd be.

The wind blew, accelerating at moments so that they felt the car shudder. At the intersection of two highways, they stopped at a marooned-looking bar and restaurant with a sign that squeaked loudly in the wind. A portion of it seemed to have been shot away. The plastic lay in big shards at its feet.

Taylor threw Charlie a long look. She felt affronted by people or places that let themselves go. As they got out of the car, an ambulance rolled onto the gravel lot with a flat tire. Charlie sent Taylor in to order hamburgers, and conferred with the driver and attendant about the best way to fix a flat with a patient inside the vehicle. Because they didn't want any tipping or jolts, they decided to unload the passengers, a white-turbaned girl on a stretcher and a freckled, tough-jawed woman in her forties with streaks of mascara on her face. The girl was unconscious. The driver and attendant had a brief discussion about whether to take her inside, but the woman vetoed the idea and directed them to place the stretcher in the lee of the building out of the wind.

"Just get it done," she snapped, holding a windbreaker over the girl for shade. It put her in green light. She looked spell cast, sleeping in a cool cave. A strand of pink hair had escaped the head bandage.

The job went quickly, the men working silently and efficiently. Taylor had come to the screen door to watch. Two men from inside had joined the tire changers as observers. When it was done, the girl was gently lifted through the rear doors and the woman scrambled in behind her. The attendant grabbed a few puffs on a cigarette, tossed it, and they were off across the last of the grasslands and into the mountains. The road was visible for many miles, which gave it a fateful and timeless aspect. They watched the ambulance move along it, west, into the sun, until it was very small.

"What was wrong with her?" Taylor asked, as they took seats at the bar.

"No one was saying," Charlie said shortly. "It wouldn't be professional to."

"Well excuse me," Taylor said. She had dark circles under her eyes.

"It's not the sort of thing you ask."

"Well excuse me again," she said, trying to sound light and dismissive so that he would know that the trip had been a disappointment to her in more than a few respects.

Charlie's aunt Petey lived in a small pink house near Butte's most spectacular sight, an immense, abandoned open-pit copper mine, its deep bowl now holding water the color of cough syrup. Most days, although she was almost eighty-five, she walked to the cliffs of the sunken lake. Sometimes she saw men in rowboats paddling around down there in the chemicals, firing guns to scare away migrating birds.

"No one wants a repetition of the swan incident," she told Charlie and Taylor. "They'll keep flying if they know what's good for them."

"They mate for life," she added with a pointed glance at Charlie. She didn't approve of his history of short-lived liaisons with women.

Charlie and Taylor had driven into Butte along hills long denuded by vapors from the smelter, then they had Petey-prepped, as Charlie put it, with a couple of drinks at the Jack Club, the bar and cafe where his father, Roland, had mopped the floor and washed dishes as a kid.

Taylor wore the beaded belt and moccasins she'd bought at the Indian museum near Glacier and looked quite sleek in her stretch jeans and tucked-in black shell, her stiff, white-blond hair pushed off her forehead with obstreperous designer sunglasses. The men in the bar appraised her automatically, like tired dogs who knew they should terrorize a cat in their yard.

Charlie pictured his father working in the place as a boy, raw-boned and jug eared, and the gray-faced miners drinking bootlegged hooch after their shifts, the floorboards fresh wet, the watery sun falling through a greasy window. There would have been squeaky snow outside, the sound of it beneath boots, and the seep of forty-below air under the door. They would have been men who had known each other for decades, had worked shoulder to shoulder in the dark and steamy tunnels, then surfaced in the same cage, drenched with sweat that turned to ice on the surface of their skins.

He tried to think where this detailed vision came from, and saw his father, Roland, sitting in a lawn chair on a tiny square of hot cement outside the house he'd lived in for so many years in Bakersfield. He sat in the white sun and told stories. About trudging in the bone-cold dawn to his job at the Jack. About the Wobbly labor organizer, Frank Little, hung from a trestle; about the huge funeral for a child who had fallen down an abandoned shaft, and an old man at the wake, afterward, singing a dirge to break the heart. That's Butte, Roland had said, adding as some kind of summation the information that his neighbor in Bakersfield was taking his schnauzer to an acupuncturist.

There was a certain rightness in getting Roland relocated to Montana, the money aside. Charlie had tried to find a facility in Butte, so Petey could visit her brother often, but nothing had worked out. Missoula, two hours west, wasn't the perfect solution, but anything was better than the ridiculously named Ocean Breeze Senior Residence in Bakersfield. The place was far from the ocean on the east side of the freeways, and had not only cost a fortune to begin with but had doubled the fees when Roland took a bad fall and was moved, at least temporarily, to the next tier of care, the confined-to-wheelchair tier.

Also, Roland hated California, something he had decided—or had decided to talk about—a few years ago when he quit drinking. It was as if the booze had been a bandage over his mouth as far as California went, and when it was off, he hated being an old man there among the Hitler youth, as he called them. Palms, hot sun, shiny muscles and fun and cleavage and waxed cars and jewelry-colored hair—Roland decided he despised it all. He liked to say that all the women had tiny cranks implanted behind their ears to pull their faces tight; that all the dog owners took their pets to acupuncturists; that the only real place on earth was Butte, Montana, though he hadn't laid eyes on it for decades and had long professed to hate it. Now he said the name with a curious reverence, as if it was the title of an important book.

Petey's house prickled with heat and knickknacks, but she was an ancient queen among it all. Thin, smoky voiced, avid. As soon as she had thrown her perfumed arms around them, she pushed them toward the couch and sank back against the crocheted headrest of her chair, smoothing her caftan across the tops of her Birkenstocks. Her skin was blurred with wrinkles, but her eyes were black lashed and vivid. Her hair was an auburn wig anchored on either side by rhinestone clips. Her hands, resting on crocheted doilies, were long fingered and ringed. On the shelf above her head there was a collection of ceramic cigarette lighters. On the wall, a crucifix. On the coffee table, a framed portrait of her brother, Roland Taliaferro, during his FBI days.

Charlie had seen a television program about the way nineteenth-century Americans liked to prop their dead children sitting up, to have them photographed as if they were still alive. His father had something of that arranged, beyond-it-all quality in Petey's photograph. It would have been taken in the forties, when things were more formal.

In the photo, Roland looked somber and smooth, a calm and untried version of the old man who was so fiercely querulous now, so in and out of lucidity. At the Ocean Breeze, the attendants had parked him in his wheelchair by a sealed window with a plastic plant on the sill. His fingers incessantly brushed his knees or the top of a shoe box he wanted always within his sight. The staff took some pains to keep him unpanicked regarding this box. Inside it were his things, as he referred to them. All except the revolver he'd kept with the rest of it before he went to the facility. Charlie had confiscated that.

The box contained a winning ticket stub for a long-shot Trifecta at the Santa Anita races in 1959; a handwritten note from J. Edgar Hoover, welcoming him to the Bureau; the papers for his long-ago German shepherd, Kid; a studio photo of his second wife, Rita Ann; a newspaper clipping about the death of a former FBI agent named Aidan Tierney; a small packet of letters with the same name in the return address; a law school diploma; a duck-hunting stamp for the fall of 1939.

Petey gazed tenderly at the photo of her brother, her head tilted quizzically. Everything she did was a sincere concoction. She had discovered very early in a hard life that style is a way to keep from being bled to nothing by disappointment. It's a way to have a hand in the aspect, if not the direction, of your own fate. She reached out with a beautiful old hand to tap her brother's forehead.

"Sweet Roland," she said. "All he ever wanted was to be a G-man."

Taylor said she thought that's what he had, in fact, been. She had picked up an ad insert from the newspaper and was fanning herself. Petey had the space heater aimed at them, though the little house was stifling.

"Yes, dear, he was. But not for life," Petey said. "He wanted to be a G-man until he was old and then retire with honors and a silver watch engraved with the dates. That's all he wanted. First he was going to go into the law and then he turned to G-man. He had a heart as big as all outdoors. Plus being a fingerprinting expert. This counts for nothing?" She had turned her palms to the ceiling, widened her large dark eyes.

Charlie felt caught in the middle of a conversation he hadn't heard the beginning of.

"All outdoors," Petey said.

"He left the FBI because he wanted to change professions," Charlie said to Taylor. "He could have practiced law after he left the Bureau, but he wasn't interested. He had a wife and kid— me—and California seemed the up-and-coming spot and he wanted a salary and regular hours, and no dealing with criminals or divorces."

"Refrigeration?" Petey demanded. "That's a profession? You're asking me to believe that a man of Roland's caliber, a man with heart and bravery and all the qualifications that go along, that such a man is going to move to Bakersfield, California, and go into refrigeration?"

"Well, Petey, as I've said before, you'll have to try," Charlie said. "Since that is, in fact, what he did."

"Mr. Smart Guy," Petey said affectionately. Her arthritic Russian blue, Romey, was hauling himself up the side of her chair, and she lifted him gently the rest of the way and placed him on her lap. He closed his eyes as if the sight of his own struggle had been too much for him. The space heater ruffled the edges of his fur.

"Nineteen hundred and forty-six," Petey said. "That's when Roland's heart broke into a thousand and one pieces."

Charlie gave Taylor a look that said *ten minutes*. Firecracker sounds came to them from a distance.

"That's the swans," Petey said. "If they have the sense God gave a baby, they'll just keep flying. Take a rest someplace besides the Pit. They mate for life." She looked hard at Charlie and then at Taylor. "And then this. They land on that water in good faith."

"Geese," Charlie said. "It's geese. The mating part." The word embarrassed him. "And I believe it's geese they're shooting away. Snow geese. They're the birds that drank the stuff and died. I believe it was snow geese."

"Oh no, honey," Petey said. "They're swans." She looked at Roland's photo as if he could back her up.

Then no one could think of anything to say because all they saw were long white wings, bent, bobbing on dead water.

Petey leaned over her cat to pick apart a fur mat on his neck. She looked up.

"Sometimes an agent's family never knows what he has been asked to do in the line of duty," she told Taylor. "Sometimes the family never knows the true extent of the sacrifices he has been asked to make in good faith." She paused, as if considering whether to divulge more. "I will tell you this. In my heart of hearts, I believe J. Edgar Hoover requested Roland's resignation and arranged for Bakersfield in order to remove him from a threat. That is my private belief. Something had happened," she said, squinting at the far wall.

Taylor gave Charlie a look that said the ten minutes were up. He extended two fingers in a V, below Petey's line of sight, like a catcher's signal. He needed a little more time.

"And then," Petey said, "Here is a new agent in the Butte office, and there is Roland on the way to Bakersfield. Pale as the shade of that lamp. And *that* is when the refrigeration phase began. And California and all the rest."

"You don't remember," she told Charlie. "You were just born."

Charlie took a breath. "How would you feel about the chance to see him more? Your baby brother," he asked her. "How long has it been?"

He told her he'd found a good place for Roland in Missoula, just a hundred miles west. He'd done some hard shopping, he said, and the facility in Missoula was the best. And now her brother was just a couple of hours away.

Petey looked at him quizzically. "I don't travel, unfortunately," she said. "People my age have invisible blood clots traveling around, and if we travel far, they can stop somewhere and clog up something and kill us." She said this as though she were explaining the way a temperamental appliance worked. "That's how my friend Lenora Wing died after her cruise."

"You're looking at an old lady here," she added. "I haven't driven outside the city limits since 1979. It's not something I do." She looked at him hard. "Or ride as a passenger either," she said.

Charlie told her about Roland hating California, and the immense expense of the Ocean Breeze facility, and his reluctance to put his father someplace where he wouldn't occasionally see people he knew. A person, anyway. After he, Charlie, had returned to Bakersfield.

"He really hated the Bakersfield facility," he said, a pleading note in his voice.

"Except for Raquel," Taylor said.

"Oh, for God's sake," Charlie snapped.

"That was his favorite nurse," Taylor said.

"Don't quote me," Petey said coolly. "But the Roland I know isn't the Raquel type." She located a nail file and began scraping at her thumbnail.

"No problem," Charlie said. He stretched. "I'm a little punch drunk from all this driving and sightseeing. I don't have the most highly developed sightseeing skills." He cracked his neck ostentatiously. "But I think we got Taylor her money's worth."

Taylor stood up. "You wanted to as much as me," she said. She stepped out to the porch. "They're your precious mountains," she called over her shoulder. "You're the one who makes the pilgrimage up there every year. I could personally take them or leave them."

She closed the door with elaborate care. Beyond the frosted glass of the door pane, Charlie and Petey could see her stretching and pacing.

It was bliss to have her out of the room and out there on the porch. Charlie hadn't realized until this moment the full weight of her. It came as a relief to him that she disliked the mountains he had driven her to see. That clarifies the equation, he thought. He wasn't sure what he meant, but it felt—the phrase—like the beginning of his way out.

Petey hummed, petted Romey. She was thinking of her boy-husband as he'd stood on the same porch where Taylor now collected herself. It was the day she'd last seen him—she did some brief calculating in her head—sixty-two years ago. Then he'd got on the train, a kid with a jarhead haircut, and then the next thing was the uniformed man at the door to say he'd been killed at Corregidor.

Young men off to war. That valiant eagerness, the sheer zest they brought to the most dire danger. You don't believe you'll ever die when you're twenty, they'll say later, but Petey didn't think that was the real explanation for the eagerness. In the case of her young husband, he simply didn't want to be left out. It had sounded, to someone whose only other option was the mines, like an adventure. And she had urged him to go, though he could have got a deferment as the only remaining wage earner in his family. She had urged him to go because she wanted external confirmation that she was marrying an adult. A person with some knowledge of the world beyond Butte.

Now, these many decades later, she had come to know something else about risk. It was a way to coax meaning from life. If you do something dangerous in the name of some large belief—in freedom, love, democracy, religion—the shock of the inevitable cost can't be borne without an intensification of the belief. So going to war is a way to believe in something large and overriding. Something that didn't exist wouldn't be able produce such suffering.

Look at her own early love affairs. For her, their importance had been verified by the pain they were capable of producing. Her second husband, Angus McFarland, had left her for her cousin. Her third, Romey Pissaro, she'd stolen from her best friend, only to find herself serving a restraining order on him four years later. Intense and protracted anguish had been involved in both cases, to the point that she prayed sometimes that she would die. Her cousin and Angus had been killed together in a drunken rollover, so they didn't even have time to fall out of love. And Romey had gone back to the best friend and they still lived in Butte, though neither had ever acknowledged Petey's existence again. When they happened to see her, even now at the Seniors, they offered not a flicker of recognition. Wouldn't it have to be something of the utmost importance that could cause such anguish and rupture?

Of course, she also knew that the connection didn't bear protracted examination. Does the shock of sticking a pen in a light socket mean the impulse was a worthy idea? Put it that way and the answer was obvious. Nevertheless. A boy loses a leg and his friends and all his innocence for a cause, and he's going to want very much to believe in the value of the cause. As are those who send him to his diminishment. Great pain adding up to nothing, for nothing, about nothing—that's what can't be borne.

She wondered if Roland had turned to drink because of some grief he couldn't extract any meaning from. He was, when he was young, so in love with logic and science and system. He was a hard one to fool. If he had stayed that way, she would have leaped at the chance to see him again. But who was this Roland of the twenty-first century?

She thought about a telephone call she'd got from him a couple of months ago. They had just put him in the Ocean Breeze and couldn't get his medications right, according to Charlie. Roland had called her to report that Saddam Hussein had ridden a tiny motorcycle into his bedroom to have a meeting with him. It was a motorcycle the size a child would ride, so the man's knees stuck way out to the sides. He wore an Arabian hat, red velvet, with his town, Baghdad, embroidered on it in gold thread.

"That happened in Butte," she'd told him, trying to make her voice calm and explanatory. She felt she had to shout at him because there was some kind of reception difficulty going on, and it made him seem to draw close, then recede. It was the phone system. Her hearing was perfect.

She reminded him that she'd sent him photos of the Shriners' parade with all the city fathers and businessmen wearing fezzes and turning circles on their miniature motorcycles the way they do.

"No," Roland had said patiently. "This person was from Baghdad. I don't know why his vehicle wasn't up to size, but he was, in fact, from Baghdad. I do know that."

There was a long pause.

"It was on his hat."

Petey wasn't sure how to proceed with the conversation. It made her too sad to know what to say.

"Let's say you were looking at the photo I sent you and then, in your mind, it came to life," she ventured.

"Okay, okay," came Roland's voice, stronger now. "Just drop it. But let me state for the record that some very odd behaviors go on in this place. I'll just leave it at that. I'll just leave it to your imagination. Which has never lacked, I might add."

The conversation had shaken her. She had felt she was talking to a stand-in for her brother, someone provisional and still learning his lines. And now Charlie had brought this person back to Montana, where she would be expected to be his only living sibling and visitor, and there would be more conversations about little men from Baghdad. Before she knew it, the old Roland—the grave government agent in the photo—would be eroded by this new one, this person who was, since his fall, so in and out.

When Roland first moved to California in 1947, he had faded into a pink haze with swimming pools and movie stars, and even during his infrequent visits home, with first the one wife and then the other—Charlie sometimes in tow but always made to feel underfoot—he hadn't been quite a real person to Petey. He had never invited his sister to California, and she had never invited herself.

The real Roland was right there in that portrait on the coffee table. The real man was the one with the stricken white face, that Christmas of 1946, when something very bad had happened. Someone had died. His friend. Yes, his friend Aidan Tierney had been found shot, apparently by his own hand. The name, coming suddenly into her mind, brought with it a feeling of something muffled, a sound perhaps. A crying child under layers of stifling blankets. Not that, but something close. And Roland, rigid, trying not to hear.

It wasn't something Petey wanted to hear either, so she focused on the porch, where Charlie had joined Taylor. They murmured in a quiet, aggrieved sort of way. People argued and fought so reasonably these days. It made her a little nervous. The way she'd been brought up, she and Roland, was more like the program on the animal channel about how bears train their cubs to survive: cuffing them, letting them fend for themselves when other bears stole their salmon, and so forth. Hard and loud and geared to sheer survival.

The murmurs stopped. Taylor and Charlie came in to say their good-byes and use the facilities.

A volley of gunfire came from the direction of the Pit. Taylor came scurrying out of the bathroom.

"There must be a big flock of them," Petey said. "They think it's strange, delicious water. They're just warning shots."

"Well, consider me warned," Taylor said acidly to Charlie. He raised his palms, a plea for exoneration. He looked, Petey thought, like a man who'd exonerated himself. She turned from one to the other, trying to decipher what was going on between them. They floated in the fog of her exhaustion.

"Give Roland my dearest love," she said, adjusting his photo. "He's a crackerjack, that one." It sounded final enough to send them on their way, an eon, now, from the moment she had started wanting them to.

As she watched their shiny car glide around the corner and out of sight, she found that she was weeping. I miss my mother, she said to herself. More than half a century later and I am inconsolable that I cannot walk into this kitchen and find her there.

"I still miss my mother, Romey," she told the cat, her fingers on her sternum, which ached. He kneaded her leg with his careful claws.

The doorbell rang, and there he was, her gentleman friend. She'd have liked a nap first, and now she only had time to change her shoes. She called him inside.

"Jim!" she said, stretching her arms to a small ropey man with a shiny pate. "My hero. My love." Romey thunked down on the floor and stalked off.

Jim parked his cane very carefully on a ladderback chair, and nodded formally to her and looked at his watch. They played Bingo together every Tuesday evening after sharing a hamburger deluxe in the bar of the new Applebee's.

"They've moved my brother up here," she told him. "They've moved him to Missoula."

He pointed at the photo of young Roland, and she nodded.

"It's a wonder they didn't kill him in the process," she said. "He doesn't do well with changes in his routine. He never did." She gazed at the photo a last time before moving it to a new spot on the coffee table.

"Well, why should he?" Jim said, checking his watch again. "Why should any of us?"

SEVEN

2003
To Missoula

"COME OUT, LOVE," ROSALIND SAID SOFTLY. "Come talk to me and Mike." She knocked lightly on the locked bedroom door.

Mike had come up from the basement to hear about the trouble, and he sat now in the living room, gazing out the big windows. His shoulders were sharp and hunched, his face gray.

A bar of sunlight trained itself on the top of Rosalind's foot. It had the warmth of a human hand. She slipped off her shoes and moved one stockinged foot and then the other into its heat.

"Neil," she called. "Get yourself together so we can make a plan. I need you out here. Please."

"Give me a minute," came the reply. He sounded almost matter-of-fact, despite the crack in his voice.

In the hallway, Rosalind had arranged black-and-white family photos going back more than a century. They studied her coolly, not a smile in the bunch. These were the braced faces of people who expected to lose children, she realized. Rosalind held their gazes. The bearded, hot-eyed men rested heavy hands on the women's shoulders. The children in the front rows crossed their cotton-stockinged legs and tried to look like no trouble.

The door opened and Neil stood before her, unmoving, blinking, as if he'd been somewhere lightless and was trying now to guess where he stood. He looked wavery in all ways. Can a person age a decade in an hour or two? That was her first thought. Oh, honey, she said to herself. You're almost not here.

His white hair was tousled and a shoe was untied. His head was cocked to the side as if he listened to instructions that were too quiet for him to make out. He blinked again, owlishly. She went to him and put her fingers lightly on his forearm and steered him into the living room to his chair. She brought him and Mike iced tea on cocktail napkins.

They began to talk. To her relief, he sounded fairly calm, as he tended to be most of the time. Except for the recent spate of serious memory lapses that she didn't want to think much about, he had retained a constancy that matched her own and comforted her. The locked door was an aberration, a brief flight from this terrifying day.

They decided to drive to Missoula, where the Valentine girl had been taken in an ambulance for surgery. "To stand by," Neil said. "Until we know the lay of the land."

Once, coming back from a bus trip to see the Winnepeg Ballet, Rosalind had been startled to see Neil in the doorway of the gas station that served as Neva's bus depot. It was almost one in the morning and he knew she had a ride home from the depot with a friend who'd gone with her to the ballet. But he had come down, four hours after he usually went to bed, so he could drive her the seven blocks to their house. He had stood stiff-legged, shoulders back, in the doorway of the small white building. A single bulb burned above his head, dropping a cone of light onto the pavement around him. He looked as if he had posted himself there hours earlier, and as if he would have waited hours more. As long as it took. She watched him through the bus's tall smoky windows. He waited. He stood by. A geranium in a hanging plant holder—an odd little note of beautification—rocked gently in the night wind. My soldier, she thought. *My old soldier.*

Now, on this stunning day, it was time to organize themselves, to move. The deadly thing was to sit and brood like the old bachelors who lived out there alone on their pitiful little farms, gargoyled by forty and folded in on themselves.

But when they were ready to go, visions of the girl came back. "What if she hasn't come out of it?" Neil said after they'd double-checked the locks. His handsome old face looked stripped.

"I don't know," Rosalind said. "Why don't we get some information before we start thinking in those terms." They helped Mike into the backseat and got into the car, Rosalind at the wheel.

"Did you empty the garbage?" she said. Neil hissed through his teeth, angry at himself; he tapped his fingertips on his head. And that's when she felt the first wave of real anger. Anger at him, at inattentions small and large, at her own deep fear.

"Sit," she said. "I'll do it." She unlocked the door and fetched the two bags of trash, knotting the ties in a couple of rapid-fire motions. At the door, she lay them outside while she relocked, then stuck them in the big bin. She heard a crackle of hard plastic—the sun-glasses she'd stepped on?—and slammed the garbage lid down hard.

"Do you think it's possible your diamond somehow got into the trash?" Neil said when she got behind the wheel again.

She turned to him, her throat tight.

"I don't know, Neil," she said coldly. "Shall we spread the garbage up and down the driveway and poke through it all for an hour or so, on the chance of that?"

He closed like a shellfish. "No need for that," he said stiffly. "My thought was that we could put those bags inside the garage so they aren't hauled off, but if you think that's a ridiculous idea, well then don't."

"I won't," she snapped. She was breathing as if she'd run up a flight of stairs. Some part of herself stood at the bottom of the stairs and watched the furious woman at the top. She backed the car out of the driveway. Mike sat with his hands on his knees.

"That diamond was never mounted right anyway," Rosalind said. "There was always something a little off in the setting, so it wasn't sitting in there right and it was just going to happen sooner or later."

"Forget it, Rosalind," Neil said.

"You sold that good saddle horse Aidan gave you so you could buy that diamond," Mike said in his low papery voice. He'd been very silent to this point in the day. "When he moved down to Missoula. He sold you a colt of that good sorrel stud he had when we were kids. That Gato."

"I know, Mike," Rosalind said, apologizing to Neil through his brother. "It's not that I don't want the diamond back. It's just that this isn't the day to look for it."

"Not a good day," Mike agreed. They took him to the Hillsview and settled him into his room. He sat on the edge of the bed, hollow-chested, hollow-eyed, and waved them jauntily out the door. They'd call daily, Rosalind promised. She'd call his children and make sure they were in touch too.

Mike and his wife, Delores, his high school sweetheart, had had four children. Three of them were scattered. The oldest, a blithe and freckled boy named Aidan after his uncle, had been killed by friendly fire in Vietnam.

When he and Delores learned of their son's death outside a flyspeck village in the jungle, Mike had locked himself in the bedroom and refused to come out. There was a revolver in the dresser drawer, and Delores told them later that she was sure he was going to use it on himself. He had always believed his brother had done it, so why not himself, now? Hadn't the propensity been there all along perhaps, like a hidden, improperly welded seam?

Delores had called the sheriff and he broke in, and all they found was a middle-aged man, hair white at the temples, sitting on the edge of the bed with his face in his hands, weeping for his son, for the sheer and sweeping waste of him.

For years Mike had run the town's single gas station, planning to pass on the business to that son. He'd finally sold it to the woman who made it into a gallery for her wheat weavings. Once a charmer and a talker and a wild one, he had become, in the years after his son's death, a recluse. Delores had moved to the coast where she eventually married a retired colonel.

Rosalind and Neil traveled some miles in silence.

Neil stretched carefully and lay his head back. Soon he seemed to sleep.

She drove. The car moved across the plains, south and west to the mountains. From the corner of her eye, she watched Neil's white head and felt a fury of tenderness. The mountains grew.

What was in store for them? Neil had spoken for an hour with the police chief, and there didn't seem much chance of any legal action. The girl had shot out to the street from behind a tall hedge. Neil hadn't been exceeding the speed limit. Her friends were witnesses. No driver could have stopped in time. All of that was quite clear. The cataracts hadn't come up.

But circumstances weren't really the point. The girl was the point. If it turned out that Neil had been the agent of her damage or end, his own life would be effectively over. Rosalind knew this for a certainty. If the girl died or was never to be right, the lens of Neil's entire life would shift so that it caught the sun and burned him up as if he were a dry leaf. Nothing before it would count. Not even their marriage pehaps.

When she first got to know him, the hometown war hero seven years her senior, it had been less than a year since her husband, Frank O'Brien, had died in the crash of the commercial airliner he was piloting. Their first real conversation took place after his brother Aidan's funeral on a bitter December day in 1946. They had murmured together in the dusky light of his parents' kitchen after everyone else had left or gone off to try to sleep. Snow had flung itself like sand against the window. They had a drink. They talked. They said nothing for long stretches. When it was very dark, she got up to leave, and he got up to walk her home. They put their hands on each other's faces, and looked at each other. They each wept, then, without making a sound. She put her fingertips to a pulsing vein on the side of his smooth neck, and she thought, This. *We could go forward with this.*

It was the last time she ever saw him cry, though he was close to it when their first child was born and, again, when his mother died. During their many years together, she had sensed always that he kept steady by fixing his gaze at a point on the horizon. That point, in its essence, was his idea of his brother Aidan, his idea of what Aidan would do in a given circumstance. He had behaved, in the large and the small, as he felt Aidan might have. For all these decades. And in the process, he had laid down layers of what might be called trust, or even faith, in a larger order of justice than the human mind could easily apprehend.

Now, though, it could all fly apart and be wrecked. That's one terror of old age, Rosalind thought. There isn't time for repairs, for rebuilding. Neil now could reach the end of his life with the terrible sense that all his gestures of trust in it had been ludicrous.

It was all being decided right now. As they had sat, just hours ago, in their sunlit breakfast nook eating bran muffins and sharing the paper, something had already been put in motion. Perhaps the Valentine girl, sleepy-eyed, had been eating her Rice Krispies at the same time, while her mother still slept. Then she had left the house with her skateboard under her arm, her mother in a dream, and she and Neil had moved toward each other blindly, on strings.

The late-afternoon slant of the sunlight across the long prairie ignited anything that interrupted it. The center stripes of the road grew so sharp and white they seemed to click as they flew past. An old corral on a rise of land was a tangle of gold. Sometimes Rosalind's eyes filmed and then she'd blink furiously to clear them. A pickup passed her with a roar. She was getting tired. Seventy-eight wasn't a good age to weather this kind of day. Ten or so miles to the Four Corners Bar, where she'd wake up Neil for a Coke.

"Someone should notify the girl's father," Neil said suddenly. He seemed, almost, to be talking in his sleep. She gave him a sharp, interrogative look. His eyes were open. Rosalind felt a small infusion of panic. He knew perfectly well that Ronny Valentine was long gone. If he now thought otherwise, it was possible the events of this day had tipped him away from her and from his own rational mind. It was going to happen sometime, to one or the other of them. This might be the moment. She might be, from this moment on, the one who would reassure and remind and keep the facts straight. It would be a loneliness.

"Her father has disappeared, Neil," she said lightly. "You know that."

Neil rolled up his shirtsleeves and sat up straight, alert.

"Ronny Valentine? He's up on the Tower, is where he is," he said. "He works an old mine up there, and sells whatever he finds to some farmer who gives him food and so on."

"You're making this up," she said. "I don't know why you are, but I can tell you it isn't going to improve this situation to be passing around folk tales or idle talk or whatever it is you've heard."

"He lives up there," Neil said patiently. "Raeburn saw him when he was bird hunting."

Rosalind tried to read him. Did he really think he'd heard this news? Was he just trying to divert himself? Well, let him, she thought. By the end of the day he might have something quite terrible to deal with, so why not let him, right now, tell himself a story. That was her first instinct. Then the anger that had jumped onto her shoulder at odd moments all day was there again.

"I can't believe you didn't tell me this," Rosalind said. "I really can't believe it."

Neil thought for a few moments, as if he were reviewing the reasons he hadn't told her.

"I thought I had," he said simply. "I can actually hear myself telling you all this at some previous time, so I'm having trouble thinking that I didn't tell you."

"You didn't!" she said. "How can you say you told me?"

She drove into the lot of the Four Corners. Large shards of its sign lay scattered on the gravel. She turned off the car and sat for a moment with her hands in her lap. "And what made Raeburn so sure it was Valentine?"

Neil squinted. "Because I believe he said he was. And if I'm not mistaken, he asked how she was. The girl. His daughter. He's been worried about her ever since he left. Raeburn told him that she was just fine."

He folded his hands and dropped his head. "This was a few weeks ago, of course," he said. Then he bent forward, as if he was dizzy, and rested his forehead on the dash, taking deep shoulder-lifting breaths.

"It's time to eat something," Rosalind said, her hand on his back. "Just a sandwich or something. To tide us over."

The barmaid was a talker. When she wasn't talking to a customer, she was talking to the overhead TV. When she wasn't talking to the television, she was talking to her cell phone or to some entity that seemed to reside in the refrigerated well that held the bottled beers.

What she talked about to Rosalind and Neil, as they ate their hamburgers, was the ambulance that had broken down a few hours earlier out in the parking lot. A day drinker at the other end of the bar corrected her. It hadn't broken down, he said. It just had a flat tire.

The barmaid listened to him, one hand on a cocked hip. Her turquoise sweatpants and top were thin, like pajamas. Above her head, on a shelf, was a cow skull with American flags in the eye sockets.

"An ambulance with a flat tire?" Neil sounded incredulous and angry. "What do you mean it had a flat tire?" His voice had risen and he had pushed away his half-eaten meal.

"I mean it had a flat tire," the barmaid said lightly. She was middle-aged but moved as if she were younger. The lenses in her glasses were an odd greenish tint. "What's to explain about a flat tire?"

"Well, what did they do with the patient?" Neil said. He was standing, retrieving bills from his wallet. Rosalind took a last quick bite of her own burger.

"They lifted her out on her stretcher and put her in the shade. Her mother was with her. She was in a coma, I believe. The girl. Wasn't she in a coma, Ty?"

The man at the end of the bar shrugged elaborately. "Maybe already dead," he said.

"No," said the barmaid. "Not dead."

"In the shade!" Neil shouted. "Did no one have the decency to bring her inside? The only building for miles and you can't even bring her inside?"

Rosalind took his arm and tried to steer him away from the counter, toward the door. He shook her off roughly.

"Settle down, sir," the barmaid said. "Her mother didn't want her brought inside. They put her in the shade. It took a few minutes, max, and they were on their way."

"Unbelievable," Neil said loudly, scanning the room for verification. The man at the end of the bar studied the ceiling, then moved off to sit himself at the Keno machine. A couple of young guys across the empty room kept playing pool.

Neil slammed the money for the hamburgers down and hissed through his teeth. Rosalind took his arm again, firmly, and steered him outside. She could feel his muscles quivering.

"Have a good one," the barmaid said.

Rosalind put Neil in the car. She started it.

"Are we going on?" she asked him. "Is it maybe a better idea to go back home?"

He peered ahead through the window, hands again on the dash. She looked hard at him. He wore his tweed driving cap and his unruly eyebrows jutted beneath the brim. His eyes moved back and forth across the landscape, the grasslands tilting up to the charcoal mountains, as if he were trying furiously to determine his and Rosalind's position.

He blinked rapidly. He bent over to check the fuel gauge. He stared at it. Then he sat back, as if he'd got the information he needed, and he said it was time to go; they should keep going. With any luck they'd be there by dark.

EIGHT

<hr>

2003
Missoula

THE LITTLE CITY HAD APPEARED AT the end of a trip that seemed, to Roland Taliaferro, very long. He and Charlie and the girlfriend, driving from California, had seemed to move up a shallow incline over a period of days. At the bottom of the hill were freeways and the odd palm tree and Raquel waving sadly from the nurse's station. Behind her, behind the fanning trees and the whirring river of cars, were the industrious white-tipped waves of the Pacific. All of it grew small and disappeared as they climbed, though you could hear the tiny whine of it for a long time. Roland studied his hand as they drove, spreading his old fingers so they would look victorious like the palms. He pressed his fingertips to the dashboard and studied the faint marks they left.

At the top of the long hill was a valley ringed with shiny mountains. They crossed a river on a concrete bridge with people walking down both sides. Charlie told him that he, Roland, might have walked along that bridge when he lived here during his college years. And did he remember doing that? Roland nodded solemnly. It was the quickest way to make people stop asking questions. They turned here, turned there, and then they pulled up to the new place, and the moving-in business began. He had a room with an attached bath and windows that looked out upon the mountains and, to the side, a hospital made of glowing blond bricks.

Charlie took him for a drive around the town, pointing out the landmarks he would surely remember: the spire of the Catholic church, the Greek Revival courthouse, the bell tower on the university campus, a Deco building that used to be the grand hotel, a turreted one that used to be a bank. There it all was, producing in Roland a series of sharp, wild jolts. He was back, and the town where he had gone to college continued busily on. It was quiet, though, compared with California's murky roar of engines and cooling systems and coded airborne information. Here there were sounds, but they were separate and buoyant, like children raising their voices with the right answer.

Charlie called the new place rehab and said Roland would be there for several weeks minimum. He had to learn some new things about balance and tasks and skills, he said. And then he could go to an assisted-living facility across town. Charlie had one picked out, a nice new one called Mallard Run. But Roland couldn't have another bad fall, he warned. Another hit to the head could kill him.

After he was settled in, Charlie wheeled him out to the common room and parked him next to a white-haired man who was sleeping on his hand. He wore a glossy black jacket embroidered with a dragon.

"These feet of yours are ice cold," said a kneeling aide who was trying to wriggle Roland's gnarled, bluish toes into a large sheepskin slipper. "You'll want to keep those toes from dropping off on the floor."

Roland studied her. She looked rosy and plump like Raquel, and this one wore silver rings on every digit but her thumbs.

"I don't want my body burned up," Roland told her.

She shook her head, rocking her long turquoise earrings. "You don't like these furry things your son went out and got for you? They make your feet too hot? Just say so, sir. Just give me a nod." Roland said nothing, did nothing. She sat back on her heels and peered inside one. Then she circled Roland's ankle with her warm hand and managed to work his foot, a little at a time, into the woolly fleece.

Down in California, on his very best days, Roland had always tried to make a pass at Raquel and he wondered now if he owed the same to this new person. Unless she was too tired or busy to muster it, Raquel had always flown into high dudgeon at his advances, knowing it would please him. His motives were similarly charitable. A hand on her thigh, an ardent gaze at her breasts, a double entendre if he could manage it, which was hardly ever anymore—they were his way of thanking her for her chatty patience with his troublesome old body and his mind that, among other fissures and failures, sometimes made the wrong words come out of his mouth when he tried to speak of ordinary things. Especially since his fall.

He would intend to ask for toast, or another blanket, or something for his acid reflux—ordinary maintenance situations—but he couldn't make his mind ship the correct instructions to his mouth. Something weird would come out, often just a single word, but sometimes entire wrong phrases. "I'd like a glass of heaven-in-all-its-glory," he'd said that morning, trying to obtain a simple container of water to rinse his dentures. Trying again, he'd said, "Bring me some glass tacks."

He knew perfectly well when he'd reached the far edge of the verbal universe. It was lonely out there and so filled with fury that all he could do, on behalf of himself and everyone else, was to go immediately to sleep.

They were adjusting his medications again, to help him recover from the fall. And now something new was happening with the words. His trivial thoughts still came out garbled, but when he wanted to say something important, he was finding the accurate words. "I don't want my body burned up." That was not what this girl thought it was: a messed-up way of saying that the slippers were too heavy and hot. It was a phrase that had popped into his mind the minute they'd driven into the city and he had seen the late-day sun rocket off the spire of the Catholic church. He said the words aloud because he was hoping that the sound of them in a room with other people would help him fill in a picture that had been taking shape since he'd left California.

They were his own words. That was certain. And he had said them, many years ago, to another agent. The room where they'd talked had a high ceiling and it smelled like tobacco and wet wool. Rain threw itself against a dirty window. They were talking about the war and about war work in South America. They were talking, specifically, about their friend Aidan Tierney, who had returned from Argentina gaunt and incontinent and fiery-eyed. He'd done something, or something had been done to him, and now his body was burned up.

Or had it been an actual conversation? Roland acknowledged the possibility that portions of his ongoing memories were things he had seen or heard in movies. For weeks, getting off the booze, he'd done nothing but watch videos. Five and six a day. There were many he had mentally stored for later retrieval. His mind worked that way. It filed things systematically and comprehensively, even when he was addled in certain other respects.

The movie that came to him now didn't have a title that he could remember. It had swishing lawn sprinklers in an early California that still had small spaces of silence in it, which was where they put the sprinklers. A man about his age tap-danced as he sold bottles of solvent door-to-door, then died in bed while his blond daughter in the next room studied herself in a mirror.

Roland gazed across the room at Charlie, who had bent his face close to the receptionist's, apparently to confide something to her, probably about the great pains he took with his difficult old father.

In the movie with the sprinklers, the unlikeliest fellow, a Caspar Milquetoast sort of fellow, kicked a little kid who was tormenting him. Kicked him until blood spurted out of his mouth. Roland clenched his eyes against that scene and wiggled his toes around in the slippers. They felt comforted. They felt as if they were in a musical, which he liked the idea of but could never watch all the way through because steady exuberance exhausted him and always had.

There were a lot of spy movies in his head. The one he kept coming back to was about a young American who'd been sent somewhere in South America to ferret out Nazis and Nazi sympathizers. As it opened, the American stood on the iron balcony of his apartment and listened to heavy church bells as he smoked a cigarette and pondered his next move. He'd been sent by the Old Man himself. In a flashback, the camera showed only the back of the Old Man's neck, but there was no mistaking that bulldog stance, the rat-a-tat delivery, the blunt fingers chopping the air.

The South American city was full of churches and plazas and women with taunting dark eyes. Heat made the light ripple like the huge river that ran through the city, its banks lined with stockyards and abattoirs. The women with the dark eyes pressed their noses to linen handkerchiefs and waved their drivers to speed on.

There was a scene in which the young spy rode in a long car to the countryside where a German industrialist had a magnificent *estancia*. The car passed horsemen in ponchos going to market, baskets roped to their high-cantled saddles and filled with figs and peaches. Leather-covered milk cans hung from the horses, and half-draped cages filled with whirring birds. At the *estancia,* the guests rode high-headed horses that pranced sideways, the silver medallions on the bridles and stirrups flashing in the morning sun, and the American was the best rider of them all.

Much later, back near the city, the American crawled on his stomach through a cold swamp toward some sort of farm. Antennas pushed like tentacles from the buildings, above the tops of the slick gray trees. Gray rain poured down. He shivered and inched forward. There was the sound of air babble. German voices, faintly, in scraps, transmitting.

Boots then, tall boots, and a hand on the American's neck. They had got him, and they threw him in a bare cell. The men with the big boots came in and there was a jagged tussle and a muffled animal cry.

Roland couldn't remember much about the rest, except that it involved, like most spy movies did, some kind of disastrous and dangerous betrayal.

The movie seemed linked in some way to the day he had come home to find an intruder in his house in Bakersfield. His neighbor had dropped him off after they had gone somewhere, perhaps to an actual movie theater, and he had turned around from hanging up his jacket to find a doper asleep on his couch. The guy was young, maybe still a teenager, and he stank of something chemical, and when he jumped up from the couch, it was as if he'd been ejected from the cushions. And then he stood there, eyes squinted, arms out to his sides as if he were walking a fence rail.

Roland didn't see a weapon on the teenager, so he turned quickly to the closet and retrieved his loaded .22 from beneath his golf caps. When he turned again, the boy was leaping at him through the air, and so he shot him in the thigh. The next thing he did was walk coolly to the phone and dial 911, and they took the burglar off screeching and bleeding to get him sewn up.

It turned out that Roland had accidentally left the patio door unlocked, but the intruder had failed to execute a theft because whatever substance he'd been taking had kept him up for a week straight and then, unfortunately for him, had dropped him straight into oblivion.

After the boy was treated at the hospital, they took him to a jail cell to await arraignment. And shouldn't that have been the end of the story? In a sane world, that would have been the end of the story.

As it turned out, the incident had a disastrous outcome. Instead of confirming his son and few friends in the idea that Roland could still take care of himself, they twisted it around so that the mere presence of the doper on the couch became, ipso facto, proof that Roland was too vulnerable living alone. That's when it all started, the gradual process of his eventual incarceration. Because they'd failed to trust him, he experienced high levels of stress, which produced inroads on his health, which produced various wrongheaded and drug-riddled treatments, which produced occasional instances of confusion, which produced skyrocketing drug bills and other expenses and insurance forms, which produced more confusion and the so-called necessity to sell his house. Well, it wasn't hard to connect the dots.

He felt still, always, deeply aggrieved by all of it. He felt that the man in the cell had been released, and he had been stuck in his place. Betrayal would not be too strong a word.

Charlie was still chatting up the pretty young woman at the computer. It seemed to Roland that his son had been talking to her for hours, so he signaled to him to come over. Charlie seemed not to see him. Then he did and he made a be-patient gesture with his hand, as if he were patting the head of a child.

The aide with the warm hands had asked him something, but he didn't remember the question. She stood before him with her shiny hair and her smile, waiting for his reply.

"He was in that cell," Roland told her. But he couldn't go on. He swallowed hard.

"Who was in a cell, Mr. Furry New Slippers?" she said. "Who was incarcerated that you know about?"

"A man," Roland told her. "A man I shot once."

PART 2

NINE

1927
North of Neva

THERE WAS A GREAT QUIET UP there near the Sweet Grass Hills, not an absence of sound but the presence of the sounds that human agendas obscure.

The egg-colored hospital where Opal nursed had just twelve beds. Around it an aggressive glittering light flung itself across the treelessness and the long spaces where people weren't. Bird shadows on the spaces. Cloud shadows like boats cut adrift. Sometimes a train, coming in from the far distance with its pitch pipe cry.

The only way to keep yourself from evaporating in that bright and windy emptiness was to insist upon something for yourself, insist long enough that a chafing commenced between whatever you might be and whatever else there was, and then you felt the friction and you felt yourself to be there.

Thus the lilac bush, forever untrimmed, outside the room with the cot where Opal lived. Attached to the hospital kitchen, the room had a small dresser, a wood stove, the cot, a splintery clothes tree, and nothing else. The overgrown lilac covered the single window, and when it was in bloom, it shattered the light into pale blotches that quivered across the floor. This she didn't mind. Leafless,

though, the dark arms reached at her and gave her the old night-
mares and she wanted it cut back; she wanted it gone. Every week a
man who did odd jobs for Doctor was supposed to come and trim
it back so it wasn't so choking. Every week he failed to show, and
when Opal was gauzy from long hours and aloneness, she became
convinced that the man didn't exist at all and his anticipated appearance with his long trimming shears was a joke among the
townspeople, the seventy or eighty of them, at her expense.

Let them have their fun.

Let them think about their practical joking when she was tending them in a hospital bed, when it was up to her to make the
middle-of-the-night decisions about their treatment. When it was
up to her to keep the germs at bay, their wounds clean, their fevers
down. To keep them from dying of fright, as some had done during the Spanish flu, their faces her own face in the parlor mirror the
day she'd left the Indiana farm. If she wasn't vigilant during those
long hours when Doctor wasn't there, then no one was going to
be vigilant.

Let them think about that when they made their comments
about a lilac-clipping handyman who didn't exist.

She appreciated the indoors part: the hospital routine, its unvarying ritual. Appreciated it because she had come close to total
evaporation, and this miniature replica of a real hospital in a real
town had pulled her back into a human shape. She lived now in the
anteroom of the gone life, and still needed official exit papers.

She was a real nurse, thirty-one years old—the city-trained
nurse in pin-striped dress and apron, in stiff-winged hat. The only
real nurse, though they sometimes called in a farm girl to watch the
patients at night, and if most of the beds were full, Valerie Ann,
Doctor's wife, came down.

Opal helped Doctor in everything. He had scientific enthusi-
asms and she assisted him in the experiments he conducted after he
treated patients and performed surgery, or when the hospital was
empty and there was no one to treat.

When he was a very young man, an older cousin had taken
him to Edison's show in New York, and he had since been enthralled

with the Roentgen rays. He had a bookshelf full of the early articles and reports: pamphlets with titles like *The Trail of Invisible Light, How to Photograph and See Through Opaque Bodies, The Old Light and the New, The Effect of Roentgen Rays on the Blind.* He had made his own Crooke's tube and used it to make shadow pictures of every condition in which the real trouble resided beneath the body's surface. It was immoral, he now believed, to perform surgery without first making a shadow map of the patient's "unknown country," as he liked to put it.

He enlisted Opal in a variety of investigations involving X-rays of the body and of other entities such as shotguns and Valerie Ann's diamond ring. Sometimes he used his fluoroscope to view an animal as it lived. Painless vivisection. Other times he made X-ray photographs, which he pinned to the wall of the lab. In virtually all of them, Opal's skeletal hand was visible, holding Valerie Ann's diamond, for instance, between thumb and forefinger.

Sometimes Doctor would become so enthralled he would spend hours at it and Opal would go to her room with a hand that prickled from the rays.

The first time she saw her hand bones, she stayed awake all night, holding herself against a terror that minced at her like lake waves. What frightened her the most was not the bones but the shadow of her mother's signet ring that she wore on her right hand, the way it seemed to hover around the bone, resting on air.

Doctor was an optimistic, curious man. Sometimes he wore a straw boater and a bow tie to the hospital, of a piece with his springy walk, cat-green eyes, and his eyebrows that looked continually surprised. Opal was used to more solemnity in a physician, something more fateful and priestly, but she found over time that he gave off some sort of energizing rays himself. They produced a feeling in others that was, if not hope, a lesser degree of wariness or despair.

His verve extended to analysis of his own diagnostic lapses, and he pored over his X-rays for shadows whose significance he'd missed. If he operated on someone whose ailment was a mystery to him, and discovered a cancer, say, then he'd go back to the X-ray plates and reexamine them for the clues. What did the X-ray show at the location of the cancer? He'd study the look of the interior cloud so that when he saw it again in another patient, he knew what he was likely to be looking at and could diagnose with some confidence. It was a continual circling back to decode the predictions implicit in the images. He called it retrospectoscopy and said it was an art.

There was a day. Early September and hot. Lindbergh, on his hero's tour, would fly over the Sweet Grass Hills, late morning, on his way from Glacier Park to points east and south. Directly over the mountains and then the town, and maybe he would drop down to buzz the scatter of buildings, the seventy or eighty residents, before he looped up to disappear.

Opal had no intention of watching any of it. She avoided airplanes and the thought of airplanes.

Two boys rode into town on a single horse. The rider led a second horse. The smaller boy sat behind the larger one with his hands on the bigger boy's shoulders. He had a bruised face, an egg above his eye. He looked sunburned and a little stunned.

Off in the distance, a drone. The boys seemed to click awake. They stopped the horses and squinted in the direction of the noise. Their faces said they heard what all the ballyhooing papers had described: the sound of a wire stretched between them and the rest of the world, the sound of aloneness and audacity moving over the fogged Atlantic with an insouciance that bordered on the comic. Hadn't he dipped down, at the end, to call a question to a French fishing boat? "Is this the way to Ireland?" he'd shouted, roaring along ten feet above the whitecaps. Hadn't he yelled that? Outlandish goals, indisputable triumph, the winged life—wasn't it, for these watchers, the best sort of dream?

They all ran into the streets to crane their necks. The plane stayed high and small, but the town cheered anyway. Perhaps Lucky didn't notice them. Perhaps he was reading his flight logs and didn't take note of this particular scramble of buildings, the egg-colored hospital, the little town—all eyes. Then the plane tipped its wings and the cheers flew skyward again.

Opal began to push through them to go inside the hospital. Her heart thudded in her ears. The crowd made her slow.

Now the boy with the bruised face stood up on the back of the horse, his hands for balance on the larger boy's head. If his foolish head wasn't already broken, he was in danger of breaking it now. Furious, pushing through the people, she called out to him to quit stunting. She shook her finger at him. He called back something disrespectful that she couldn't hear. A taunting yipping sound, like something untamed.

Inside the hospital, Opal rested the side of her face against the cool calcimined wall. She listened to the noise, the cheers, then the sound of the machine becoming a humming dot on the horizon before it disappeared.

She consulted her watch and saw that she was behind on her rounds, and would be all day. She had a feeling of being tricked. Also, the lilac man should have been at work several hours ago. She walked quickly outside to check. No evidence of him. Soon the branches would be bare of leaves and closing in. She cracked off one of the smaller branches of the lilac and threw it on the ground. She pulled off another. One of the semiwild dogs trotted by, studying her over its shoulder. She lifted the branch and the dog snarled and growled and lowered its hips like a hyena.

In the evening, after rounds, she briefed the farm girl and took a walk. In Doctor's window, the pretty wife Valerie Ann and two boys sat around the table in a warm light. They were the boys who had ridden into town this morning, the smaller one climbing to his feet atop the horse. He had a bandage now. They were all laughing and alive as Valerie Ann, her blond hair in a long braid, drew something in the air with her hands. The older boy had his arm casually over the younger boy's shoulder. Opal felt like an urchin at a store window and paused in her walk to hate them all for doing that to her.

Back at the hospital, a truck rumbled at the door and the driver waved her over. He and another man sat in the front with something between them mummied in a blanket. It turned out to be a slim young man, a boy almost, and he was broken, bleeding, and unconscious. The blanket had large irregular patches of fresh blood. She directed them briskly inside and sent the helper for Doctor.

The men who brought in the beat-up boy were grim and rather young themselves. They were a rancher's son from up north, Frank Mix, and the ranch foreman, Glen Phillips.

"This boy got himself in over his head," Frank Mix said. The man Glen said nothing; wouldn't even look at her, just grimly did the carrying, the listening. "This boy is my brother and he got himself into a fight he couldn't finish," Mix said.

Doctor went outside with them to talk, and they all got down on their heels and some kind of serious something got said, the man Glen gazing off to the side.

"Well," Doctor said later that night, as he adjusted one of the boy's splints. "He'll wake or he won't. And if he wakes, he can be a freak or he can straighten out."

He lay there on the high white bed for weeks. She saw by the chart that he marked his twentieth birthday in that bed. Infection set in, intensifying the head injury, and it didn't look good. Something about his young silence was deeply familiar to her. She stayed at his bedside, hour after hour, calmly urging him to stay the course, patting cool compresses on his smooth brown forehead. Sometimes she sat by him late into the night and early morning, and she murmured to him stories she had heard of others who had survived physical damage and mental removal, had come back bony and alert to take up their place in the ranks of the sentient.

For that long time, he didn't respond, though she began to detect a relaxation of his facial muscles when she spoke, a clenching of them when she applied the hot poultices to draw out infection.

She took those responses as evidence of interest and receptivity, and then of a compatibility between them that was so innate it existed apart from wordlessness and surface damage. After a few weeks, he would sometimes open his eyes, say a few words, then sink back. "Glen," he said first. Then, "Glen. You listen." His eyes fluttered open and he stared ardently at her, then slept again.

She began to talk to him in those early morning hours when he seemed most unconscious. At first she recounted small things from her life on the Indiana farm: the mailman's daughter with red braids to her hips; the antics of her dog Stormy, who was born during a tornado. She told him about the rigors of nursing school, about the baby who died in her arms. "Not mine," she assured the unresponding boy. "In the city hospital. When I was training."

One night she told the sleeping boy about the day the biplane, canvas and wood, had come roaring out of the sky, toward their farm, on its way to Tell City. How she had stood at the window, laughing with happiness at it and at the prospect of the daredeviltry they'd all see at the fairgrounds in the morning—the loops and death dives and ocean rolls. How something in her laugh had made the cloth of her blouse feel too thin and when she turned around, her uncle was looking at her as if she'd finally said yes. Her mother sat deaf in her chair, eyes on a letter from her husband, who was about to be dead of an infection in an army tent in France.

Opal had run outside to feel high and audacious like the airplane, and she saw immediately that it was too low. There was the barn—the grainy light-shot barn, her refuge—and there was the airplane, flying toward it. She felt the shadow thrown by its wings. Her blue mare was in the barn, tied to its stall. Her blue mare and the cat, Bailey, who sometimes slept on the mare's back.

There was a cough and a lurch and terrible long silence. She saw the pilot throw his arms across his face inside the silence. And the plane dove into the top of the barn and made it a cloud of fire.

It burned silently in the memory, roared without sound, and the ashes of everything—her pony, the cat's blanket, her dying father—fell onto her thin white blouse and when she brushed at them, there was a smear.

She told all this to the boy in the bed.

By the time young Porter Mix was fully awake and the fever had broken, she had told him everything. It had been emptied into him. And he, too, as he spoke more and more—in fragments, but ever more scrutable—had, by the time he was fully present, given her his impossible situation: the ranch foreman, Glen; all the horrible aftermath; certain torment if he stayed and certain heartbreak if he left; his cousin's offer of a partnership in a combination furniture store and mortuary in Lewistown; his desperation for an ordinary, calm life.

Then he was ready to leave, pale and thin and wild-eyed, but alert and on the mend. She felt that they'd crossed a lake in the same rowboat, a lake that covered an entire city they'd constructed themselves. His parents approached the little hospital in the Ford, a golden cloud of dust that was to take him back to the ranch. She and Porter sat on the white bed together and watched them draw close, and stop.

"Porter Mix," Opal said. "I think we should marry, and move."

TEN

1927
Butte

BEFORE DAWN ON THE DAY THE hero was due, Roland Taliaferro and his father, Nick, walked together down Mineral Street to the Jack Club. They wore old sweaters against the chill and walked without speaking. It was the quietest time of the day, after the last racket of the night and well before the mine whistles at eight. Only now did the little city abate and the streets breathe easy before they filled again with the clatter and bray of the day. Though always, in the noise or in the brief silence, there lived the possibility of the worst sound of all, a sudden shriek of the mine sirens when something bad had happened down there. And then the women would come flying out of the houses and shanties to mill around the gate, shawls over their heads, wailing, or silent and rocking.

For Roland Taliaferro, age thirteen, daylight usually meant the impending furies of the schoolyard, the gangs, the pantsings, the blows, and the taunts—all of it the codified mimicry of, and rehearsal for, their adult lives ahead. But today was different.

A sleepy-eyed paperboy shuffled past, his canvas bag hanging to his knees, two ringworm circles on his burred red head. Lights were on in the houses, cool sparkles on all the gray hills, as the next shift drank their coffee and their wives wrapped lunches in waxed paper. Some of the men sat on their front steps or the broken walls along their streets, breathing in cool air, reminding themselves of it before they stepped into the cages that took them to the stifling dark corridors below.

Roland slowed his step to his father's. He could feel himself trying to push his way into this day of such extravagant promise, trying to get this first dull part behind him. Here was a day that held Lindbergh and his valiant silver plane. Roland's father walked even more slowly than usual. He had risen wheezing and pale, and hadn't even bothered to smooth down his peppery shock of hair with a handful of water. He looked newly amazed at what his lungs were doing to him, and Roland knew enough not to talk. He felt more uneasy than usual with the old man because he had made one of his rare attempts to initiate a conversation with him the night before, and it hadn't worked. Nick had barked a curt response, then opted out. And yet it was Roland who felt guilty now, as if he had, by his overture, stolen his father's energy and made him unusually unfit for this new day.

He had tried to talk about fingerprinting. He wanted his father to know about the FBI's new repository of fingerprints, about science and systems, about the existence of coolheaded methods of dealing with violence and anonymous random evil. Roland loved the idea that each human had his own unreplicated arrangement of whorls and grooves, and that you left your signature on everything you touched. For a while, newly in love with the idea, he had gone around touching things he wanted to possess: the fender of a rich man's car; the doorknob after a beautiful girl had passed through (his fingerprint atop hers, the swirls intermingling); the money in the Jack Club till; Ernie Koski's baseball glove. He left his quiet marks everywhere.

He thought, too, about falling out of the world the way so many did; how the body of a hobo could be found and you'd never know who it was; the way you could live a life and then blip out so utterly from the record. But if everyone's fingerprints were recorded somewhere, a system could be devised to match dead anonymous people against those files and determine who they had been. Most exciting were the criminal applications. Police in some of the big cities were already starting to solve crimes by matching prints on weapons to the fingertips of suspects. You left your mark wherever you went.

Roland liked the idea that it might be possible, working backward from the crimes to the fingerprints, to come up with a kind of predominant criminal pattern. You learned to know, by the outcomes, what predictors you had been looking at. Did all cold-blooded murderers, for instance, have similar whorls? Could you stop disasters before they happened?

"Maybe you can stop some disasters before they happen, but not by pressing pinkies on ink pads," his father had said, his voice cold as the moon. "You're pathetic if you think it's that easy," he had added, looking straight at his son. Always, the gratuitous twist. Then the old man had left the table to cough into his rag, and Roland's mother had turned grim and teary, and his sister Petey had left the house in a new red coat she'd got somewhere—she wasn't saying.

Roland would have liked to have felt a simple, clean hatred of his father, but he didn't. He was burdened with flashes of empathy. He believed he understood the source of his father's griefs and rages. Young as he was, he could imagine how it was down there in tunnels filled with the gagging dust from dry drills. Years down there in the clanging heat and the dark, disaster always a moment away. He even dreamed moments of his father's life, especially that early terrible day when his best friend and partner at the Mountain Con mine was killed when a hoist man failed to cut off the engine in time, and the ascending cage passed the surface, forgot the surface, and flew upward into the sheaves. Where it threw the man out and down, a thousand feet to the sump at the bottom of the shaft. A human pulp with a few bones sticking out. That's what was left of Romeo Verdi, age twenty-four, late of Palermo.

The hoist engineer, a Latvian and rumored Wobbly, had got a visit from the Palmer boys the night before to be told he was getting deported in a week. He'd been confused and distracted at work—hadn't deciphered the shouted English in time—and he got on a ship a week later with his crying, bedraggled family feeling himself a failure and a murderer for life.

That's how it had started out for Roland's father. That and the Wobbly Frank Little swinging from a rope and the Speculator fire sending its terrible smoke and gases down the shafts and the drifts to topple all those young men in their tracks. That was 1917, a year of local and global cataclysms, the year Roland was only three.

Their boots squeaked. They stepped over a drunk sleeping it off against a low stone wall; stepped into the Jack, where a couple of customers slept on their arms and a woman in the corner, in a booth, laughed sweetly at someone they couldn't see. The Greek owner, Yannis, had hired Roland's father when he'd heard that the company had nothing for him. Nick and Yannis were old friends, had both been friends of the dead Sicilian, and had in the circumstances of his death the locus of a mutual understanding of the nature of rage.

In the Greek's case, the rage hadn't physically consumed him, as Roland felt it had consumed his father. Gnawed at him, shut him down, turned him to ash. Though the old man's arms were still ropey and muscled as he plunged them into the sudsy water to wash glasses. First he washed glasses and put them up on the shelf. Then he dealt quietly with the bootlegger who came around with a wagon full of milk jugs just after six. Then he mopped the floor slowly, moving at his own pace, stopping to take slow, scraping breaths. It was Yannis who had suggested that Roland work alongside his father, the expectation being that Roland would do the whole job himself on mornings when his father wasn't up to it.

Old Seamus Reilly sat at the lunch counter, his mangy dog sleeping at his feet. He spent most of his day and night at the Jack because he was afraid to sleep, convinced that dynamite gas would get to him and steal off with his life if it found him unconscious and alone. He drank for courage, and the drink gradually bled off all his courage, and so he drank more, feeling the lack. Every year, on Christmas Eve, he recited the long last paragraph of Mr. James Joyce's story "The Dead" so soulfully and beautifully that the listeners had to briefly rearrange their idea of him to an uncomfortable degree, and so they let him finish—*His soul swooned slowly as he heard the snow falling faintly through the universe and faintly falling, like the descent of their last end, upon all the living and the dead*—and then they laughed. Laughed at him and bought him a drink in order to bring back his familiar discountable self.

Roland's father washed the glasses, the wings on his back working. Roland ran the filthy mop over the floorboards. The smells of pasty dough and eternal mutton stew floated damply from the kitchen.

Nick Taliaferro began to cough, close-eyed. He worked faster. From the back, he looked very old. He dipped the glasses in the gray water and placed them wet on the papered shelf. Yannis left. Roland finished his mopping and noticed that some of the floorboards had dried with long white streaks on them. He went for a fresh bucket of water, but his father, still coughing, signaled that it was enough. It was all enough. It was time to go.

As an apology for the night before, Nick spoke very calmly when he caught his breath. "Go see your flyer," he said to his son. "It's a big day. Go see what the hero looks like." He himself had no intention of joining the hubbub.

They left the Jack together. Roland set off toward the flats at the bottom of the terraced hills, where the crowd would gather to watch for the plane. His father walked the other direction, very slowly, up the crooked road. At one point he stopped to let himself down on some broken stoop steps. He saw that Roland had stopped to watch him and he batted the air, sending the boy on his way.

Roland stopped for a moment and thought. He circled the block, went down the alley and inside the back door of the Jack. He refilled the bucket and remopped the floor. He filled the sink, begging extra hot water from the cook, and carefully rewashed all the glasses. Seamus Reilly smoked a pipe and watched the boy as he held each glass up to the light to examine it for smudges and fingerprints. Reilly had a little glitter to him, as if he were watching a secret.

When he was done, Roland took delivery from the bootlegger,

who was late. He slipped one of the bottles into his rucksack to stash in his secret place. Every couple of weeks he did this, and had since he was twelve. When something bad happened, or he was afraid, or frightened, or saddled with his old man's despair, he drank some. Not much. Just enough to calm him and lift him. He thought of it as his tonic, his medicine. It gave him distance and perspective, made the world and its troubles seem the way they would from an airplane. Small, busy, far away.

The *Spirit of Saint Louis* was supposed to be silver, to sparkle in the sunlight, but there was always a haze of smoke here, a brown fog of it, so there was no gleam. The Viking of the air dropped to the city in a small, dull, unlit-up machine. But the crowd cheered ecstatically and threw hats into the smudged sky, and when he stepped out to be a hero for them, he carried, Roland thought, his own shine. He was tall and long limbed and blond. His clothes were so clean they gave off a light. Even his teeth did.

His movements were calm and economical. He tipped his head graciously to the dark and blocky welcome committee, and they pumped his gloved hand. He wore an expression of reserve and politesse, though he didn't seem to be sealing himself off from the heat and excitement, the yips and shouts and banners and oompahs, so much as he breathed cooler, clearer air as a fact of his nature.

Roland wondered if Lindbergh had ever been a boy. He believed that he himself, though only thirteen, had never been a boy. He could not lose himself in the swim of a day, a moment, the way a boy was supposed to. Not even at this moment, which he thought he'd been yearning for. Not even a little drunk, as he was. Carefully drunk, and all he could do was measure and evaluate. How did the cool golden hero stack up against these people, this place? Why was Roland so embarrassed for everyone who milled around the man, including himself? It had something to do with the way the flyer seemed to stand apart from chaos, from dirt and dimness, from the extravagant danger and striving of this place, a place where disaster lived in the pauses, waiting to fly down.

His hair ruffling in a breeze, Lindbergh gave a speech about his vision of the aeronautics future. Every American city would have an airport, he said. Mail would travel by air. Ordinary people would move from place to place in airplanes, as easily as they do now in automobiles. The day of the unsafe airplane was fast receding. Commercial aviation would be a fact of life—it would!—and it was up to America to lead the way. This brought indulgent cheers and more hat throwing. It was another reason to love him, that he could posit the fantastic with such clear-eyed trust in the future. Was there anything in store for him that he couldn't imagine?

After Lindbergh had been escorted off the field to a banquet with a thousand mucketies, Roland and his friends Dexter and Hugh hung around talking to the men who would refuel and examine the plane before the tour resumed. One of the mechanics, a young guy with a single front tooth and a red scarf like a pirate's around his head, let the boys come close to the plane if they didn't touch it. They could walk around it quietly, and Hugh, a natural draftsman who carried paper and a pencil with him always, could draw it if he wanted to. Roland managed, during the drawing, to move closer to the plane's silver body, and at the moment when everyone was briefly distracted by a vicious dogfight halfway across the park, he pressed two fingertips to the cool metal.

When Roland finally walked through the door, his mother had cleared the supper dishes. She caught his eye in a warning, but he couldn't see where the danger might come from. His father read the newspaper. Petey lay on the floor on her stomach, hands folded, skinny legs scissoring, listening to the radio so raptly she seemed to be praying. The pages of the newspaper didn't turn. Roland looked around curiously. He cleared his throat to tell them about Lindbergh, though of course his sister and mother had been somewhere in the enormous crowd. They wouldn't have missed that. What he would tell them about was the plane itself, up close.

"Had a chat with Reilly," his father said, lowering the newspaper. "He's a snitch, you know. Why do you think no one speaks to him?"

"Where?" Roland said, disoriented.

"Went back down there when everybody was worshipping Lindbergh, and there was Reilly, of course, bolted to his stool, his foot on the head of that mangy dog."

Now it was coming, whatever it was. Roland touched the door frame for ballast.

"He said you appeared to have a problem with the quality of my work," Nick said. His voice was very low and very cold. He stood up. He wore old carpet slippers. His T-shirt was stained. A quaver rocked him. He steadied himself with one hand on the chair back.

"I don't have a problem with the quality of your work," Roland said. He detested the plaintive, conciliatory sound of his voice. "It's just, a lot of people would be coming in today after Lindbergh. It's just . . . the place, the glasses, I thought. I thought it was a big day and maybe we'd forgotten that there would be all those people, and you want . . ."

"What do you want?" his father almost whispered.

Roland closed his eyes. "Clean," he whispered back. "You want things, some things, to be clean."

The blow caught him under the chin, so that his teeth snapped down hard on his tongue and blood poured instantly from his open mouth onto the floor. His mother screamed. Petey blinked awake and shut off the radio and walked, coatless, straight out the front door.

In the night, his tongue swollen so large he felt he couldn't get a full breath, he lay awake in a state of icy fibrillation. A distant, almost convivial, voice in his head remarked that it had always thought hatred was hot, when it was actually a kind of sentient ice. Here it was in full, finally, and this is what it felt like. He finally drifted a little and as he did, he thought he heard a mosquito sound a long way away, the sound of a small silver plane climbing above the mine gallows, above the city, above the mountain ridges, and out. Then he could sleep.

The next morning, Hugh told him Lindbergh was up hunting

and fishing in a secret place the company had, up in the mountains with the mucketies. He was taking a break. The plane, of course, awaited his return.

Roland walked out that evening and found it. He was calm and drunk. It had begun to rain, a drizzle. A couple of guards played cards in a white tent a few yards from the machine. In the dirty twilight, the plane looked old. It looked as if it had been tethered there for a long time. Roland squinted. It seemed cobwebbed already.

One of the guards came out of the tent to piss luxuriously.

"Hey!" Roland called. "What's that plane doing here?" His voice sounded slurry through his huge, bruised lip, and his tongue hurt to form the words. The man buttoned up and moved toward him, peering through the gloom.

"I heard it taking off," Roland yelled, though the man was just a few yards away.

"What you heard was yourself bumping into someone's fist," the man said, not unkindly.

Rage engulfed him again, made him prickly ice. He scooped up a rock and in a single, fluid motion lobbed it at the wing of the plane. It missed. And now, to his relief, the long day was broken open. He was running. The man ran after him and in the first few seconds, Roland could almost feel fingers on his neck. Then the heavy feet fell back in a wake of gasping and curses, and when Roland darted into an alley and over a splintered wooden gate, through a ragged patch of dirt reeking of latrine, out the other side and into the rainy night, he knew he would stay uncaught.

ELEVEN

1939
Missoula

Smoke from the mountain fires crawled into the valley heat to give everything—the heavy-leaved maples, the smooth Hudson at the curb, Wendell Whitcomb careening past on his ridiculous bicycle—the malignant glow of a photo developed in chemicals gone bad. It was, this light, the hectic and doomy flush of tuberculosis, Opal Mix thought. Something in it of that. She had been shopping most of the afternoon and needed, now, to bring in the wash and tidy up the house. The bed sheets she lifted from the line smelled like Porter's clothes after a campout with his Scouts.

Wendell Whitcomb wobbled past again, pumping his huge bicycle like a high-stepping cartoon. He was quite small for his age, and the seat was too high for him to sit on without losing the pedals, and so he pumped. As he passed Opal at the clothesline, a wild boy's body inside a device, he managed somehow to lift a thin wrist from the handlebars and say something to it. Then he shot her a long look, filled with loathing.

"You watch your mouth," she called as he wobbled around the corner. "Perhaps your mother would like to know about your mouth."

Before he got the bicycle, Wendell had prowled the neighborhood on foot, cutting through yards, peering into windows, scribbling in a small notebook. You'd see him squat suddenly to stare at the dirt or the grass, and sometimes he stood on the sidewalk and yelled indecipherable accusations and commands at Opal and Porter. He called them fiends and public enemies. He ordered them to drop, and reach, and get their hands out where he could see them. On one occasion he actually clutched his chest and fell to the ground, where he rolled in the dirt like a person having a fit. Then he jumped to his feet and walked on, calm as you please. It was pathetic.

Opal had felt it her duty to alert Wendell's mother, a child herself by the name of Edna, to the boy's mental difficulties. The girl had been impregnated by a traveling salesman, so the story went. She was local, but her parents were dead and she had no obvious friends. Her shiftless brother, a good-looking wastrel who did odd jobs when he could get them, was the boy's only male relative, and his appearances were rare. The child needed a real father model. He needed an example of high-minded behavior, someone of a different caliber from Edna's brother or the men she dragged home from time to time for some sort of tawdry interlude. Older men, often, in frayed and shiny suits.

Porter had been more than willing to make contact with the boy. Twice, at least, he had tried to recruit the child into his Boy Scout pack. But the mother, a slutty little thing with eyes that looked right past yours when you spoke, refused to allow the boy to join. And so her son, quite possibly insane, ran amok.

Now he was back, and shouting. His reedy voice screamed that she had been found out. Opal turned in his direction, but couldn't see around the pile of sheets in her arms. "I know what you are!" the boy was shrieking. "You can't fool me, lady! I know what you both are."

She watched him, the linens heavy in her arms. He was a cockroach, skittering crazily through her clean life, and she wanted, at moments like this, to flatten him.

Inside the house, she sat for a moment at the dining room table, her chin on the smoky sheets. She was drenched. The heat and her erratic female humors joined forces several times a day to burn her up, then leave her a sodden rag.

There was a hush. The thick heat had pushed the day, the town, into such a stupor that all but the essentials of daily life— selling food, tending the ill, keeping the peace, preparing the dead—were muted or stalled. Her clubs and Porter's were dormant because it was August, and so the orienting rituals of social life had evaporated too. The Chamber, the Knights, the Shriners, the Legion, the Lions, the Scouts, Professional Women's, Matrix, Nile, the Tuberculosis Association, the Hoo Hoo Club—between the two of them they went to four or five meetings a week during every season but summer. And then August, and nothing.

Deaths increased in heat that went on for days, as this spell had. If Porter wasn't here soon, she'd walk over and help him finish up. He'd been suffering some sort of ague for a few days and would have liked to spend a Saturday in bed like any Joe Blow with chills and a bad stomach. But there were no weekends in the mortician's life.

He had three today: a young hobo with a bashed-in head; Priscilla Withers, dead of a stroke at ninety-one; and the premature Raynesford baby. As the county coroner, he'd had to spend some hours yesterday making a determination in the hobo case. It seemed as likely as not that it was a drunken fall. The fellow reeked of vanilla extract and his body was stretched out next to the railroad tracks. A fall on the iron rail then. The police had received no reports of any trouble among the hoboes, no ruckuses that anyone saw. And if it had been perhaps a rock or a bottle that had hit the man—a very young man, it was clear; early twenties, quite likely an Indian—well, there was no sign of the weapon. The likeliest sort of perpetrator, a fellow vagrant, would have slithered back into the shadows, onto a railcar, across state lines. It wasn't worth exercising all the imaginative possibilities when you had these sorts of people involved, Porter said. His verdict: Probable Accident.

After the egg-colored hospital, she and Porter had gone to Lewistown, where he trained with an uncle who was a mortician, then here to the college town, which seemed to them very fast and wild at first, as if they had stepped from a barge onto an ocean liner full of hopped-up people and electric lights. Twenty thousand citizens in a mountain valley, a number that allowed you to know those you wanted to know and to ignore, and be ignored by, those you didn't. A waste-filled river ran through the center of town and trains too, and so it seemed also to partake of the larger world, to have fast liquid links with it.

The idea, never articulated but fully understood by both, was that they would mitigate the past and its damage by becoming involved and hearty citizens. They were undertakers, though. Takerunders, as they jocularly referred to themselves in private. The mortician and his lady attendant. It was a profession that did not preclude becoming social pillars—certainly they had done that—but it had taken a while to put acquaintances at ease. There were people who found it difficult to look you in the eye because they couldn't erase from their minds the undertaker gazing down on their gone selves.

A day ago, Opal had sat across a bridge table from Priscilla Withers. Tomorrow, Opal's husband, recovered from his stomach trouble, would finish preparing Priscilla for the grave.

She would have a tepid bath and put on fresh clothes; do it now, in fact, and then soon, walking loose-limbed up the walk would be Porter, done for the day.

"Hello, Mother," he would say.

Because the lurid day and the heat had produced in her a slowness of mind, he seemed already to present himself in parts that could be contemplated one by one: the look of him, the sound of him, the words he was saying. When had he begun to address her that way?

"Hello, Mother." The heat didn't wilt him as it did her, but seemed to intensify his dark eyes, his frank and handsome face. He had vitality, fuel, and it showed in his fast clean hands and his mobile mouth. Eleven years younger than Opal, he sometimes seemed to her eleven years younger than any adult she knew. He spoke in a

resonant tenor voice. He moved like an athlete. He laughed at terrible jokes, and seemed much of the time to exist in a realm of necessary self-involvement, like an adolescent.

They lived as brother and sister, and always had. This was their
central understanding, the one on which the other, lighter under-
standings rested.

By the kitchen sink she found a note from Doc Stanchfield, their
neighbor. *Porter came home ill and called me. I thought it best to put
him in the hospital for observation,* he'd written in his elegant copper-
plate. *Recurrence of influenza in eastern part of state and want to rule
out same.* Opal felt a jolt of disorientation—influenza in the state?
Porter so sick he'd called a doctor?—then irritated illumination.

Stanchfield was an old friend and a seasoned medical man, but
he was prone to an almost fiendish scrupulosity. She thought it was
because of his own sad experience, this quickness to find and ferret
out medical danger. His youngest son had died at a boys' camp of
a nail wound in his foot. The poison had set in and carried him off
before anyone saw the danger. They'd brought home a boy's body
that was tanned, lithe, and—she could see it on the table now—so
tensile it seemed to be faking sleep. A small body surprised.

She was tempted to walk to the hospital to retrieve Porter, then
decided to drive in case he was wobbly. She changed her dress and
turned back the coverlet on his bed.

She calculated the time it would take to persuade Stanchfield
to let her husband and his stomachache come home. Perhaps by
now the temperature would have been taken, the organs palpated,
the heart sounded, the reflexes verified. Stanchfield liked to articulate the worst, thus giving any condition short of the worst the
glow of reprieve and grace. He was like news of a foreign disaster.
The effect was to make you feel not worse about one's human
prospects and the suffering of others, but mildly relieved to inhabit
a separate, temporarily invulnerable realm.

She would therefore have to listen to him say it wasn't cancer
for this reason, and it wasn't a ruptured appendix for that reason,
and it wasn't a grinding chronic ulcer or terminal food poisoning

for yet others. It was simply, obviously, a stomachache and a stretch of unseasonable heat and too little rest. She would nod sagely—the nurse now—and thank him, and Porter would laugh with her later at the way Stanchfield had managed to shanghai him from home, where he might have obtained a little rest.

Porter should have known better than to call. Most likely he'd done it simply for some advice, and hadn't anticipated a visit and then an order. There would have been no real resisting at that point, because their own livelihoods were linked with Stanchfield's. He would recommend their professional services when the occasion arose. He did that on a regular basis. So if he wanted to haul Porter over to the hospital to exercise his scrupulosity upon his old friend, well, there was really no simple way to say no.

As she started the Hudson, Wendell Whitcomb appeared in the mirror. Now they were letting him tear around off the sidewalks, in the streets. He pulled closer, a shock of blue-black hair standing straight up, and pumped crazily past her, pulling close to the car at the last minute to strike the mirror with one quick hand. Even in motion, he seemed to perch like a gargoyle in the corner of her eye, skinned knees next to his ears.

The whooping cry of the fire engine sounded on the far side of town. Wendell's mother, down the block in a tarty little dress, called for him. Opal pulled away from the curb.

This was preposterous. Not satisfied with smacking her car mirror, the boy now followed her on his ludicrous big bicycle. She was driving slowly because she always drove slowly—she felt, still, as if a car were some kind of beast that must be checked and reined or it would tear off on its own—and there he was, screeching and pumping behind her. It was past time to have another talk with his mother. Opal had seen versions of this boundarylessness before. It almost always resulted in an adult with criminal proclivities. It was the sort of thing that had to be nipped for the child's own good.

One night last week when the forest-fire smoke was almost intolerably thick and they had closed all their windows against it to sit baking inside, Wendell's avid little face had appeared at the window as she and Porter tried to divert themselves from their own sweltering by listening to the radio. Hitler had made a nonaggression pact with Stalin and was poised to invade Poland. Porter had been involved for a year with Legion efforts to identify local Nazi sympathizers, and nothing about all of Europe flaring into war seemed to surprise him. As he leaned toward the radio, he even suggested to her that Lindbergh was pro-Nazi, a charge she wasn't, of course, prepared to refute but which filled her with a kind of leaden unease because the appearance of that glittering little plane, up there by the Sweet Grass Hills, had coincided exactly with the appearance in her life of Porter, who had brought her everything she knew about possibility. And now he was blotting out that little plane while Wendell pressed his face and the palms of his hands against the window. The flattened nose and mouth, damp and spilled-looking, had made her shriek at him, had made her run to the door with a broom.

Porter had been infuriatingly impassive. He had simply looked up at the boy, swiveled his eyes to another part of the room, then back to the radio. She was the one who'd had to do something about it, and the thought of Porter's blankness now swept her again with fury.

The sun had dropped behind the mountains, and the sky had taken on a lavender tinge. Brief rain had fallen, they said, on one of the bigger fires up the valley. Perhaps the worst of the heat and heaviness would soon be over. September was around the corner. The days would blink awake again.

Last night, before going to her own bed, she had arranged the sheet on Porter as he slept, and had adjusted the shutters so that a faint breeze made its way into the room. Then she had gone to her own room, where she read a silly romance and watched the curtains lift in the midnight wafts, and she thought about the time when she and Porter would be old. At some point in middle age, she decided, every small illness or injury becomes a reminder that longer trials are to come. In two decades, say, when Porter came down with a stomachache, she might have trouble climbing the stairs to their rooms to tend to him. It was possible. And without children, whom would they look to for the care they might need? He had not spoken to his family since the day, a dozen years before, when she and Porter had left the little hospital near the Hills.

In the night she sometimes heard him moan. His dreams did that to him, not infrequently. The dream, when he remembered it, was often an adventure that he was not quite up to. He would be a bronco rider in a rodeo who could not spur his horse into action. The gate would fly open and he'd sit there raking the sides of the animal, but nothing would twitch, nothing about the animal would move, and he had to finally step down onto the dirt of the arena to the uproarious, inexhaustible roars of the crowd.

Or bears. He is leading the Scouts up a river drainage, three or four of them, and through the underbrush crashes a big grizzly that simply flattens one of the boys, tips him over and stands over him, that huge paw on his chest. Porter tries to coax the bear off the boy. He holds out a candy bar to it. He *reasons* with the bear. The other Scouts scatter and it is finally Porter, the bear, and the terrified boy beneath the bear's paw, and Porter stands there with the pathetic candy bar extended, and the bear throws back its big snout and laughs.

In the long light the hospital was elucidated, brick by dark brick. A nun floated up the front steps. They seemed to have wheels beneath their long wool, even some of the older ones, so smoothly did they glide.

She half expected Porter to be sitting in the lobby, smoking a cigarette with Stanchfield, but no one sat there except a farmer in overalls, capless, his white head against the wall. He slept as if he'd set himself at sleep like a hard job to be done. Each gnarled, huge hand clenched a knee.

She knew the nurse at the desk from the TB association, and felt oddly embarrassed to be asking her the whereabouts of her husband. The nurse was one of those professionally hearty types and so it shouldn't have bothered Opal that the information was offered so buoyantly, but it did. This nurse could use a few tips from the mortuary profession, she thought. Nothing made worry or pain worse than the loud good cheer of another.

In room 312, a corner room, Porter slept. A nun at the other end of the corridor began the evening rosary, praying aloud. Porter slept, in his hospital gown, under the sheets, on the far side of a room with the shades drawn. She raised the blind and shook him softly.

"Hey, lazy," she said. "It's time to go home." Porter opened his eyes. He looked very young and very pale. A sheen of sweat covered his top lip.

"Why has he got you all settled in?" she said.

Porter smiled, shrugged.

"Well, why?" she said more sharply.

"My stomach."

"What about your stomach? I had no idea he was serious about this. Why the hospital? What about your stomach?"

"It still hurts," Porter said. Then he sat up as if he had just wakened. He shifted to the edge of the bed, his narrow white feet dangling to the floor. "But not so much, I think." He smiled slowly. "He thinks it might be appendicitis."

Opal snorted. "Of course he does. Isn't that what he said the last time you got the ague?"

"I don't know," Porter said. He lay back down and closed his eyes.

"Does it hurt in a different way than it has hurt before?" she asked. "After that Scout campout two years ago when you thought you had food poisoning? Does it hurt worse than that?"

"I don't know," Porter said.

"Did he give you something?"

"I couldn't say," Porter said. "Maybe. Yes."

Opal gathered up his clothes rapidly and placed them at the foot of the bed. The nun had moved farther away, down another corridor, and she heard only the cadence of her prayers now, faintly. The hospital was extraordinarily quiet. Someone a few rooms away coughed dryly.

"Please get dressed, Porter," she said rapidly. It was time—it was past time—for the day to revert to normal. It was getting away from her.

"It's time to get out of here. Let's leave." She began to help him on with his clothes. He seemed to move underwater. She gave him a light slap on the shoulder to hurry him. The cougher called out a rather conversational request that a nurse stop by. He waited. He coughed.

Because she couldn't bear the thought of the hearty nurse at the front desk, she took them down the stairs and out a side door. She'd phone the hospital when they got home. She also had some things to say to Doc Stanchfield, but they could wait. Now it was time to be home. To wash, to eat a little soup, to sleep in their own beds.

There was a note stuck in their front door. A day of notes. Opal tucked it in her pocketbook, let herself and Porter in, and told him to rest in bed while she made them a light supper. He seemed ethereally passive. Anything she suggested was fine with him. Stanchfield had given him something, she knew. Phenobarb? He was always on Porter for overscheduling himself—the mortuary, the clubs, the youth activities—and it may be that he had given him something because it is quicker to induce relaxation in someone like Porter than to argue him into it.

In the kitchen she unfolded the note. It had been written with a blunt heavy pencil. *I quit. You know why. You owe me seven dollars. Give it to Father Darraugh at the Catholic Church. He will mail it to me. Basil.*

Basil Marley was the teenager who lived at the mortuary. The caretaker. Also the driver of the Buick Eureka, which did the removals, but also, when the hospital's Eureka was in use, served as a backup ambulance. Basil didn't like to drive it when it was an ambulance. The people who were transported got too upset.

Many of Porter's Scouts, including Basil, didn't have normal homes. They lived with grandparents or cousins or one desperate and struggling parent. Scouting, as Porter pointed out, was their lifeblood. Like many of the others, Basil was subject to rapid mood changes. This was due to his rootless upbringing, his lack of a real home.

At an Eastern Star meeting one evening, Mabel Dodgeman had quizzed Opal about the boy, making some kind of vehement and thoughtless comment about what a shame it seemed that a young man's first real job would put him in such close proximity to the dead and the grieving. Shouldn't he get a more *uplifting* job than that? she had wondered, no offense to Opal. Opal had no patience for that sort of thing. What Basil had, she told Mabel, was a job. A job, when many who were older, who were responsible for others, would give their eyeteeth for a job. That's what Basil had.

It wasn't necessary that Porter know, right away, what the note said. He'd be upset. When a boy he'd known or worked with or Scouted with took a bad turn—it happened from time to time, the word sometimes arriving from some distance if the boy in question was well grown—he took it personally. It was as if some version of himself, a dormant but worthy aspect of his own personality, had become twisted and given in to misfortune. On occasion, the boy or the grown man gave in to a wild misplaced anger. *You know why.* That sort of thing. That was the inept fury of a boy who had wanted a real father and had got something else.

There was Doc Stanchfield, no surprise, tapping on the screen door.

"I kidnapped your patient," she said, beckoning him in. Stanchfield was corpulent and smelled of cloves. His face was cherubic. He wore a straw boater and his sleeves were rolled. He removed his hat and dabbed at his sweaty pink forehead with a folded handkerchief.

"He's fine," she told him. "I was just about to call the hospital. Now I'll let you do it." He nodded. He opened his mouth as if he was about to ask a question, then seemed to forget the question.

"Well," he said briskly. "How are you doing this evening?"

"I'm just fine," she said. "But you want to know about him." She pointed at the ceiling.

"Oh yes. My wife sent me over to check. Check on the patient. The hospital was a bit frantic."

"The patient," she said, gently mocking his odd formality, "is resting comfortably. He had a stomachache from the heat and too much work. You didn't need to haul him off to the hospital."

"I suppose not," he agreed. His voice was unanchored, drifty. He seemed very slightly disoriented, though perhaps it was simply his own exhaustion. Faces like his were cruel to their owners. Signs of weariness or grief were so at odds with the serene plumpness that they seemed manufactured and false.

"He's fine. He's probably sleeping," she said.

"The raveled sleeve of care," Stanchfield said faintly. "Yes." His perfectly round blue eyes blinked rapidly. He smiled graciously, his mouth a little bow.

"And so my dear, I shall take my leave," he said, as if it were the last sentence of a long speech. And he replaced his boater and walked out the door into an evening that was, after two weeks of smudge and smoke, finally clearing a little. Moving toward the sweet lavender color it could be. *Of a mountain summer's eve.* The phrase assembled itself slowly.

His mind, as it happened, had for some time been blinking out. Yet he retained such formidable social skills—he could always think of a workable and genial greeting, a riposte, a question that flattered or encouraged another to talk—that his lapses of comprehension, logic, and memory were often masked or glossed. He could still recite all of "The Lake Isle of Innisfree" word for word. And he had been a physician for so long by the summer of 1939 that the sequence of an examination, of most simple procedures, had stayed with him so far, though his nurse, who knew him well, saw the gaps and hesitations and she had taken these worries to Stanchfield's wife, Myrna.

Myrna had always thought the nurse minutely if chastely too interested in her husband and an emotional hypochondriac to boot, and so she didn't listen very earnestly to the details of the nurse's concern. Her husband was getting absentminded, yes, that was clear. But not, she told herself, in a way that warranted dissection.

This evening, upon his return from the Mix house, he offered Myrna his angelic smile and eased his round and tired body onto the sofa. He kicked off his shoes and carefully placed his boater on the end table and sighed hugely.

"What's wrong with him? " she asked. "With Porter?"

At this point, Charles Stanchfield began a strenuous interior assembly effort. He began with the most recent images that seemed to apply. Opal Mix saying something reassuring. Their sternly ordered little house. Something above their heads that Opal was pointing at. Well, yes, Porter. Porter up there in his bed above the doctor. Porter asleep.

He had no memory, none at all, of Porter in the hospital. When he tried to think *hospital,* the black-bricked horror in Saint Louis where he'd done his training came up and was all he could seem to see, though he did know it was the wrong thing, that it had jostled the correct hospital out of the lineup.

"What's wrong with him?" he echoed, trying to sound rhetorical, stalling for time.

"Why was he in the hospital?" Myrna said. "Why did you have a call in to the surgeon?"

He made another run at the hospital, trying to make it take shape. And then it did, his hospital, but he could not find himself in it in recent hours, on this particular day. He had no idea what he had said to Tom Murray, the surgeon. But he did remember that he himself was known for a certain overscrupulosity regarding his patients. It came into him in a sweet rush, that knowledge. And so there was that. And there was this waiting woman, his wife of forty-one years.

And there was, at the last possible moment, one more thing. An image with words. Opal Mix's oblong fingers on his forearm and her calm deep voice: "He's fine."

Charles Stanchfield looked up at his wife, who had a wary aspect to her face that was new to him, as far as he knew, and that would be repeated time after time until his oblivion in two years and his death in five.

"He's fine," he told her. "He's just fine."

TWELVE

1939
Missoula

WENDELL WHITCOMB SPENT THE LONG SUMMER days prowling his designated domain, performing surveillance. What he looked for was federally felonious behavior or a tendency toward it. Counterfeiting, conspiracy, sheltering public enemies, widow bilking—those crimes were his bread and butter. Now, though, they'd been superseded by espionage. He searched now for Nazis. They might be spies who were forwarding coded messages to Hitler, or Germans who were sympathetic to the spies and had offered their assistance in the transmission of information. Either or both, Wendell wanted them in his crosshairs.

Asked by an admirer to describe his working conditions, he might have compared surveillance to riding the huge dented bicycle a brief gentleman friend of his mother's had given him. Daunting tasks both—the bicycle, the G-man duties—but expertly accomplished when the practitioner's confidence in himself was, as Wendell's was, complete.

As for information that was leaving his Montana valley for the Reich, Wendell suspected it had to do with the paper mills and the university. Perhaps spying scientists at the university were collaborating with people at the mill to make a special paper for enemy agents. Say you didn't have your invisible ink on you, or it had run out. You'd just write something on the special paper with regular ink, which would disappear almost instantly, to be reconstituted when the recipient moistened it.

A smart spy would also write something in pencil, which did not get sucked up by the paper, something ordinary like a reminder to himself to buy his mother a birthday present or ask her again for a new dog. Behind the pencil marks would be hidden measurements, observations, overheard conversations, speculations, data.

And there were trains. Every train that passed through town was a potential relay instrument. In the rosy dawn, a treasonous brakeman steps off to have a smoke and stretch his legs while the engine huffs and stamps. He buys a newspaper inside the depot and carries it to Chicago or Seattle, where he hands it to a customer next to him at the lunch bar who needs something to read with his pie. Inside that newspaper is a piece of notepaper holding invisible diagrams and words.

With a ten-block radius to work with—limits set by his mother, Edna—Wendell had to adopt an intensive, rather than extensive, approach. And so it was fortunate that he had patience for detail. He had a brief image of himself, soaked to the bone in an April rain, his ear to the listening device he had attached to a suspect's windowsill. He had another of himself with a flashlight under his bedcovers, running newspaper ads through his cryptographer's frequency chart. And the time, after his fingerprint powder got damp and clumped, that he had spread it with infinite care, almost grain by grain, upon sheets of paper to dry. Tolerance for the painstaking. That was his gift.

X-29 was his professional name. It was the name he had given himself the day he found his puppy, Lucky, dead in the street in front of his house on the twenty-ninth day of June. The official verdict from Edna was Hit by Car, but Wendell didn't buy it. Lucky had been an extraordinarily curious and vigilant dog and, in fact, had detected something untoward in the yards of three houses within a four-block radius of Wendell's own, to the point that he,

Lucky, had begun intense excavations in those yards several days before his death, and had clearly paid dearly at the hands of someone who had something to hide.

X-29 lived only to avenge Lucky's death.

Mr. Mix, the mortician who lived across the street and whose yard had been Lucky's first target, topped Wendell's list of potential murderers. Mix had what an experienced G-man might call The Tinge. This was a quality—the best spy hunters felt it in their bones—that signaled the existence in a suspect of a clandestine life. Wendell would have been hard put to say exactly what alerted him to The Tinge, but he recognized it. As Lucky surely had.

The other thing was coffins. Coffin removal. Wendell's mother had told him that it was not unusual for Mr. Mix to embalm a body, haul it down to the train station in the Buick Eureka, and ship it off to waiting relatives elsewhere. Here was a perfect opportunity for a mastermind to transfer blueprints, guns, and any number of things to a fellow mortician/traitor someplace else.

Wendell hated his ten-block domain. But he stuck to it most of the time because Edna had threatened to turn him over to the hoboes if he ventured farther. He was able to recognize her customary hyperbole—she was only sixteen years older than Wendell himself and not yet blessed with anything like adult calmness—but there were times when she sat at the kitchen table and wept so disastrously, so inconsolably—her knees poking through her thin skirt—that he saw in her the potential to take desperate measures in the interests of another life. And he wanted no part in provoking something like that.

The boys at school who had fathers seemed to be allowed to roam at will, or within certain very loose limits. Wendell had an acute sense of smell and he could often tell where they'd been, these untethered boys, by the odor of their clothes. If they had been selling newspapers in the bars, they smelled like tobacco smoke and stale corn. If they had been hanging around the river, they smelled like metal and wet leaves. If they'd gone to a movie over the weekend, their sweaters smelled of overheated popcorn oil. A tinge of incense, and they'd been to the Chinese shops on Front Street.

Smell sensitivity was a distinct attribute in a G-man because any target conveniently wore a record of his immediate past activities. But to a twelve-year-old without any friends to speak of since Tom Zelinka had moved to Portland, it was also a provocation. Boys who might be his friends carried on them the evidence of the activities and freedom, the sheer boyness, that separated them from himself. And all of them, to Wendell, smelled wonderful.

Tom Zelinka had, in Portland, gone deep undercover. It was extremely dangerous for him to communicate anything in writing, even using secret ink or the code he and Wendell had perfected over the previous summer. Several years older than Wendell, Tom had been his mentor as well as friend, bringing him up through the G-man ranks with rigor, sternness, and affection. Then Tom's father had found a job working under a shirttail cousin in a rendering plant, and the family had decamped to Portland virtually overnight, leaving Wendell so bereft he'd almost abandoned sleuthing altogether. His heart for it was gone.

Tom had eventually sent a letter urging Wendell to carry on for both of them. He wouldn't be able to keep close tabs, he said, because Portland was a viper's nest of treason and schemes and he had his own work cut out for him. This, therefore, was the bottom line: If Wendell didn't hear from him again, he had gone into deep undercover. Wish me luck, pal, Tom had written.

Wendell went further than that. When Edna brought home a gentleman friend who had once been a preacher near the Gulf of Mexico, they prayed over the ham dinner—the preacher resting his fat hands on the heads of Wendell and Edna—and then the preacher requested the names of specific people on whose behalf he should exercise his connections with the Almighty. Tom Zelinka, Wendell had mumbled. Tell him to keep Tom Zelinka out of danger.

Edna had looked at him quizzically. His little friend, she explained to the preacher, as if she'd only just recalled Tom's existence herself. Cute little towhead, she added. Not the sort to get himself in any trouble. But go ahead, she said. Pray for him if you like. And so the preacher did, and when Wendell heard his friend's name in the stranger's voice, floating cloudward through the smell of baked ham, he felt such a wild sadness that he had to jump up and run from the room.

In an attempt to share a part of his life with some potential friends at school, a few of them Junior G-Men like himself, Wendell one day took with him his letter from J. Edgar Hoover. Though the FBI chief was canny enough not to acknowledge explicitly Wendell's counterespionage efforts—Wendell sent him regular reports—he did make it clear that Wendell was an operative whose age gave him a particularly effective cover.

Dear Mr. Whitcomb, I speak for myself and the FBI as a whole when I commend you and all Junior G-Men for your patriotism and your concern that the American way of life be protected from those who would seek to undermine it. It is the youth of America who hold the keys to the continued exercise of democracy on our shores, and it is reassuring to know that fine young citizens like you are among their number. Sincerely, J. Edgar Hoover.

Two weeks later a wild-haired girl in his class, Janie Quist, brought a letter to school that J. Edgar Hoover had sent to her father, the editor of the newspaper.

Dear Mr. Quist, I speak for myself and the FBI as a whole when I commend you for your patriotism and your concern that the American way of life be protected from those who would seek to undermine it. Those in the nation's press who reassure the public that their safety is ensured by the agents of the FBI perform an invaluable service in the interests of democracy, and it is gratifying to have the evidence, once again, that you are among their number. Sincerely, J. Edgar Hoover.

Wendell wasn't fazed by the similarities in language. Mr. Hoover was an extremely busy man. He wasn't going to think up new and colorful ways of saying things every time he wrote a letter. Wendell, however, had to acknowledge that were he the chief, he would enjoy finding new ways to say things. That was something else he did besides spying. He had won a thesaurus at school for his exceptional spelling, and he liked to find words that were off to the sides of the words people generally used.

After school got out and the summer began to heat up and the distant forests burst into bright flames, giving everything in town a muffled glow, Wendell realized one day upon waking that he was entering upon the riskiest phase of his surveillance of Porter Mix. For two weeks he had kept an eye on the house, noting the departures and arrivals of both Mix and his wife. He wanted to ascertain whether either of them came home at off-hours to operate a radio transmitter.

The wife generally left the house at seven and came home by four. Her departures and arrivals were consistent over the course of the two weeks. Mix's day was more erratic. He had his mortician's duties and his coroner's investigations, so he left the house at all hours. What Wendell was after was a consistent return at the same hour, a stay of a short duration, and exaggerated vigilance on the man's part as he left the house again. Something like that would suggest the presence of a radio transmitter and the use of it to update contacts in the field.

Wendell's vigilance paid off. For three of the past five days, Mix had returned around two in the afternoon, stayed for periods of time ranging from twenty-one minutes to forty-seven minutes, and left with his eyes swiveling around the immediate neighborhood. He was clearly receiving transmissions and probably decoding them on the spot.

What Wendell had to do now was get inside that house and catch him in the act, or at least get a glimpse of the equipment. A bright trickle of dread moved across the back of his neck. He didn't know what might happen if he was caught. Wendell suspected that ice ran in the man's veins, but he didn't know what that ice implied in terms of steps the mortician might take.

He knew that he had to be prepared to act first, to jump Mix and tie him up so that he could interrogate him. Ideally, he would employ the lie machine he had requested in writing from Hoover, and when Mix protested his innocence, lights would flash on the machine and there might also be an alarm. Wendell couldn't remember what sounds and lights the best lie machines had.

Hoover had not yet responded to the request. X-29 found himself maddened sometimes by the grinding slowness of officialdom. He needed speed. He needed flexibility. He needed, more than anything else, to stop the mastermind as he spun his web. On behalf of Lucky and democracy, he had to do this. And the time was now, machine or no machine.

As insurance against his disappearance, should it come to that—what better hiding place for a murdered body than a casket!—he dashed off a note to Hoover.

Dear Mr. Hoover, I am going in. Results will be forwarded to you via letter, to be sent within five days. If you do not receive same, complications have occurred. In such a case, please know that I regret nothing. Sincerely, X-29.

Because he wanted to remind Mr. Hoover that he was somewhat outside the mold, as far as his facility with the language went, he got out his thesaurus and changed the last sentence. *In such an eventuality,* he wrote, *please perceive that I am remorseless.*

The street, the neighborhood were very quiet. Smoke from the fires had erased the nearby mountains. The valley felt like a large dirty room. Wendell was drenched with sweat. It was two-twenty, and he had made two circles of the Mix house, pretending to be looking for a new dog he didn't have. Every time he rounded a corner, he called or whistled for a Labrador/German shepherd cross named Lucky Junior. Several windows were partly open and gauzy white curtains hung transfixed. Frail though they were, they blocked a view of anything inside, and Wendell was too nervous to reach for the low ones and push them aside. Also, it was close to the time Mix tended to showed up.

One last whistle for Lucky Junior, and Wendell scooted back to his own house to sit on the front step. Mix drove up, as if on cue, and went inside. Wendell gave him time enough to get a drink of water and go to the radio transmitter. He felt in his pocket for the card Post Toasties had sent him as a member of the Melvin Purvis Law and Order Patrol. It was there and it reinforced him. He walked across the street, the blood in his temples thumping frantically, and knocked hard.

Nothing. He knocked again, insistently. His plan was to ask Porter Mix if he had seen his new dog, then gain ingress to the house by requesting a glass of water.

He listened. Nothing. The transmitter must be in the basement, he thought, or in a closet deep inside a room. Perhaps Mix was watching him that very moment through a hidden peephole in the door. He studied the wood, the fixtures, to see where the peephole might be. He fingered his Junior G-Man badge, pinned to the inside of his shirt. He slapped at a bead of sweat that ran down the inside of his arm. He hummed, trying to ward off the nightmarish feeling he got when he waited for sharp new knowledge. He saw his little unmoving dog, felt the terrible hush before you know everything. He hummed louder and studied a spot of peeling paint on the door.

And when Porter Mix's shadow fell over him, Wendell grabbed the doorjamb, feeling shot.

"Why are you out here?" he squeaked.

Mix stood next to him, smiling. He had rolled up the sleeves of his crisp white shirt. His hands, quite hairy and dark, were folded at his belt buckle.

"I was out back," he said. "Heard someone pounding down the door." He smiled encouragingly.

"I was looking for my new dog," Wendell said. "I thought maybe you'd seen him on your way home. He's black and white with a patch over the right eye. He has a limp. He hasn't been home for three days."

"Why don't you ask a friend to help you look? Four eyes are better than two."

"I did. He's looking over by the university," Wendell said miserably. Everything out of his mouth sounded false.

Mix studied him. "Are you making the best possible use of your time this summer?" he asked. "Come out back for a minute. I want to talk to you about something."

Wendell recognized a diversionary tactic when he saw one: anything to keep him out of the house. He also knew what was coming, because Mix had tried the same thing last summer. He was going to lecture Wendell about joining the Scouts, which his mother had told him seven hundred times that he couldn't do, because it cost money—the outings and so forth—and because he was her only child and she was afraid he would, in the pursuit of his badges, step on river glass or get eaten by a bear.

Porter directed him to a bench in the shade of a big maple. Wendell sat down and watched the leaf shadows flutter on his feet. Porter stretched his arms over his head. He groaned and patted his stomach. His face was flushed.

"The times, Wendell," Mix began, eyes closed, "call for discipline. We live in an era in which it is crucial to learn skills, to learn discipline."

"That's what Scouting is about," he continued, "though most people wouldn't look at it that way because it's also so much fun. Scouting is about skills, about discipline, about fun." He emphasized each point with a tap of two fingers on the boy's dirty scabbed knee. His eyes were still closed.

He droned on about the times, and being alert, and Germany being a bully that was kicking sand in the eyes of everyone else on the beach, and was about to invade Poland. And then Britain would come in—they were blood pals to the death—and the world would start to change forever.

Very clever, Wendell thought wearily. Give me your patriot's speech. You don't fool me. He also heard in Mix's cardboard tones the sound of a man who spent too much time with corpses.

Now the man was sighing, audibly sighing. Something about Germany made him sigh. He patted his stomach. He tipped his head back and watched the sky. He had left two fingers on Wendell's knee.

"Ow," Wendell said, carefully. "My scabs."

Mix lifted his hand. He fixed a slow smile on the boy. "I'm so sorry," he said, as if mocking the way you were supposed to say something like that. And then, to Wendell's horror, the man's eyes filled with tears. And he took Wendell's hand, looked at it, regarded it as if it were the rarest object he had ever seen. Wendell tried to pull it back. Porter held it, turned it palm up, and placed it, in his own, on Wendell's lap.

"You're a beautiful human being, Wendell Whitcomb," he said.

Sometimes in his spying efforts Wendell felt that he lived inside the radio, the hero in his own G-man show. Now he had the sense that Porter had climbed inside the radio with him.

Moreover, the man was weeping. More accurately, he was blinking back tears with a strained, tight look on his face, his gaze focused on something in the distance, as though someone were sending him a message by tin can and string, and he couldn't decipher it. His mouth pinched and unpinched.

Wendell jumped up. He waited a moment so he could know what to do. Mix studied him, red-eyed. "Charming," he said gently. "Charming indeed." It sounded like a line from a song Wendell didn't know. He pretended to catch sight of his new dog. "Lucky!" he shouted, and he ran.

It is the afternoon of August 30, 1939, in an ordinary town in an ordinary part of America. Three hours have elapsed since X-29 successfully infiltrated the Nazi apparatus and escaped to tell about it. The suspect Mix subsequently received a male visitor, an older fat man in a boater hat, and the two left together in the stranger's car. An hour later, Opal Mix, on foot, entered the premises in her lady attendant's garb: gray cotton dress, sensible black oxfords, streaked hair rolled back from her long face in sausages.

Now she is pulling sheets from the clothesline. X-29 waits patiently across the street, pretending to examine a small leak in his bicycle tire, then leaps onto the pedals and starts toward her. He bends his head to the miniaturized two-way radio strapped to his wrist. "I've got her," he murmurs. "I'll handle this one alone." He touches his badge for luck. "Wish me luck," he tells his wrist.

Riding full speed past the traitor, hiding now behind her sheets, Wendell calmly gives her notice that he is on to her. She stammers something in return. He speeds on and turns the corner, where he throws down the bicycle and flops on a lawn, gasping.

After a time, he gathers himself to do what he must do. He rides around the block and rounds the corner to find Opal Mix trying to get away. Why hasn't Wendell registered a crucial fact before? Every time the woman leaves the house, she carries something: a paper sack, a handbag big enough for a sheaf of documents or a handgun. Something.

She reaches her small inconspicuous automobile, starts it with a roar, and moves down the street, nervously watching the mirror.

She spots him! Quick as a cobra, she opens her pocketbook with her nondriving hand and reaches for her revolver. X-29 speeds straight into the danger and smacks the mirror on her car to destroy her aiming capabilities, then veers sharply away from the vehicle. She shoots wildly and screeches down the street. Wendell hits the ground, rolling so blurringly she wouldn't get a bead on him if she was standing a foot away. When he stops, he's got his own gun out and her tailpipe in the crosshairs. Bam! Bam! Bam! Hot lead shears off the pipe, but it's too late to bring her down. His vehicle doesn't have the German engineering that hers does.

"Charming!" he screams. "How charming would it feel to have .45-caliber bullet holes in your lungs, neck, and brain!"

The G-men assisting him wait for her at her destination. "She's yours," he says into his radio. "The chicken squawks, but not for long." He snaps off the radio, washed with exhaustion.

"He called me a beautiful human being," Wendell reported to Edna when he had thought it over. She was wrestling with the wringer on the washer and her cheeks were bright pink. Her dark hair framed her face in damp ringlets. Usually her brother came over on wash days to help her wring the big items like sheets and haul them to the line, but he was indisposed.

"Well, he's more generous than I am," she replied, wetting her finger and running it across the dirt on his face.

"I don't think he should say something like that," Wendell said.

"He doesn't know how to talk," she said. "He thinks he should sound like a preacher. Inspiring." She kicked the bottom of the machine, like a child. "Don't you feel inspired?" she said, loud and mocking.

Wendell was weary. He hated it when his mother acted like a teenager, a pal. At those moments he felt decades older than she was.

The red sun glared through the smoke. Wendell took a last spin on his bike. Past the Mix house, past the grade school, past the creamery, and back.

He thought about Mix's voice and knew what he had heard in it. He had heard his own voice on that endless day when he had searched and searched for his missing dog, Lucky. Hope and dread were in both voices—Mix's and his own—a terrifying blend of wondering and knowing.

Certainty waited in a quiet place ahead. Meanwhile, you called. And you called.

THIRTEEN

1939
Missoula

RAIN SCRUBBED THE SKY, FINALLY. IT fell mechanically for several days and when it was done, the last of the forest smoke lay way up the valley where the mop-up work was going on. A curtain lifted on cool blue, on clouds that were airy gestures of dismissal.

Roland Taliaferro stood at the window of his room and yawned hugely. He had worked half a day at the student store, gone to his estate-law class, studied for a couple of hours, and was getting ready now to go with Aidan Tierney to the campus convocation where the FBI man from Butte would speak. Afterward, the agent wanted to meet with students from the law school. A reception would be held at the dean's.

There was a buzz and crackle underfoot, a delicious sense of event and consequence that made every ordinary thing iconic. The pretty clouds became something to feel tender and nostalgic about. The sounds of the day—the landlady sweeping the porch, the church bell tolling the half hour, a tree full of birds—seemed as naive and referential as the atmospherics of a radio play.

Hitler had invaded Poland, the last-ditch missives had failed, the chessmen had moved to their new squares, the headlines blared, Europe was in a condition of full-blown war.

Roland wouldn't have said aloud that he was enthralled by it all, but he was. The thought of ten million soldiers mobilizing to stop the screaming, voracious heel clicker and his machinery of state was a drama of such proportions that all of his own life, to this point, seemed shabby, scrambling, and pocked with undersized hopes. The thirties in their entirety did. But the thirties were almost gone. Out there, now, was a perfect enemy and a wide new day.

He buttoned his stiff shirt and squinted through the treetops at a squirrel on a phone wire. He sighted. "Boom," he said, and the squirrel lifted and froze, all but its frantic metronome of a tail.

He could hear Aidan Tierney whistling as he dressed. It was a loud whistle, stridently off-key, and he employed it at certain times only: in the shower and before he went anywhere in the evening. He had two songs in his repertoire, "The Road to Mandalay" and "My Wild Irish Rose," and he liked to intermingle them to produce a single, ridiculously sentimental march. Every time Roland heard the mishmash—and he heard it often—he felt lighter.

The two of them, both in their last year of law school, had taken rooms in the same boardinghouse the year before. Two other men in their class had rooms as well. Their landlady was a tiny little person, a professor's widow whom they called Mrs. Tuttle to her face and Tinker Bell behind her back. Tink.

They'd been in school a long time now, and owed money on loans. Every summer they had managed to find jobs where they could work overtime and sock away enough for the next term or two. Roland, this past summer, had been down in the mines. Dirty, stifling, dangerous work. And he had promised himself when he rode the cage up the last time, sweat-soaked, and stepped into the smoky hot night and then into the Jack Club, where old Seamus Reilly now slept on his arms most of the time, that he was done with Butte forever. Done with such work. He bought Reilly a whiskey, drank his own down fast, and walked out.

He would never have worked the mines if his father had still been alive. He would have signed on with some gyppo logging outfit or taken anything else he could get, because he wouldn't have been able to bear whatever his father's reaction to the mines would have been. Vindication, disdain, jealousy? Fear for a son, down there in the killing dust? Whatever the response, it would have been too fierce. But the old man was gone, five years gone. And all Roland had to deal with now was the fact that they'd never made it right between them—never come close—by the time Nick Taliaferro lay gasping and dying like a fish on a riverbank.

What a relief it had been to get back to the leafy college town, back to school, back into a white shirt. And what relief, too, to be close to some kind of self-chosen life. After years of the books, the grind, the grueling or tedious jobs, you want something on your own terms. You want to go out and be a player. And here was a stage, now, that was larger than any of them could have imagined, even a few months ago.

Sometime late in the summer there had been the news story about a mother and two children leaping from the thirteenth floor of a Chicago hotel because the woman, on a temporary visa, thought they were going to be returned to Czechoslovakia and Hitler's invaders.

There had been the shock of the German-Russian peace pact. There had been the torpedo attack on the British liner with a couple hundred Americans aboard.

Strands were connecting, then winding like fast-spooling thread around the globe.

There was espionage and sabotage to think about, and Roosevelt had put the FBI in charge of all of it. This, following on the heels of the Bureau's stunning arrest in August of Louis Buchalter, head of Murder, Inc., the most hunted man in America. Coolly, the men had stopped Buchalter in his tracks before turning to the defense of the entire nation in a time of impending war.

All of it gave Roland the feeling that he was riding the back of a massive animal that was shifting its body, readjusting its position. And he was adjusting his own position, too, entertaining a new and secret hope. The Bureau needed more men. And it needed analytic, information-sifting men, not just bold high-level cops. What were the chances that they might want him? And what were his immediate prospects otherwise? Low-level lawyering in some Podunk town, at least when he was starting out. Maybe a run at local political office. Helping small-town men with their small-town matters: deed transfers, sorting out mineral rights, suing a neighbor. Maybe a little criminal law. Lock up the local bad guys, if you could find any.

One of their friends had already set up a law practice in his hometown up north. He and Aidan had driven up to see him, and there he was in a cramped office with a rag rug supplied by his mother, and a bust of Lincoln, and his diploma on the wall, sitting very straight and moving papers around on his desk.

No. That wasn't what all this effort should add up to. The prospects for the best of their class—and Roland and Aidan were the best—could include lives as G-men. When he thought about that, about the distinct possibility of it, he felt a brief, ridiculous glaze of tears.

He prayed that the war would not come to an early end. He badly needed this war to stay, and to grow.

They were taking Lenora Wing to the convocation with them, though Roland felt it was a mistake. Not because she had shifted her affections from Roland to Aidan—a switch that had produced in him muddled feelings of humiliation and deep relief—but because she was so unapologetically Lincoln Brigade and anti-ROTC and anti-FBI that he could hear, in advance, her crisp disdain for the Bureau man and anything he said. She was going to the convocation as an undercover agent, she had brightly told them.

Lenora was sharp tongued and quick witted. She had a lithe build, shiny chestnut hair in a bob, no-nonsense ankles, and eyes that quite literally flashed when she was inflamed, as she often was, about a political or ethical abstraction. Roland had met her at the student store, where they both worked part-time. He had mistaken her avidity for sexual license of the frank, no-nonsense sort he required in any girl he was going to bother to spend money and charm on, and the dismal consequences had left him feeling bumbling and angry for a time. Angry with her. Angry at some kind of

sexual illiteracy he felt in himself. But they had, surprisingly, remained friends of a sort, and when Lenora and Aidan began dating, a delicate equilibrium among the three of them quickly took
shape.

The year before, Lenora had worked on the staff of the college
yearbook. Aidan and Roland still liked to tease her about the intro-
ductions she had written for its various sections. The graduating seniors, she predicted, would look back *upon the sudden nearness of
the world outside, the cardboard hats, the long robes, and the longer
speeches of the final flutter.*

"The final flutter!" Roland had crowed, hands in a choke hold
around his neck, and she had smacked him lightly with the yearbook on the back of the head. It became a joke among them. "That
felt like a flutter," Roland would say when he sneezed. "The final
flutter?" Aidan would ask solicitously.

*Who knows what portent the headlines of today threaten for to-
morrow?* Lenora had written for the brief section on the Military
Department. *European war clouds cast shadows on the campuses of
American universities. Did our elders tell us that youth, blind and
overenthusiastic, was the raw material?*

The men didn't comment on that one, except to agree between
themselves that Lenora had what Aidan called a poetically extravagant sensibility.

Special agent in charge F. X. Travers of the Butte FBI office calmly
removed his hat and hung it on his chair, shot his cuffs, examined
the line of his tie, folded his jacket, rolled up his sleeves. Then he
gazed with feigned alertness on the American Legion president who
had taken the lectern to introduce him to a packed auditorium.

The Legion man summed up Travers's career and his major ar-
rests; he reminded the audience of the importance of the Bureau in
this time of war and espionage. The FBI, he said, had stepped front
and center, and its mission had broadened from the apprehension
of known criminals—the Buchalter arrest got a run-through here—
to the identification of potential criminals. What it boiled down to
was the preservation of democracy, pure and simple, and the audience

should know, he said, that the Bureau had not been idle as hostilities heated up abroad. The country could be reassured: The cool know-how of the G-man already had been at work.

"Let's let the agent have his say," Roland muttered. He'd been watching a boy in the front row, a skinny, wriggly kid with blue-black hair sticking straight up in front. He wore a big Junior G-Man badge and was loudly tapping his pencil on the notebook he had on his knee. His mother, a pretty young thing with violet circles under her eyes, slapped his hand lightly. The boy sighed very loudly. You and me, kid, Roland thought.

Now the Legion guy was on to some extended anecdote about the previous Legion president, who'd died in such an untimely fashion a few weeks earlier. Porter Mix, coroner and model citizen, had succumbed to the effects of peritonitis, leaving everyone who knew him a little poorer. Just a week before his death, the speaker remembered, he and Mix had driven together to the Legion stag party up Rattlesnake Creek. The best party yet, he remembered fondly—movies and boxing and roast ham and potato salad, which the men had eaten out of mess kits.

Travers had taken out his pocket watch and appeared to examine it curiously. He gave the face a polish with his white handkerchief. The kid with the electric hair looked alertly at the agent, then at his mother, and he polished his G-man badge with the cuff of his thin shirt. His mother yawned, two fingers to her bright mouth.

The Legion man took his seat to loud, relieved applause and the G-man stepped to the podium. Someone dimmed the lights a notch and brightened the spotlight on the man.

He talked very rapidly, and punctuated his points with small chopping motions. His accent was Boston Irish. He seemed to be running down a detailed outline he'd posted in his head, complete with humorous asides. Though he spoke without notes, he'd left nothing to chance.

The relief of it, thought Roland, especially after that meandering legionnaire. Potato salad in mess kits! They were boys playing at being men, playing at risk. They seemed more childish than the kid there with the badge, listening with every fiber of his scrawny body. Leave it to the professionals, the director himself had implored the Legion men, the NYPD, every other kind of amateur spy hunter trying to land a Nazi or finger a sympathizer. Leave it to trained agents who know how to proceed in a cool and systematic fashion.

The G-man reviewed the FBI's evolution during the past decade. The refinement of fingerprinting. The director's close ties with the president, and the concern on both their parts that espionage in this incendiary world be nipped, at home, in the bud. The new and expanded role of the Bureau with the outbreak of European war. From the best cops in the world to the best sleuths. From responders to illuminators. Pruning away the weak and rotted branches so that the tree of democracy, and the uniquely American virtues of freedom and family, might flourish unimpeded.

The boy in the front row was lolling in his seat. The big picture was boring him. What he wanted was escapades. The agent wound up his speech and entertained questions from the audience. Hands shot up all over the auditorium.

"You, young man," Travers said, pointing at the front row. "You with the badge. What's on your mind?"

"What do you do if you know that someone important is a spy?" the boy called out strongly.

"What do you mean, *important?*" the agent asked, leaning over the podium in a confiding posture.

"Well, someone who has lots of friends and clubs and everyone thinks he's regular? And he owns a business, maybe, or is the principal of a school or maybe a preacher?"

The young woman was looking at her boy intently, patting his shoulder now to say, Enough. He shot her a look of fury.

"Keep your eyes open," Travers told the boy. "Trust your instincts." He looked up and moved his eyes around the big room. "That goes for everyone," he said. "They're here. We'll find them. And we do need your help. Your good eyes. Your good ears. Tell us what comes to your notice. The actions, though, you need to leave to us."

Lenora, sitting between Aidan and Roland, sighed hugely. "Everyone gets to be a snitch and feel good about it," she murmured. "No one has to worry about silly little things like someone else's privacy, presumed innocence, freedom to say whatever. It's a funny twist, isn't it? Take away freedoms to keep the world free. I think I'm missing something here? Could anyone please explain?" She tapped each of them on the knee, Roland and then Aidan.

They left her at her dormitory and walked over to the dean's big Georgian house for the reception. The evening had a vague look to it, something ashy again that fuzzed the outlines of the mountains and the big trees in the night light. The moon burned rosier than it should, as if lit by the roaring heat from the other side of the world.

"They're still putting out the last of those fires," Aidan said. "I can smell it sometimes."

To their surprise, they were among only five law students at the reception, the rest of the group faculty men and deans.

Their dean, a handsome, canny man with a froth of white hair, introduced them to Travers. They shook his hand, one by one. They complimented him on his talk. And then they waited for him to say something.

What he said was that he wanted each of them to consider a career in the FBI after they graduated. They'd have to be checked out, but they seemed like the sort that the Bureau could use now. The director had called upon all his field men to find the best. Think about it, he said. He'd be in touch.

For Roland, it was as if the huge door of an airport hangar had been pushed back, and there, inside, were the steel wings that would take him out and up. He was so agitated as he and Aidan walked back home that he kept shrugging, his nervous habit, until Aidan, laughing, had to tell him to stop.

They had a drink of whiskey in Roland's room. Four Roses. A couple.

"Someone told me he won't take you if you're showing any sign of going bald," Roland said. "He won't have it."

Aidan stretched his legs out and felt his thick hair, as if to make sure it was still there. "Well, you," he said to Roland. "With that pelt of yours, you could lose a handful every day and it wouldn't show until you're drooling in your rocker."

"And you can get fired if you drive around in a dusty car," Roland said.

He had heard these things from an acquaintance who'd interviewed with the Bureau and decided against joining. Though he was trying to speak offhandedly, the odd and fastidious rules worried him a little. Not because he objected to them, but because he was afraid Aidan would.

"Here's the thing, Roland," Aidan said, swirling the last of his drink slowly. "None of that matters. It's a kind of encryption. It's code."

"For what?" Roland said.

"Well," Aidan said, "You do certain things, not for their own sake, not because they are important in themselves, but because they . . ." He paused, and finished off his drink. "Because they signal your general intent." A quizzical look ran across his face, as if he'd heard the statement from someone else and was trying to make sense of it.

"So for instance," he said. "We've all got these nasty little thugs inside us that are jostling for advantage. Yes?" He threw Roland a wry and knowing look, and all Roland could see then, for a few moments, was himself at his most driven and furious. He saw every experience that had made him shameful to himself—with women, with booze, with whatever it was that had produced his father's fist to his face—and he saw his own gift for encapsulating those episodes and throwing them as far as he could from his apparently affable and productive life; and he watched them creep back, as they always did, and call him Fraud. All of it, in a moment or two.

"Well," said Aidan, almost laconically, "I think that the only way to keep them from running into each other and making a big mess is to get them to send a delegate out there who appears to keep faith with what's fine and true and good." He said the words with just enough skepticism to give them some weight.

"So that particular self—the delegate—he makes sure he washes his goddamn car!" Aidan said, grinning. "Not because he believes in the shiny car as something fine and true, per se, but because keeping it looking good is a way to say, in code, that you subscribe to something big and untalkable that is at odds with the slovenly, the careless."

"There's a theory for you," Roland said. "One problem with it. Why pick a good guy to go forth on your behalf if you're a thug who's doing the picking?"

"Oh," Aidan said, dismissing the subject with a flick of his hand. "They're okay, those thugs. They foul things up, but their hearts are sort of in the right place." He felt around for his own heart, feigned a moment of panic, and sat back satisfied, his hand over his sternum.

Roland lit a cigarette. He thought about Aidan getting up early, whistling his goofy medley in the shower, and heading off to early Mass. Almost every day he did it. Roland knew where he went, but he'd never been able to ask him why. He felt as if he had caught him in some embarrassing, needy, helplessly repeated act, and had tried not to think much about it.

Now, though, it seemed an almost reasonable practice. It seemed gestural and rather casual, like tipping your hat to a stranger. He felt a little rise of tranquillity. It might have been the whiskey, but he didn't think so.

He was going to apply. He had the stuff, and the agent in charge, Travers, had seen it, and now the future was clear. It might be Roland Taliaferro, one of these days, who would blow into town to recount his adventures to a crowd of a thousand.

"I'm going to sign up and see if I can make the grade," he said. *The thugs have spoken.* He almost laughed aloud. *The thugs are sometimes okay, and they've sent their man forth.*

"I wonder what Lenora will think?" Aidan said, and the comment made Roland so happy he could only lift his glass in a high salute. It meant that Aidan's mind was mostly made up. They'd both apply. They had the stuff, and the agent Travers had seen it.

"I think we don't need to wonder what Lenora will think," Roland said. "Lenora feels a certain disdain for government agents, you might have noticed." He took the chance. "Hell, she feels a certain disdain for government itself. I'll go that far. But then, she's a poet, yes? And your poets are a different breed of cat, so to speak."

"Well, she is and she isn't," Aidan said. He leaned back and blew three perfect smoke rings. "She's not one of your lady poets. She's not one of your sentimental sorts. We need to give her that."

"I have no problem giving her that," Roland said. "I have no problem with Lenora at all." He could have been speaking of a girl he knew in grade school, so far away did she feel from the contours of this new life, so cleanly taking its shape.

The second day of duck-hunting season was the next morning, the season opening a month earlier than usual. Aidan and Roland were dressed and ready to go at dawn. They whistled their imaginary full-blooded Labrador, Rowdy, into Roland's old Ford and headed to Ninepipes Reservoir where, in a couple of hours, they each bagged their limit of ten.

Driving back into town, they stopped near the bridge to watch a pack of undergraduates enact a pregame ritual that involved a mud-and-flour fight. The river glinted blandly. It was low, lower than it should be. The warriors stood on the bank wearing approximations of gladiator gear. Several canoes contained the weaponry: tubs of the flour/mud combination and makeshift catapults. Lying atop the tubs of one canoe was a dummy wearing the colors of the football enemy, the Bozeman Bobcats, splayed and wrecked looking.

The teams paddled out to a small island thirty or so feet from shore. They set up their positions, the dummy on the ground between them, and began to sling gobs of white mud back and forth. Both catapults jammed, so they resorted to heaving the stuff at each other as they ran forward roaring.

Roland and Aidan and the others on the bridge cheered them all on. Two boys emerged with the dummy. They sprinted with it to a tree at the island's end, their teammates defending them, and hung it by the neck until it was dead.

Half of the bystanders on the bridge cheered; half booed happily.

A car pulled up beside them and idled loudly. A young guy who looked like a slimmer, faster version of Aidan—same straight, black eyebrows and thick, inky hair; a variation of the same full grin—leaned out the driver's side to call hello. This was one of Aidan's brothers, the one they called Neil. He had worked on the railroad all summer for good pay and had just pledged a fraternity. Two other men and a couple of young women packed the car.

Roland had met Neil just briefly, once before. The brothers, he knew, ate dinner together somewhere downtown every Wednesday. No matter how much studying he had to do, Aidan rarely missed a week. He told Roland he had to keep the kid lined out, but he returned looking as if he had laughed a lot, and it gave Roland a pang of jealousy. His own family, his mother and Petey, seemed to belong to a different social organization entirely. He couldn't imagine a casual evening with either of them. It was out of the question.

Neil, Aidan said, wanted to be a pilot. He was taking lessons out at the airport with the flying school and had signed up this week for the new civilian pilot training program at the university. They were taking thirty students tops, and he was sure he was in. He'd study with math and physics professors, learning navigation, meteorology, theory of flight. He'd fly a minimum of thirty-five hours with those barnstormers and coyote hunters out at the flying school. When he'd get the time to study regular subjects, Aidan didn't know. But the kid was completely gung ho, and when he was gung ho, there was no stopping him.

And he'd be good, he added. He had a quality of utter focus and a certain fearlessness that would, he hoped, keep the boy decisive, alert, and safe.

"He might get the chance to fly straight into a squadron of Fokkers," Roland said.

"He might," said Aidan. "It's hardly out of the question now, is it?"

The comment had the effect of slowing their walk back to the car. They ambled. They looked around. The leaves of the maples glittered like coins. The river carried the wispy white clouds on its back. Horns honked. Sun rocketed off the copper spire of the Catholic church. One of the warriors ran past, hoisting the dummy aloft. Aidan and Roland took stools at the railroaders' bar for a couple of beers, and then they took themselves and their ducks home.

They sat on the stoop behind the boardinghouse cleaning their birds. It was taking a long time because the carcasses had so many pinfeathers. They dipped the birds in a can of melted paraffin, let the wax harden, and pulled it off. That took some of the barely started feathers with it. They plucked at the rest with needle-nose pliers. The twenty birds lay in soft limp piles, heads lolling. Loose feathers drifted across the floor of the stoop. Feathers filled a big cardboard box. The glossy entrails were piled high in a wash pan, and there were drops and splashes of blood all over the rickety porch. There'd be hell to pay with Tink.

Roland counted the small pile of clean birds. It would take hours at the rate they were going, but neither was willing to leave a single pinfeather unplucked.

Roland wiped his forehead with the back of his bloody hand. It was chilly on the stoop, and the sun was almost down. The maple leaves had dimmed and the trees were dark, patient things against the violet sky. He was hungry.

As if on cue—he had the thought, and there she was—Lenora came around the corner of the house with part of a chocolate cake on a plate. The remains of someone's birthday, she said, and then she looked closer and saw their hands and the mess, and she put the cake on the step and lit a cigarette.

She bent forward to look at the bigger pile of ducks, at all the black dashes on their pale loose skin.

"It was the heat," she told them. "It was in the paper. The headline caught my eye, the way those strange ones on the back pages do. Many Pinfeathers This Season."

"It was the heat. The summer was so hot, and the season is early, and the feathers didn't get a chance to grow out." She squinted at the pile. "What are you going to do with so many ducks?"

"Want a duck?" Roland said.

"No," she said.

She picked up the cake and made her way through the mess and into the dim kitchen, where she put it on the counter. Beyond the kitchen, Tink sat in a circle of light next to the radio, listening to her Saturday shows. She waved, straight-armed, at Lenora as if she and her radio sat on a far-distant bluff.

Lenora took a seat on the step again and wrapped her arms around her plaid woolen skirt. Roland felt he should try to say something to push off the gloom she'd brought, but he couldn't think of anything. Aidan focused intently on the paraffin he was pulling off his bird.

She studied him for a moment. "Do you want me to help you?" she said. "Should I hold the duck while you do that?" Her voice sounded wistful. Roland wondered whether Lenora had got bad news about her mother, who lived in Butte and suffered from some kind of long and unnamed illness.

"I'm fine," Aidan said quietly.

"How's your mother?" Roland said.

Lenora looked at him, eyebrows high. "My mother?" she said. "My mother's fine. As fine as she ever gets." She stood, as if to consider the question from another angle. "Which doesn't mean I'm not going to be scurrying home to Butte one of these days to watch her take some kind of endless turn for the worse."

If Roland had heard this strand of bitterness in her voice before, he didn't recall it. She heard it too, and moved away from it by touching Aidan on the shoulder. She left her hand there for a few moments.

In the distance they heard a low roar of voices—rhythmic, chanting. It quieted, then rose into a sharp, hammering chorus.

"The bonfire," Lenora said. "It's huge this year. They had it all built, but not lit, a half hour ago." They all listened.

"They invoke their pagan gods to vanquish the brazen Cats," Aidan announced in an announcer's voice.

Tink's radio audience laughed at something.

The light on the stoop wasn't reaching the far corners anymore. They had a half dozen ducks to go.

Lenora seemed to be watching something in the almost lightless sky. She blinked to see it better. Then, as if she'd got the information she needed, she stood up briskly and pulled the sleeves of her big sweater down over her hands.

"I'll go see what the pagans are doing before it's all over," she said. Aidan sneezed hard. He said nothing.

"Pick away," Lenora said jauntily. "I'll bet I've got better things to do than watch you." She toed the higher pile of limp birds. "Have yourself a time," she said.

Aidan thanked her for the cake. She didn't turn to respond. On her skirt, near the hem in the back, there was a deep splotch of black-looking blood. Neither he nor Roland was careless enough to say a thing.

PART 3

FOURTEEN

2003
Missoula

As he rode the stationary bicycle, pedaling in starts and stops, Wendell Whitcomb tried to identify what exactly he was feeling on his left side, the affected one. He looked around for the aide who had placed him in this torture device, smiling her impervious smile. She had ordered him to pump the bicycle one hundred times, paying particular attention to the muscles of his left leg, eyes ahead, as if something interesting were moving along the horizon.

He had "leftside neglect." That was their term for it, a rather peculiar one when you thought about it, as he couldn't help doing now, since there was, in fact, nothing interesting along the horizon unless you counted a big wall with some sunflowers painted on it. *Who* was neglecting that side? *Who* had abandoned it? If you have a neglected side, someone or something has walked off the job vis-à-vis that side. The term had blame in it. Maybe he would bring this up with the rehabilitation staff, this nomenclature. Or maybe he was being paranoid. Maybe it was actually a word that forgave the person suffering the neglect. Something larger had failed to keep that side going, keep it up to par, keep it unneglected.

He'd reached twenty-nine. One hundred revolutions was a

joke. Perhaps they would like him, next, to scamper up the Matterhorn.

He threw back his head in exasperation and disgust. There were huge butterflies affixed to the ceiling. He'd seen them when he entered the room for the first time, but someone had dimmed the lights a notch and now the butterflies, three-foot wingspans at a minimum, looked more intense, the way a summer day will look when the sun has tipped just enough toward autumn that every color looks a little drenched.

He thought about his neglected side. It had felt far more neglected just after the accident happened. The cerebral vascular accident. That side had, at first, felt so . . . what? So essentially unincorporated. Like a stranger who takes your arm at an intersection and walks you across. The person is at your side, assisting in the act of your personal movement, but in no sense is he you. You had to watch him to know what he would do next.

That was the point of all this work, these bicycles and balance bars and splashing around in the pool with old ladies. It was all to convince his neglected left side that it wanted to rejoin the rest of him.

He'd looked at his face in the mirror that morning and the droop was less pronounced. This was an immense relief. It was still more somber, that side of his face, but not undistinguished really. In some respects it was closer to his customary interior state than the right side was, which had a lot of laugh lines and a jaunty tuned-up aspect to it. And all of it was still rather handsome in an aged and craggy way. Any man in his mid-seventies had to be grateful for that.

The aide returned at last. He'd pumped eighty-one times, to his mild amazement. She patted the handlebar and congratulated him on his progress. She had sturdy inexpressive hands. He told her he had done about as many as he was going to do; that one hundred was quite unrealistic at this point. She told him to keep going, smiled that horizonless smile, and moved off to help another aide get a portly man to his feet for the balance bars. Wendell kept going, until ninety-eight, and then he stopped, though he had a few more in him.

He walked in a slow circle to let his heart collect itself. What a strange place this was. The silvery floors were polished to such a high shine that he felt he was walking on water, that he'd look down at his feet and see bright fish swimming beneath them.

His aide returned and congratulated him profusely when he told her he'd made the limit. As a reward she helped him on with his linen jacket instead of making him work it on himself. He liked to wear his interesting jackets—the linen one or the silk one with the dragon on it—because they helped him feel that he was residing for these several weeks in a spa in some exotic part of the world. I'll be here in Tangier for about two weeks, they tell me, he'd said to his neighbor Flannery, who was going to assist him when he got out of rehabilitation.

He couldn't think about Flannery without seeing her bent over his fallen body, the tiny bells on her earrings pinging in some far-distant universe.

It had started with the UPS man knocking at the door while he was doing his Tai Chi. He had ignored the knock, though he moved the curtain an inch to verify that the young man had left the package inside the screen door. Wendell had watched him, in his brown shorts, leap into the truck, and felt every minute of his age. Even older. It was a day in which everything felt a little wrong and queasy from the moment he'd opened his eyes.

He was at grasp-the-bird's-tail, hands slowly warding off the invisible enemy, then the rollback, the press and push, and now the single whip and the arms lifting and opening in the lovely white-crane-spreads-wings. He closed his eyes to see the moving bird, and opened them upon his mother, Edna, on the mantel.

Edna was sixteen years old in this sole photo he had of her, taken the year he was born. She wore a sober, intent expression, and her pale hair was bobbed and frizzed. Already, in the set of her mouth and the shape of her eyes, there was a disappointed droop, something that said she wasn't going to fight back hard enough, that she didn't trust her own vitality or expect much luck. As indeed had been the case during her short life.

The drawn curtains, unfortunately, were a must. Just once he had done his Tai Chi with them open, and one of the beefy college boys from the duplex across the street had come striding over to ask if he was signaling for help. For help! It was pathetic. The kid had a big rolling walk and a rich father who had bought the duplex for an investment, and now there were two equally unsavory roommates in there with him from someplace in the Midwest, most likely. They had that blocky dimness about them. Pale eyelashes and blotched skin and chip-and-beer guts. Well, live and let live. Except that this particular trio were definite public nuisances with all the noise they made: cars backfiring in the middle of the night, girls coming and going at all hours, and even a huge bonfire once in the front yard, all of them leaping around it, drunk as fiends.

Old age was supposed to be a desert of loneliness, but, in truth, it wasn't easy to get left to your own devices. Logic would dictate that a person might ignore a knock because he is taking a nap, on the toilet, reading without his hearing aid, or doing his Tai Chi. But they won't leave it at that, the helpful types, because you could also have suffered a fall or a stroke, and be lying flat out and helpless on the floor or crawling pathetically toward the phone à la *Christina's World*.

Which, in fact, is what happened. Flannery said she saw the UPS guy knock when she knew Wendell was home, so she went over to check on him, and there he was, having his cerebral accident and trying to crawl.

She had the ambulance there in minutes, and rode in the back with him to the hospital, holding his hand and murmuring reassurances. Then there was the hospital bed and test after test, and she had visited every day and translated the medical talk for him and made the arrangements for his posthospital stint in Rehabilitation Services.

It had been a confusing time, and Wendell hated feeling confused. He hadn't worked as a newspaper reporter in his hometown for forty-seven years in order to feel confused. There were probably only a handful of people in the entire town who knew more than he did about the place and its history and where all the bodies were buried. For a few weeks after the stroke, though, much of that information seemed to slink away to some locked place he didn't know how to open. Then it came out, came back. Most of it. And it was only his neglected left side, that bottomless weakness, that needed to be addressed. That, and some bursts of rage and sorrow that washed over him at times and threatened to throw him to the ground.

He hoped he didn't do any literal collapsing in this place because, although he couldn't have attached names to the faces, there were people undergoing their own rehabilitation who looked familiar to him. The town wasn't, finally, that large. Everywhere he looked in his daily life, he saw people he knew, or sort of knew, or knew about.

He also hoped that his recovery would be complete enough that he could continue to write the children's science books that had been his bread and butter since he'd left the newspaper. Flannery had offered to help him with the research and the typing, so it seemed quite possible that there would be no major interruption.

She was his apartment-complex neighbor, and now might be an ongoing collaborator. Something about all of it seemed preordained, or at least fortuitous.

She was in her fifties somewhere, he supposed, though she had a strange combination of physical traits: She was slim and blond and young voiced, but also stiff moving and rather bent and possessed on certain days of a harsh and worn look, as if she hadn't slept much or was finding it a task to execute the details of her life. He knew very little about her background or current circumstances, and didn't ask, though he did see her furiously kicking the fender of her car once, and she sometimes came over to drink gimlets with him and talk politics or war, or about the latest shenanigans of the big jerks across the street. There was a strident, aggrieved quality to her at times. It made him want to say, Well, just go do it, or change it, or quit trying. She was, at her worst, like a revved-up car, rocking in a ditch, tires smoking. Still, he liked her. In some manner, he recognized her.

At first he had thought she was a lawyer. She carried a briefcase

all the time like a lawyer, although she tended to wear very un-
lawyerlike clothes and jewelry, like the earrings that had tiny bells
attached to silver owls. As it turned out, she had taken early retire-
ment from a public relations job at the university, and was doing
research for some kind of poetic or essayistic book that explored
the resonances between underground missile systems and the lives
of spies. Something along those lines. The whole idea sounded
ridiculous to Wendell, something that would never see the light of
day, so he had enlisted her help in the book he was writing about
the history and principles of X-rays. The UPS man had delivered
the galleys on the day of Wendell's stroke. The editor wanted to
call it *A Professor's Amazing Discovery: The X-Ray.* Wendell wanted
to call it *Mrs. Roentgen's Hand,* because he loved that first X-ray
with its terrifying image of a wedding ring floating around the finger bone of a person who was alive. His young readers would too.

At the central desk he buoyantly asked if he might have some tea to
take to his room. They were very nice about it and asked him to
wait a moment while someone got it. He had a half hour before occupational therapy, which was plenty of time to enjoy some tea,
even if it was the instant kind.

The central desk was arranged in a large circle, the corridors
fanning off from it like spokes. The rooms closest to the desk were
occupied by those in the worst shape, including the ones most
prone to impulsive behavior. These were the people whose cerebral
accidents or traumas made them screamers, streakers, wanderers—
the ones whose brains were giving them visions and apparitions,
and the need to escape. In the old days, Wendell supposed, they'd
have been strapped down with big leather belts if they got uncon-
trollable. Now they were simply encased in their beds in a wide
tube of something like mosquito netting. He'd seen one of them
through an open door, sleeping like a damp new butterfly in a
gauzy cocoon.

After he'd asked for the tea, he waited before going to his
room. There was something else he'd meant to request, but it
wasn't coming to mind. He pulled down the cuffs of his shirt so

that they protruded just the half inch he liked. This took a little while because his left arm had some trouble making the fingers obey on delicate work like cuffs.

As he attacked the problem, he felt the heads of the people in the center area snap up, become alert. Several of them were getting up and moving toward the mouth of the corridor that was behind him and to his left, out of which flew an elderly lady with a neat helmet of dyed black hair and nothing on above the waist.

She moved very rapidly for someone so old, her shoes clicking on the water-colored vinyl. She had a purposeful, happy look on her face, as if she were running after a bus that had stopped to wait for her. Her bared torso was thin and tissuey, the neat breasts like small deflated balloons, the arms ropey and veined and surprisingly competent looking.

She caught sight of the staff coming at her and hung a sharp right, speeding directly past Wendell, so close to him that he could hear her excited breaths and smell her scent, which was something citrusy on top and deep and meatlike beneath. And then she was clicking down the corridor that led to the chapel and administrative offices, a hall Wendell tried to avoid because there was a print hung on its wall that he didn't like. It was supposed to be serene and scenic, but it had an effect on him that he would have described as the sensation that his breastbone was lined with lead. It was simply a lake at sunset with an empty canoe on the near shore and a bunch of purple cloud shadows on the water. Very purple clouds on the water. Just that, really. But it scared him quite a lot, the canoe in particular.

She was past the print now, but they were gaining on her.

"Who was that?" asked a sleepy-voiced aide who'd just returned to the desk from the orthopedics-rehab corridor.

"Mrs. Wellington," one of the nurses told him. *Janie.*

"Ah," Wendell said. *Janie Quist Wellington.*

He now had the sleeve positioned correctly, but his hand wouldn't move from the cuff. He said the name to himself. Wellington. A low hum began in one ear and then the other. A switch in his head had been turned on and first it was the ears and now it was everything, his whole body. He reached out to steady himself on the counter.

Roy Wellington's profile against snow lit by an old streetlamp, and then, later, in the small glow of a cigarette lighter. And their breaths. And their lost, unmoving car.

That particular land mine he hadn't stepped upon for a long time. But they were everywhere across the long tableland of his life, waiting to leap up and ignite in him a long and humming phosphorescence.

"You okay, Mr. Whitcomb?" the ortho aide demanded.

"Absolutely," Wendell said.

The other aide returned with a lidded cup with a straw.

"Iced tea for you," she said. "You can carry it yourself to your room. Any spills, you won't get singed. Iced tea is a better option at this stage."

"Perfect," Wendell said. He let her place the cup in his right hand, the strong one.

"Do you happen to know her first name?" he asked her, pointing the cup down the hall where the old woman had gone, a couple of staff people on her trail. "It's possible that I know her. That I knew her a long time ago."

"It's Jane," she said. "Or, as she likes to insist: Jane Quist Wellington." The weariness of a long day came through and put a little edge in her voice, though she was trying to make herself sound affectionate and funny. She studied Wendell. "Is that the person you know?"

"Oh, I don't think so," Wendell said quickly. "Jane doesn't sound right." He made himself appear to be thinking hard. His heartbeat was thudding behind his eyes. "It would have been a very long time ago, if it is, in fact, the same person."

"Well, she just moved back up here from Sun City to live with a daughter, I believe," the nurse said. "She hadn't lived here for decades and decades. Here maybe a week when she had her CVA."

Her cerebral vascular accident, my cerebral vascular accident.

We're all blowing gaskets. Wendell saw a cartoon of a toppled robot with smoke pouring from its ears.

He had to hear the other name. He had no intention of residing much longer with this subject, but he did want to hear the name.

"And what was her husband's name, do you know?" They'd had enough of him, he could tell. But perhaps they viewed his attempts at recall as therapeutic, and they wanted to give him a reward. Because, a little grudgingly, the female nurse pulled out a drawer behind her and withdrew a file. "I can't tell you personal particulars, of course," she said. "But the husband's name? Let's see. She's widowed. Deceased he is." She looked up at him. "Roy Wellington," she said. "That was her husband."

"Ah," Wendell said. He felt ripples of heat run through both hands. "A Roy Wellington I knew slightly."

They were bringing Jane Quist Wellington back now, wearing some kind of nightgown thing on top. She passed him again, so close that she would have recognized him if she was going to. She lurched a little to the side, and bumped his arm. Iced tea jumped from the straw and dribbled onto his jacket. She watched the tea stain grow and looked up at him, smiling. "Isn't it time for us to go?" she said before they hustled her toward her room.

He stared at her retreating back. His eyes felt a little wild and he knew he should move away quietly, to his room and his tea. "It could have been a Jane I knew," he told the desk nurse brightly. "Jane wouldn't be out of the question."

In his room he sank into the chair by the window and stared out at the frippery of the big willow and, beyond the leaves, at the expanse of the golf course traversed by a few tiny golfers. *A veil of green. Veils of green.* Another phrase hooked itself briefly on his mind. *Something vaguely terrible on the increase.* He sent it away and examined the stain on his jacket so he could feel nothing but frustration and anger at Janie Quist.

He wet a corner of a towel with warm water and a dab of soap. He spread his jacket across his knees and kept it in place with his weak hand and scrubbed at it with the dampened towel. What had he heard about tea stains? Were they the ones where you used salt? Or was that wine? Was there a particular kind of salt? Sea salt? How distant and impossible sea salt sounded. How could he walk around this place with a shred of self-containment and style if he had a tea stain on his jacket the size of a child's fist?

He dabbed, blotted with a tissue, dabbed again, jabbed.

She clearly hadn't recognized him just now, even when she spoke. But when he thought about it, she hadn't fully recognized him when they were both nineteen and dating, either.

He counted the years on his fingers. Five and a half decades since he had last seen her. And those many, many years streamed like a widening river from the single small spring that was a December night in 1946. Or so it seemed to Wendell as he thought about it. A single night that had in it Janie Quist and Roy Wellington and his own mother, home in her bed. And the Flame restaurant and bar, and a snowstorm, and a conversation with the thin young assistant county attorney. Aidan Tierney, his name was. Sad story, Aidan Tierney.

That was the night when Wendell had begun to give up any notion that he would move through his life in a manner that was conventional and safe. He would not marry, not have children. Some men could go where he had gone with another man and come back, but he was not one of them. Roy Wellington could go there and come back and marry Janie Quist and live for another half century as a handsome, booming husband and father, but Wendell wasn't Roy Wellington. And, all told, all done, he knew that he wouldn't have wanted to be.

In a rush, and quite suddenly, he was exhausted. This he had been told to expect. He let the dampened towel drop to the floor and leaned back in the tall plastic chair, spreading his jacket across his knees the best he could, and then something inside him became unplugged, the humming went away, and the residue was warm unsurprising tears falling down his face.

"Here in Tangier," he told Flannery later on the phone, "jigsaw puzzles are the rage." In fact, he said, he was doing one at this very moment, in the common room, with a little help now and then from one of his fellow Tangierines. The person he was doing it with didn't care about the finished picture on the lid of the box. He seemed to think it was more fun to simply plunge in, not knowing exactly what you were trying to re-create. Just focus on the shapes of the pieces, the way the ancient Chinese calligraphers focused only on the motions of their brush tips.

"I think consulting the finished picture is how you make any progress at all," he said crisply to Flannery. "But Roland here does seem to get results."

Roland Taliaferro nodded. He was uncannily good at jigsaws, as it turned out. Nothing about his fall, nothing about whatever his brain had suffered in his fall, affected his ability to match a shape to a shape, to discover exactly where that match might be hiding among all those colored pieces. Not right away, of course, but he always, eventually, seemed to find it. Right now he was working his way through one called Buster the Redcat: The World's Most Difficult Jigsaw Puzzle. It was double sided with the same artwork on both sides—rows of cat faces—but offset 90 degrees from each other. And the puzzle was cut from both sides so you couldn't identify front or back from the bevel. Wendell had no idea how Roland did it.

It was later in the Day of Janie. After the forty-five minutes of occupational therapy, after the long restorative nap. Now a wind had come up and was throwing the willows around, dervishes in the tall common-room windows. Looking at them made Wendell feel a little drunk. Roland seemed oblivious to the weather. He seemed to devote all his energy to concentration, the object at times something in his head, at others something not far from his head, like the jigsaw.

Roland's son, Charlie, a high-voiced, amiable, hyped-up type, was in and out of the rehab center a few times a day, rushing around. Guilt has a very distinctive physical aspect, Wendell thought. It looks like eagerness.

He, the son, had told Wendell he was staying in Missoula for a short while in order to get his father settled. He'd sent his lady friend home to California by plane, and appeared to be dedicating himself, now, to doing too much for everyone. He was on his stomach at this moment, examining the wiring under the television set in the corner. There had been some odd buzzing sounds during the news the night before, and this had somehow come to the fellow's attention, so he was writhing around there like a fool, trying to be helpful. His father, not three feet away, seemed not to notice him.

Wendell handed a puzzle piece to Roland to see what he might do with it. As soon as he'd met the old man, had learned his name, he remembered him in the company of Aidan Tierney all those years ago. Big man, Taliaferro. Big head of hair. An FBI agent. But the rest was fuzzy, like a photo in a chemical bath that had begun to come clear, then had stopped. Wendell could see broad shoulders, blunt hands making an emphatic chopping motion to punctuate a point. But not much more. The countervailing presence in the memory was Aidan Tierney, the ailing attorney who had died shortly afterward during the long blackness that held Wendell's young mother's death. Tierney's voice came to him now. *"Hasta la vista,"* it said. "Talk to you after the holidays."

The whole rehab center was a ghostland in some respects. Shades and apparitions and evocations everywhere. The realm of fleeting evocations.

When he'd tried to remind Roland that they'd met when they were both young, Roland had given him a long unreadable look. Now he was asleep, sitting straight up, two fingers on a jigsaw piece. It was a small phenomenon, the way he didn't lean or tip over.

Across the room, Russell Pretty On Top was talking to a young girl who had been moved from the hospital to rehab a day or so earlier. She was on a walker, clearly working on some balance problems. Her head was shaved and bandaged. Tied like a talisman to the walker was a tail of hair, colored a strange pink.

Some old man in a big car had hit the girl while she was skateboarding, someone had told Wendell. She'd had brain surgery of some kind, but was making a fairly amazing recovery, considering how close she'd come to getting killed.

Russell, from the Blackfeet reservation, had been injured in

Iraq. Spine and brain both. Some paralysis, sleep problems, anxiety, and difficulty concentrating. He was scheduled for a second brain surgery soon, and meanwhile wore a football helmet to protect the place where they'd gone in first. He kept blinking deeply. He had glossy hair pulled back in a ponytail and acne-ravaged skin over a sharp-angled, steely face. Huge liquid eyes kept him looking like a boy. The rest of him was taut and constricted, muscular. He worked at his exercises like a demon. Wendell had seen him.

One evening, in the common room, he'd heard two of the pool players talking about Pretty On Top. He'd been injured on a reconnaissance mission north of Baghdad. His convoy had been hit by a mortar, and in the aftermath, a child with a Kalashnikov walked out of the rubble of a house and shot him.

They'd given him a Purple Heart when he was still in the hospital. Pinned the George Washington profile to his hospital pajamas. Russell had taken a good long look at it, then unpinned it and handed it back. This, Wendell learned from Pretty On Top's mother. "Just took it right off," she said, demonstrating, "and handed it back. He didn't think you should get a medal for getting shot by a terrified little kid."

"I told him, 'Russell, you're gonna get in a bunch of shit,' but those military guys just took it back and pretended they'd never handed it over. And there's been no trouble with his rehab reimbursement or making him go to a VA. They just want him to shut up and get better enough that he'll go away." One of Russell's sisters, at the center with her mother that day, had laughed raucously at the story.

"Hey, Russell," she'd called out. "You going to just clam up and go away?" A very small smile appeared on Russell. He expertly whipped his chair around and headed back to his room, away from them, shaking his head in a way that made them laugh again, verified.

PART 4

FIFTEEN

1946
Missoula

CLOUDS RAN ACROSS THE MOON, MAKING boats on the white mountains. Opal Mix, at her bedroom window, watched their imperious glide across the snow. It was a rare still thing she did, this sitting, this watching, because she had found since Porter's death, seven long years ago, that if she didn't keep her mind occupied with the ordinary business of the day—if she let it stare—it could veer off into directions that made it a stranger to her and left her exposed.

It was her birthday, though, and there was a small puzzle she needed to solve in connection with that event. So she watched the cloud ships, which were only clouds to her, and made her calculations.

She was fifty years old. The puzzle had to do with the fact that the data, the fact of being fifty, didn't strike her as being her actual age. She felt that the lineaments of her life had imposed upon her a different age than fifty, but she wasn't quite sure what it was. Surely a person's experiences had something to do with how old they could accurately be said to be. Certain extraordinary events could double, even triple, the rate of your ordinary aging. As could physical suffering. She knew this well from her nursing days.

She herself had been mostly exempt from physical woes. She didn't notice her body particularly. Except for an occasional twinge in her knee, it was not an interference. This must, in some sense, make her younger than fifty. However, Porter's stunningly quick death had undoubtedly pushed her in the other direction. For a few years, at any rate, her aging must have burned out of control.

So let's say Porter's death canceled out the youth-enhancing influence of good health. You then had to factor in children, or lack of same. Whatever the gratifications they might offer certain people, they would have to be, overall, aging accelerants. She had no doubt about that. Look at Edna Whitcomb down the block, and what that Wendell had done to her coarsely pretty face as he grew to adulthood. The girl looked exhausted.

It followed that Opal, childless, might reasonably reduce her biological age to the midforties. And there was heredity to consider. Several great-aunts had lived into their eighties and nineties— immensely long lives—rocking away on their wooden porches. In fairness, then, Opal could reduce her real age from the midforties to the low forties or even slightly lower.

The men who had returned from the war. Some of them were so much older than their years. They might be just five and six years older than the boys attending the university, but they looked as if they had moved into their fathers' generation. Uncertainty, fear, rotten living conditions—those were the things that added years. You could be twenty-six, twenty-eight, thirty-one years old, and because of what had happened in the war, because of that vehement condensation of experience, be closer to forty.

She was, then, in the same age range as certain men who had gone off to war. If they had been badly damaged by it, then she was, perhaps, just slightly the younger.

He was so pale, Tierney was. Pale and black haired and with a sort of fastidiousness in his expression, a look of attention to the possibility of the distasteful, that she found interestingly at odds with his somewhat brusque manner. Porter had possessed a similar evaluative demeanor. Tierney's suit trousers were cinched around his waist with an old good belt that had been notched in several times. His shirts were stiff and white. He smelled faintly of Old Spice, that lawyerly smell, and sometimes, discreetly, of something else that she called, simply, Hospital.

He took his meals at the hospital. This she knew.

She knew he took his meals at the hospital because the chief dietician was a member of Nile and Professional Women's. Opal had asked her what kind of diet they'd put him on—asked her as a fellow medical professional—and she hadn't liked what she'd heard. She had some real reservations about the efficacy of a low-fiber diet in tough cases like his.

What he needed, really, were regular hot meals in a relaxing environment. A hospital was never relaxing. And anyone who was taking his meals at the hospital would be in the company of others with intransigent digestion problems or outright malnutrition from any number of dire situations—there were probably former prisoners of war at his table each night—so the environment was going to be stressful, and stress, as anyone knew, exacerbated any sort of chronic gastrointestinal situation.

He worked a few hours a day in the county attorney's office but didn't have the stamina for more.

A bachelor was not going to know how to cook healthily for himself, and Tierney probably lived in the sort of place, one of those bare-bones bachelor places, where he might not even have an oven. Actually, she realized with a pleased start, she knew where he lived. In the Alamosa. Portia Tooey, the apartment manager, had told her that at a Nile meeting. She'd forgotten that fact. The nicest fellow you'd ever want to know, Portia had told Opal, though she knew that Opal knew him in a professional capacity so the comment seemed gratuitous. Opal knew who was nice and who wasn't, and it wasn't as if she was going to take exception to Portia's remark, so why did Portia make it in the first place?

A hot plate might be it for him in the Alamosa. And restaurants? Not an option either because they were too expensive to patronize on a daily basis and, in any case, served all the wrong sorts of food.

Oh, and hadn't Porter always loved her pot roast? When you

cooked it on a blanket of root vegetables and added both tomato sauce and a good dollop of Worcestershire a half hour before you took it out of the oven, you had the perfect meal. Substantial but enticing, which was key in a situation like Tierney's where eating enough was as important as eating the right food. Hospital food was institutional food; there was no way to gloss over that fact. And institutional food was unenticing food.

That pot roast she made for Porter. She smelled its brown-roasted spicy aroma, and it was the smell of safety; it was the smell of an ordinary couple fitting seamlessly into their ordinary busy lives, moving unnoticed within the rituals of domesticity, and unassailable there. She clenched her eyes tight until the pain wave passed.

Had anyone ever introduced himself to her in as stern and courtly a manner as Tierney had? Doubtful. Very doubtful. Almost exactly nine months ago, it would have been, about the time she had examined the body of a dead veteran they'd found up in the mountains, and there had been all the trouble afterward.

The deputies had brought the body to her when she was not herself. In the morning she had been living a day like any other. And then had come the presence on the doorstep of Basil, their long-ago caretaker at the mortuary, his long sly face and those obscenities and accusations coming from his mouth. Shaking, she had slammed the door on him, but the rest of the day was one in which she was very much not herself. All she could see when the stained body of the dead veteran presented itself to her sight was a big bear with a paw on the man's chest.

It was one of those quick visions you remark upon to yourself, and which mean nothing, really. But it had been pounced upon by those moronic deputies. As if she had not seen, as well, the pellet holes in the body. Some bear, one of them had said, that fires a 12-gauge.

Had Aidan Tierney been there, the deputies would have been shamed into some modicum of decorum. She had no doubt about that. There was dignity in the man. From the first day he came to work at the county attorney's office, it was evident. Fresh from the

FBI with an honorable resignation for health reasons. Something in his manner had let it be known to her, instantly, that he had heard about the behavior of the deputies and shared her sense of outrage.

When he shook her hand for the first time, he sent a sort of message to her, via a slight smile, a lift of the eyebrows, that said he had some sense of what she put up with, day in, day out. And he had conveyed a personal greeting, too, from his uncle, who turned out to be Doctor Chesterfield, from the little hospital up by the Sweet Grass Hills, where she had got her start as a nurse. Up there in the great quietness where she had met Porter and discovered their compatibility and helped him realize that a life together was best for them both.

It seemed more than coincidental that she and Aidan Tierney had that link. Give her my very best, Doctor had told Tierney. Ask her if she wants her old job back. She and Tierney both got a chuckle out of that. It was like asking if you wanted a professional life on the far side of the moon.

She wanted sometimes to say to Tierney: I know your trouble. It doesn't matter to me. I am a nurse. I am a mortician. The body does not, in its griefs and limitations, dismay me. She had the idea that she would convey that message to him when the time was right. Perhaps the way to do it was simply to invite him to dinner. It might well turn into a routine, one that was undeniably to the benefit of his health. She saw no way that it could be otherwise.

The prosecutors wanted a second copy of her final autopsy report on the murdered veteran, the submarine man, because the vagrant boy who had done it had turned himself in and was standing trial. They needed it for sentencing purposes and they knew she did her reports in triplicate.

Nine months, she hoped, had erased all misconceptions about how she had handled the postmortem. Street cops were so quick to jump on what a person said in the course of beginning the painstaking work of doing a proper autopsy. Essentially, a person at that point was speaking to herself, just running down the line of possibilities. She shouldn't have let them hang around when they'd brought the body to her. She never would again, you could be sure of that.

It had been a bearish body, bulked up and efficacious, with a soft tire around its middle. A bear minus its hide and fur. Late thirties. A four-inch scar on the right thigh. The tip of his right ring finger missing. Strong intact teeth. Approximately two days of exposure.

Tierney worked sometimes in the evenings, the dietician had told her. He would take his evening meal at the hospital, then have a rest, then try to chalk up another hour or two at his desk so he wouldn't fall far behind everyone else. Walking past the courthouse once, on an evening when her mind wouldn't stop staring, she thought she saw him through the slats of a second-floor blind, dark head bent over his work. It was a wasting disease he had acquired in the war. Someplace in South America where he had volunteered to go. Something down there had infected him. When she first met him, she thought: He looks like someone who has lost what he had never, in his wildest dreams, imagined he could lose. In that way, they were very much alike.

She telephoned. He was there. The verdict was just in—guilty, of course—and the sentencing would probably happen soon after the holidays. But he supposed it wasn't a bad idea to have a second copy of the autopsy report on hand. If she wanted to bring it over, why not?

She walked the four blocks to the courthouse, the snow squeaking beneath her galoshes. He met her at the east door to let her in. The place was dim, sepulchral, lofty. A janitor plodded across the shiny marble with his wide broom, whistling through his teeth. The smell of the large Christmas tree inside the front door infused the air. A steam heater behind one of the frosted-glass doors clanked loudly.

He followed her up the curved staircase to the county attorney's suite on the second floor. She climbed briskly. No particular aches or pains. She walked a lot and so her legs were strong. My legs are still strong, she thought to herself as she climbed. I have the legs of a person twenty years younger than myself.

She liked the courthouse far better at night than she did during the day. During business hours there was too much clatter and

smoke, and the girls who still worked in the offices were always cel-
ebrating something. Every week it was a birthday or an engagement, the engagee ready to leave the work-girl world for the new
husband, though sometimes she'd come back in a year, two, with a
baby to show off and then they'd have another cake, chocolates,
and the gooey, cooing baby would pull them all close, filings to a
magnet.

It had been better during the war, less frivolous, more focused.
People pointed themselves outward to the danger, the enemy, their
eyes farsighted and alert. Afterward, everyone paired off. She tried
to think of anyone she knew who was not married or about to be
married. Widowed on the eve of the war, she felt widowed again
when it was over.

He had made a point, when they first met, of introducing himself with a grave and courtly handshake. His uncle had told him,
he said, that she had left his employ somewhat precipitously.

"He said you ran off with a patient," Tierney had said. "Not
that there is any law against running off with patients."

"The patient was healed and ready for discharge. He came
from a ranch in the area and felt it was time to move on, as did I,
and we decided to make a life together," she had said crisply. "If
you can find a scandal in that, then you are looking too hard for
one."

"No scandal," he had said, his hands mockingly up to defend
himself.

"I am a person who thinks things out. As was Porter. You can
be sure of that."

"Quite sure," Tierney said. But there was a tone of mockery in
it, or perhaps banter.

"The patient in question was my husband for twelve years, and
a respected member of this community. This was before your time
here, but surely you knew about him. He died quite suddenly. Peritonitis. A ruptured appendix. A tragic misdiagnosis."

"The patient in question," Tierney had said, as if he turned the
words in his hand and found them curious. The conversation
seemed to be at an end.

"I like it up there," he had said. "I spent many an hour up there in the Sweet Grass Hills. My kid brother, Neil, and I. Days at a time. We knew that area like the backs of our hands."

When Opal thought of the little hospital, those long-ago days at the sunny, windy end of the earth, she didn't like the thought at all. She had felt, almost always, as if something were going to reach down and toss her away.

"Don't you find it distracting the way courthouse business seems, these days, always to get caught up in someone's marriage arrangements?" she said now, as she retrieved the report from her folder.

He looked at her as if he was waiting for her to finish the thought.

"This pairing. So frantic. Almost at random, it seems. You have real doubts in some cases whether the couple is compatible, wouldn't you say? Whether they have a certain compatibility that is the key to a successful marriage."

He said nothing. He said nothing the way lawyers say nothing when they have you on the stand and are waiting for you to say the thing that is going to trip you up.

"That was my experience, at any rate," she said, pretending to examine the report to see that all the pages were there. "A sensible sort of routine. Compatibility. The sort of pattern that holds up over time."

A big hatless man with snow in his hair barged in. The tock of his footsteps had been loud in the hall, but it was still a surprise when he stopped at this office and crashed in.

"Christ," he said, slapping his gloves against his pant leg. He had a cloud of frigid air around him. "Had an idea I might find you here. I stood out there and waved like a madman at the janitor, and then he made me show him identification. Good man, I said. Can't be too safe. Stopped briefly at the Elks to see if Hanrahan had nailed down his barstool for the night, and you should have seen the gyrations I did to get out of there." There was something carefully buoyant about him, as if he knew he should monitor himself.

Aidan introduced him to Opal. His name was Roland Taliaferro, one of those Butte names, and the two of them had been in
law school together. Joined the FBI together. Roland was still an
agent. He held down the fort, he said, over in Butte.

Roland walked around the room, pretending to examine the
book titles behind the glass doors. He was making puddles of melted
snow everywhere like a big oblivious dog.

Tierney regarded him with an affectionate, sardonic smile. They
were night and day. How did this sort of pairing, this sort of friendship, occur? Opal wondered. Her own acquaintances tended to be
similar in most respects to herself. Volunteers. Club people. Good
citizens. Ordered and abstemious, with neatly kept homes and
agreed-upon rituals of interaction. They brought you a flower
arrangement and a casserole if you were ill. They voted for conserva-
tives of either party. They followed the news—not in depth but
enough to have an opinion about any major development from the
national level on down. They didn't trust unpredictable people or
"personalities." They were, most of them, Episcopalians or
Methodists. But they didn't take church home with them.

Tierney was reaching for an overcoat that hung on a hook. She
felt stung. Was she being dismissed? Perhaps they were going out
for a meal. Perhaps Tierney had not eaten dinner, had not gone to
the hospital. Perhaps his health was improving. That thought produced a small blast of bleakness.

Taliaferro said he had to see a man about a horse—he'd be
back in a jiff. He made a brisk, get-the-show-on-the-road gesture,
a chopping gesture with his hand.

"Have I met him before?" she asked Tierney when he was
gone.

"Not if you were lucky." The small smile. "He's an old friend.
Not the most couth, the most elegant person on the planet, but he's
an old friend." He seemed to hear a tentative note in his voice that
he didn't like. "And a good one," he said.

"Will you be going out to dinner?" She pulled on her gloves
and adjusted her woolen muffler.

"He might eat something. That wouldn't be the worst idea in

the world. I take my meals at the hospital for now. For the time being. A temporary arrangement."

"You know," she said. "I'm a nurse."

His face latched closed. "I think I did know that," he said.

"Do you want to review that report quickly, while I'm here?" she said as if she'd just thought of it. "You could catch up with your friend in fifteen minutes or so."

"I'll call you in the morning if there is anything confusing. Anything else we need to know." He was putting on his gloves. She began to button her coat.

"Mr. Tierney," she said. "Because I'm a nurse, I know what kind of food they serve patients with special needs at the hospital. I'm informed about those matters. I keep up."

He was looking for something in his desk drawer. It was as if he hadn't heard her.

"I keep up," she repeated. "And I will say this. It is essential that any person with a chronic gastrointestinal situation eat extremely carefully, in a setting that doesn't produce stress. In a setting in which the preparation of the meal is knowledgeable and the serving of it is not in the institutional manner."

She had decided to press forward, frankly, the way she used to do with men in the hospital who were reluctant to let her bathe them. You had to be very brisk. That was the only way.

"I have an idea that your situation might be helped in no small way if you took your evening meals, several times a week at least, in a home setting."

He had turned away from her to put something into a file drawer. "We could make an arrangement. You would eat your evening meal at my home. It would be a medical arrangement. I know what needs to be done in these matters."

It felt reasonable to talk to the back of his suit. It all made sense.

When he turned around, his face was white, with two sharp points of color on the crests of his cheekbones. He stood behind the desk. He put his hands on it and leaned toward her. His voice was very low.

"Mrs. Mix," he said. "I'd ask you to understand that my situation is a complicated one. I find it very unlikely that you could understand what it is or what needs to be done. Let me be perfectly clear: I need or want nothing from you. Is that very clear?"

He kept his eyes on hers. They had coldness in them.

"You're making a large thing out of a small one," she said at last. Her voice wobbled. She could hear Taliaferro clumping down the hall, whistling.

"I think it's time for you to leave, Mrs. Mix," he said. "Thank you for bringing over the report."

He opened the door and held it.

"Good evening," Taliaferro said like a movie butler. She pushed past him and walked as rapidly as she could. *Keep your hand on the banister. You'll fall headlong. Then they'll jump on you and hurt you.*

She could feel the big paintings that lined the wall peering down on her. At the bottom of the stairs, in near darkness, she caught her breath. It was rasping. She chanced a look upward to see if they were standing there. Nothing.

But she heard something. She heard murmurs. She strained to listen. The janitor called to her from across the foyer. He'd been invisible behind a pillar. He pushed his broom out ahead of him. Very jaunty this one. Top of the evening.

"Did you let a man in here who was knocking at the door a few minutes ago?" she said in a sharp whisper. "There is a man upstairs who has no authorization to enter a public building simply because a janitor says he can."

"Lady," he said patiently. "He's FBI. He can do anything he wants to."

"We'll see about that," she warned him. He shrugged. "Showed me his badge," he said. "You can see about it though, if you want," he added solicitously.

She heard them then. At first it was just murmurs, men's murmurs, which didn't seem to be coming closer. But she heard them. Perhaps they were in the shadows at the top of the stairs. There was an intimate conspiratorial tone to the sounds. She could make out no words. It seemed to take far longer to tell the story than it ought to. And then one of them laughed. A big released laugh, echoing through the entire building.

It was Taliaferro, the friend. The old good friend. He'd just been told something that he thought was amazing. This wasn't lazy, desultory laughter. This had that incredulous bark.

People can carry a kind of evil within them, she thought as she walked rapidly through the frigid night. There will be a smooth, charming, friendly surface perhaps. An intelligent surface. A gift for seeming frank and concerned. And really it was all a mask. Beneath it? Sheer cruelty, a willingness to hurt.

She'd noticed this in more than a few people, especially since the war. Some of the men who came back seemed to be practicing a sort of civility and ease that was not natural to them. Perhaps they watched the movies to see how it was done. How a Cary Grant, a Spencer Tracy did it. A wry, confident, athletic, ready-to-laugh way of being in the world. A capacity for concerning yourself with trivia. A capacity for simple cheer. They might have wanted those qualities, but they had no access to them. She had noticed that right away. Some were trying to get it back, that interest in the quotidian, in the weather, in wives, in children, in cars that ran well and socks that matched.

Others, a few of them, were like cobras in lidded baskets. Ready to strike. Furious and pale and rattled. Somewhere in there.

Aidan Tierney was the last person she would have suspected. But there it was. A strain of pure venom.

"Let me be perfectly clear," he had said. "I'd ask you," he had said. She'd heard a little hiss in it.

She welcomed the familiar smell of flowers and formaldehyde. The hushed, churchlike feel, the thick carpeting. Nothing to jar. No loud noises.

Two cool ones in the back. She went to the workroom. Turned on the lights. Turned on the radio. She worked with music usually. Or a radio drama. It took her head to another place, kept it occupied, while she went through the rituals of preparation: the draining, the powdering, the sewing of the eyes.

One was a woman in her early forties, dead of an apparent heart attack. She looked a little like Edna Whitcomb, her neighbor, though this one was a few years older. She thought about Edna and all those men, and the boy Wendell who had run so wild. What a horror he'd been. Even now, though he was a reporter in a fedora, probably twenty years old, she avoided him.

The mother and son were central to Opal's memory of everything going wrong very fast. She would think of that time and she would see Wendell tearing up and down the street, screaming at her. And then, so soon, just a vast silence that had never really gone away.

She studied the face on the table. A little pouchy but basically unlined. There was something stalwart about it, even in death. That slight jut of the jaw. Plump hands with recently manicured nails.

A man had stopped by the mortuary, earlier in the day, to view this woman. Then he had sat alone in the grieving room, and she had heard gulping sobs. Huge, unseemly sobs.

She picked up the lipstick and dabbed it on the lips. Jabbed it. It smeared. She stood back and examined the smear, and left it in place. She made another small mark. A big band was playing on the radio. Couples danced across a glassy floor, a pomaded bandleader smiling down on them benignly.

"You look a little disheveled," she told it. "You should be a neat lady. You should be neat as a cat." She drew a long red whisker.

"Have I hurt you?" she murmured. "Have I done something to hurt your feelings?"

She wiped away the whisker and the lipstick smudges. She tweaked the collar of the blue dress. She examined the stitches in the eyes, making sure that they were hidden by the fold.

SIXTEEN

1946
Missoula

WENDELL WHITCOMB SCRIBBLED FAST IN HIS reporter's notebook as a sheriff's deputy told the court about a call he'd got early on the morning of March 4. The caller, a carpet salesman, said he had seen a young man—maybe a teenager—in a checked woolen jacket sitting cross-legged beside the flames of a campfire built in the middle of the highway. Right on the center line. The fire was quite large and the man stretched the palms of his bare hands toward it.

Because it was such a disorienting vision—the light and its human leaping out of the midnight black—and because he'd been driving exhausted, the salesman thought for a moment that he'd fallen asleep and had veered into a meadow or a farmyard, someplace where a person might more reasonably build a fire. Then he was coming up on it fast, and he swerved and felt his outside wheels tip into the barrow pit, but he managed to keep the car upright and steady.

Back on the road again, chasing the narrow lines of his headlights, he checked his mirror to verify the existence of the apparition. It flickered and glowed and grew small. He had come close enough to the man to reach out and touch his woolen shoulder. His legs felt rubbery, then numb. He kept driving. He drove faster.

By the time the deputy got a chance to check it out, a watery sun had lightened the landscape but not illuminated it. Everything looked old, silent, and cold. The highway bisected a wide hay meadow there, and the humps of old stacks rose at intervals. Beyond the meadows were low, heavy-shouldered mountains. The blackened sticks of the campfire were warm on their undersides. There were boot prints, a gum wrapper, a couple of struck matches.

The deputy walked up and down the highway at its edge, looking for more of the story. The boot tracks ended at the tread of a big truck that had pulled to the very edge of the road and pulled back onto the concrete again. The fire maker had got himself a ride.

Two days later, up in the mountains, a forester found a dead man under a tarpaulin, not far from a box tent. He had been shot at close range. The gun lay under a bush, forty paces from the body. In the tent were two bedrolls. Around the camp were two sets of human prints and a dog's. Also, a 1939 Ford pickup that started right up. The shot dog was found in a nearby creek bottom. Someone thought to check the boot prints against those around the fire on the highway, and there was a match.

The body was identified via the wallet as a man named Calvin Rydell, who worked in a local hardware store. Coworkers said he had lived in the woods in the tent because he had been a submarine man during the war and vowed never again to sleep under a solid roof. He drove the pickup twenty-five miles to town every day to work. He was quiet, a loner, no trouble to anybody—the sort of guy who would help you fix a flat tire or work your shift if something came up, though he wouldn't say much while he worked and he waved away all thanks.

The lone surviving relative, an aged father in Salt Lake City, was notified. No one had seen the victim in the company of another. Nothing in the camp yielded a clue. The blankets of both bedrolls were the dead man's, and the rifle too. The boot prints were a common brand and an ordinary size. The salesman who had almost hit the boy and the campfire could offer nothing more than the checked wool jacket, the young vague face.

A bulletin went out all over the country asking truckers to report any hitchhikers in the vicinity around the time in question. Nothing. The case grew very cold.

Seven months later, in Hartford, Connecticut, an eighteen-year-old house painter named Jerrold Leary turned himself in and confessed.

He had hitchhiked west after a violent falling-out with his father, and Calvin Rydell had picked him up and offered him a place to stay in the forest.

What had he done after he shot Rydell? Well, he told the officers, he had shot the dog as it began to slink away, had heaved the rifle somewhere into the bushes, tried without luck to start the pickup, followed the victim's tire marks out to the highway. It took him hours to get to pavement, he said.

Had he done anything else? Yes. He had built a campfire to warm up. Right in the middle, on the dividing stripes. He didn't know why, exactly. Perhaps to make it harder for anyone to pass him by. The highway that night had the emptiness of a dream. A car passed him and kept going. Then a truck. Then another truck, but it stopped.

The location of the campfire had been withheld, so the boy's statement clinched it.

He couldn't live with himself, he told them. He was ready to face the music.

As the sheriff's deputy told the jury about the campfire in the middle of the road, he was thinking about a similar incident a few years earlier when he had worked as a snowplow driver up north, near Glacier Park.

It had been the dead of winter, thirty below and blowing. He had inched around a hairpin curve to see, fifty yards ahead through the moving veil of snow, something dark and still. An animal, he thought, or something fallen from a truck. He drew close and climbed down, shocked by the sting of the snow, the erratic fury of the wind. The form didn't move. It was a boy, an Indian, in a big army coat in the middle of the road. His bare head was bowed. His legs were spread on either side of a small dead fire. He had long braids, three of them, gloveless hands. Between his legs was a knife and a damp stick with one side shaved into curls.

Two miles away, his beat-up car had slid off an icy curve into a deep ravine. He had crawled out of there, walked through the blizzard down the road, stopped at a junction of two small highways up there in the mountains.

Had he calculated his odds, decided his best chance in a storm was a fire and an intersection? That visibility was his best shot, and it outweighed any off-road shelter from the wind? Who knew?

He'd managed to make the fire. Expertly. But the storm had continued, and the roads piled high with snow. He had looked calm and almost alive, as if he was poised in the middle of an ordinary task.

The image haunted the snowplow driver even after he became a deputy and gained more experience with death and mayhem. He didn't know why. He brought it up sometimes with his wife or friends, hoping he'd find in his own words an accurate description of what he felt when he'd seen the campfire and its maker on the concrete, which was a sense of having witnessed a time collision so violent it threw certain humans away.

Wendell Whitcomb leaned against the desk of an editor named Max Templeton, his predecessor on the cop beat. Templeton had been moved to the copy desk, where he could clip the wire, double-check addresses, tipple discreetly, and stay out of the way.

What was Wendell like at nineteen years of age? Slim, handsome, eager, fast. Twitchy with coffee and smokes. Overtly hungry in the job. Unable to affect the leisurely reassurance of an old news hand, the sort of cynicism and laziness that promised sources they risked nothing. If there was a story lurking under a scrim of slick talk, Wendell would try to get it.

He and Templeton were reviewing again the night that Calvin Rydell's body had been brought in to be examined by the coroner, Opal Mix. She had taken a quick look, pressed a finger to the bloody flannel shirt, and announced that the man appeared to be the victim of a bear attack. She hadn't read, yet, the preliminary reports of the site investigation.

"The coroner, for chrissake," Templeton said with a dry smile. "I wonder what else she's missed over the years." But he didn't wonder, really. He was a slow-handed, heavy-faced fifty-year-old whose disgust with manifestations of official ineptitude lacked even a trace of curiosity. He expected it, he remarked upon it loudly and at length, and he felt his profession to be helpless in the face of it and deluded if it thought otherwise.

"It's all cooked." That was his favorite expression. "You ride in on your white horse; you ride out on your sad ass." That was another.

Wendell was different. He was curious, tenacious, and dogged. He hated ineptitude, particularly in people who had some power in the community, and he felt he was in the perfect position to expose it, if his editors would just leave him alone to do his job.

Already he'd written stories about political cronyism, real estate deals, and sloppy city-hall bookkeeping that had caused something of stir. His next target—and the damaging stuff against her was accumulating fast—was coroner Opal Mix.

"She's incompetent, a loon, a public menace," Wendell said. "I live across the street from her. I've kept an eye on her for years. And if she wasn't always a loon, she was goddamn strange. You should have been there when Snead told her to turn the body over. Ping, ping, ping. Buckshot all over the floor. 'Oh,' she says. 'We appear to have a new scenario here.'"

"Word on the street," Templeton said. "They're gonna send her packing. End of the year. Around the bend, our girl. Word on the street." He never went out of the newspaper office. Ate his ham roll and hard-boiled egg at his desk.

Wendell liked the story more each time he told it. "Snead says to her, all respectful: 'Well, ma'am, we've got a new scenario unless you know about a bear who carries a shotgun and has the consideration to cover his victims with a tarp.' She doesn't blink. Just stares at him. See you at your funeral, copper, she says with those big buggy eyes. Gives me a slow chill up my neck."

Wendell ran his hand slowly up the back of his neck. It was a languorous, unconscious gesture that seemed to embarrass Templeton. He bent over a page proof, yawning bitterly.

Wendell was going over to the jail. The case had gone to the jury, and he had permission from the court and the defense lawyer to interview the teenager from Connecticut. It was a low-ceilinged, spitting-snow sort of day, and he wore a heavy woolen overcoat, collar turned up, and new leather gloves. Good ones. He checked his cigarette supply.

At the jail he asked curtly to see the prisoner, as arranged. Jerrold Leary sat on the edge of a steel cot writing a letter. He had thick auburn hair that wouldn't smooth down, and the blue-white skin, the pale eyes of a certain kind of Irish. Not big—maybe five foot eight—but dense and muscled. Son of a millworker, youngest of nine, saint whatever high school, a little earlier trouble, aimless vandalism with the buddies, a night in jail for a ruckus at a roller skating rink, mother dead of TB, Jerrold himself married for about five minutes and divorced. The teenage mother raising the baby.

He pulled the chair over to the bars, and Wendell took a seat on the other side. He lit a cigarette and took out his notebook.

"How long do you think they'll be out?" Leary said. He had a high, offhand voice, and sounded bored to death. Wendell shrugged. If it didn't bother Leary that he was looking at forty to life, it didn't bother him. He wanted this over with.

Leary wrapped a hand around a bar, as if for ballast. He told Wendell he'd sum it up again, the circumstances and the reason and the aftermath.

Someone in the next cell was keening. A phlegmy voice ordered it quiet. The sound rose, then fell to a tiny moan, like a tea-kettle barely at the boil.

He'd been hitchhiking west, he said, trying to get over the breakup of his marriage and a bitter fight with his dad. The victim picked him up, took him up into the forest where he lived. It took forever to get there, and it was dark, and then there was a white tent in the darkness and wind like a big river through the tops of the trees. The guy built a good fire in the stove. He didn't say much. Heated up some beans. Told Leary he could stay as long as he wanted, earn his keep by doing a few chores around the camp: sharpening the saw, gathering firewood, that sort of thing.

Each day the fellow went off in his pickup to town. Each night he came back.

He himself was a Hartford boy, Leary told Wendell. City kid. And there he was, all turned around, up on the North Pole somewhere is what it felt like. Snow everywhere and black pointed trees tall as buildings with stars between the branches that flew around and made you dizzy. Every sound like a shot—the fire, the ax on the wood. Wolves too. You heard them way off there, stalking around with the bears.

He was riding the trolley when he was four, he said. Alone. True story. Not a matter, any of this, of having guts or not. But you get out there in the North Pole and you're depending on this stranger to know where you are or get you out of there, and it does something with your mind. All he did, he said, was pine for his new girlfriend and wonder how to get out.

"I was desperate," Leary said in a distant, practiced voice, as if he were telling the story to someone else. "I had to get out or die trying. And then the fool pickup didn't start. He had some trick to starting it."

"Why didn't you just ask him for a ride out?" Wendell said.

"Wouldn't have happened," Leary said flatly.

"Well, you could have asked," Wendell said. "Instead of shooting him before he had a chance to say yes or no. A shot man is going to have some trouble giving anyone a ride. It's hard to drive when you have," he consulted his notebook, "shots in your throat, your chest . . ." He looked past the prisoner at something on the far wall. "Your buttocks."

Leary glared at him. "I'm writing a letter to my girlfriend," he said. "Could we wrap this up?"

"Of course," Wendell said. "Your lawyer clearly wants you to tell me something he can use at sentencing, so tell away."

"There were extenuating circumstances," Leary said. "They got slid over in there, I thought. Some of the details. The guy was a fruit. I knew it the first night. He said something to me. I couldn't believe what I was hearing."

"Tough city kid that you are," Wendell said.

"I couldn't believe what I was hearing," Leary repeated in elaborate sardonic tones, "in the place where I was hearing it. Some wilderness somewhere."

"But he didn't follow up. That's what you told them."

"Didn't lay a finger on me," the kid said triumphantly. Wendell put his pencil down and pulled his chair a few inches closer to the bars. He lowered his voice. "So his sin was that he didn't lay a finger on you? That's what got him shot?"

"He would have. He was going to. You don't sleep in the same tent for three nights and not know what he's planning. And I was trapped. Didn't know where the hell I was. Knew he'd tackle me if I went for the pickup. I had one last chance. And I took it."

Wendell started laughing. Leary sat back, startled. A slow flush crawled up the side of his white face. Wendell couldn't stop. He laughed longer than he needed to. Shook his head hard. Stood and pulled on his gloves.

"You know," he said. He consulted his watch. "If you and that lamebrain lawyer of yours are lucky, that jury will stay out more than, oh, twenty minutes. Just to make it look like there was a case. Just to be polite."

"He was a fairy!" the kid screamed. "A flaming fairy twice my size, and I was threatened and I resisted. Defended myself. End of story!"

Wendell turned his back. Leary had huffed across the room and plopped himself on the thin bed. He breathed heavily.

"What do you think a jury would do if it had been some girl in my position?" he called out. "You think they wouldn't say self-defense? Especially if no one ever would have known she done it, and then she turned herself in from remorse?"

"If you know you're right, you don't go all remorseful," Wendell said softly, over his shoulder. "Not in Hartford, or Montana, or Timbuktu. That's number one. Number two: The accused in this case is not a girl." He hit his pencil lightly on a bar. "Is he?"

As the jailer let him out, a heavy man in a canvas coat rose from a bench. He had flaring white eyebrows and deep, doggy eyes; big gnarled hands with a couple of missing fingertips. A sentimentalist and a sadist, Wendell thought. He had a habit of tagging strangers in his mind. The man walked hugely and exhaustedly, but he wore a look of alert vindication. Something right had happened.

"The pop," said the jailer, when the door had closed behind the man. "Out here on the train from Hartford, Harvard, one a them."

"The pop," Wendell said. "Harvard man."

"Going in to see junior there. Says junior did the right thing. Junior's a man. Junior, he says, would shoot the guy all over again." He spit cheerfully into the garbage can.

Wendell waited. He was sweating and drained, and didn't know why. If someone had asked him at that moment how he felt about the prisoner he'd just met, he'd say he hated him. Fully.

"Submarine man, the victim," the jailer went on. "Did you know a year on a sub makes your physical age eleven and a half years older than your actual age? They're like time machines. That go forward."

"Who told you that?"

"My girl. Audrey. The one that has the raccoon, the pet one. The one that lives in the bureau drawer?"

"Oh, shut up," Wendell said. He was starting to feel better.

"It *likes* the drawer," the jailer said. "It's warm. It's protected. Why not?"

"Why not," Wendell said.

"Its name is Rudy," the jailor said. "Because it used to be rude. Very rude. Prior to the drawer."

Wendell added three inches about the jailhouse interview to his trial story, and the jury was back in just under a half hour. The story ran on page one:

Guilty Verdict in Shooting
Youth Claimed Self-defense
Feared Motives of 'Samaritan'
Told Court He'd Do It Again

When he got off work, Wendell checked on his mother, Edna, before he changed his shirt and headed to the Flame to meet his girlfriend, Janie Quist. He tried not to think about the way Edna had been the last few days, with those blue circles under her big eyes, a slowness in her walk, as if she had sprained the small of her back hauling the laundry from the line. She said it was just a twinge, something not quite right, some female thing, which was far more than Wendell wanted to know. She sent him to the drugstore for aspirin. She wore an intent, pained look, as if she were listening to a tiny voice yelling insults at her, and she could make out most of the words but not all. Her breath when she adjusted his tie was stale and bacterial.

He told her she should get some tonic, thinking of the revitalized people in the ads. It was the only solution he could think of for unsavory female malfunctions and body griefs. Maybe I will, she said. Her face was a little hectic.

He told her to drink a hot lemonade and go to bed early. She said maybe she would. After she practiced her typing, she would.

She had been taking some typing courses at the commercial school and was more hopeful about the prospects of a decent job than she had been for a long time. Now that the war was over and the men were back, women were leaving the workplace in droves to make way, but there was still a certain sort of office job a man didn't want to do: the secretary/girl-Friday sort of job. Some women who'd had those jobs were getting married now and going home, so Edna had plans to step into the breach.

"There will be some vacancies for a career woman like me," is how she put it to Wendell when she'd got a high score on her first typing test. She practiced on a piece of paper with the typewriter keys drawn on it. She told him she had thought for a while that she'd try to find a decent breadwinner to marry. But that hadn't panned out, and Wendell was basically on his own now, so what was the point?

"No breadwinners to be had!" she had said boisterously. "And now I'm getting so old that any suitors"—she gave the word a quick sardonic slap—"look like death on a cracker." Edna was, this early winter of 1946, thirty-five years old. She had been Wendell's mother for half her life.

"What a nitwit," Janie Quist said when Wendell told her about Leary. "What would make a person haul himself to prison because he *felt bad*?" This was a typical sort of question for Janie. She was, at her core, coldly and cheerfully pragmatic in a way that Wendell admired immensely. It wasn't as if she had rebelled against the idea of moral principle, finding it too complicated or onerous. She had simply been born without a sense of it.

Being with her was like being with someone who was blind in one eye. Only occasionally did you notice that she navigated without a shred of depth perception. She was also extremely volatile and given to elaborate dramatics. Her father was the editor of the newspaper, long a widower, and she was his only child. Her absolute confidence in the power of her own whims made her wildly attractive to almost everyone she knew.

She had initiated Wendell, in a matter of days, into a rambunctious variety of almost-all-the-way sex. He couldn't quite believe it—her outlandishness and obstreperousness; the way she was so at home in her thin, minimally curved body. Without that mop of curly auburn hair, she would have looked like a boy. Straight as a stick. She had a clear frank face, but it was the hair that edged her toward any prettiness. Her reputation preceded her but didn't interfere.

She quite literally threw herself at Wendell, conducting explorations that amazed him and on several occasions left him gasping and aghast. He felt at times like the keeper of an animal that had been shipped from a part of the world he'd never heard of. He let the beast do things because she was used to it and seemed to want to, but he felt always as if he should be imposing rules on her for the good of them both, though he had no idea what those rules might be.

His mother was no help. She'd never stayed with a man longer than a few months, and the criteria, if any, for conducting relationships were inscrutable. She'd had just a few words for her son: Don't knock anyone up.

Janie liked to incorporate fevered narratives into her antics. On one occasion, she decided that Wendell had taken another girl to a

movie in another town. On Wendell's payday, she'd decided, he
and the girl had hopped on the train and ridden a hundred miles to
Butte, where an underground theater showed banned movies. They
had ridden the train, eaten a steak dinner, and watched Hedy Lamarr
in *Ecstasy,* all behind Janie's back. She based this scenario on nothing
and put her energy into it simply because she was bored. They had
club steaks with mushrooms, she told him.

Wendell, of course, denied the story in its entirety, which was
her cue to be outraged, which launched the next installment of her
drama: little hatch marks on her wrists, the barest scratches really,
made with a penknife. Delicious.

Wendell never knew what Janie saw in him. He'd certainly
never been in her bright orbit before. Only later, long after she was
gone, would he figure out that he had been a growth environment
for her, a sort of petri dish in which her particular ingredients could
expand within a border before she claimed them for herself and
stepped out into adulthood.

Her effect on his social life was to bring him out of the room
where he felt he had been standing alone all his life. For the first
time, his former classmates, his contemporaries, noticed him. The
boys who had ignored him all these years, or tormented him in
small rote ways, seemed now to blink their eyes and see him.

It helped that he had become tall and deep voiced, very handsome, if a little too thin, according to both Janie and his mother.
And he had a job with real money and visibility. Not box boy. Not
lawn mower. Not farmhand or clerk. He was a reporter. He wore
a hat. He asked the bigwigs importunate questions. He talked to
cops and judges and jail keepers and coroners and firemen, and
they talked back. But it was the popular, madcap, anything-goes
Janie who really opened the door for him.

His former classmates now honked as they passed in their cars.
They talked to him in the movie lines. They gave him the thumbs-
up, the sardonic tipped hat, the fellow-horndog looks. Even Roy
Wellington, who had battered Wendell's face into the schoolyard
gravel in the sixth grade and called him a pansy, even Roy was dis-
concerted into a quiet kind of watchfulness by Wendell and Janie.

When they first began to date, Wendell woke up each morning and thought, amazed: I love my life. He had never thought he would love his life. The idea had never occurred to him. Now, though, each day brought Janie's latest piece of high drama to wonder about. Each day, for her, was a kind of snowdrift, to be vehemently attacked with a shovel, to be roughed up and broken and made into a new shape. And there was also her latest attack on his person to wonder about, though thinking about it too often brought a wash of sadness and unease. And that was not normal. He knew that. He didn't know if he would ever muster exactly what it was that she was after. He felt like a damp match.

He wondered when she would turn elsewhere, and then he grew panicky. It couldn't end, because then he would be back where he was before, invisible. Even his fancy reporter's job wouldn't save him. Once she had concluded he was a damp match, all the lights would go out.

At the Flame they sat in a booth across the room from Roy Wellington and his date, who was only sixteen but looked twenty-six. Roy always looked as if he had been running in the cold. That high color. And his early gangliness had turned into a strong, filled-in, slender look. His name should be Tyrone, Wendell thought, as he shot a high wave across the crowd.

"Don't you think Roy's name should be something like Tyrone?" he asked Janie.

Janie looked at him, and he wished he'd said nothing.

"I don't think anything about Roy's name," she said quite loudly. "Roy Wellington isn't someone I care to think much about." Wendell shushed her.

"Don't order me around," she said, raising her voice to her I'm-a-devil pitch. She lifted her drink as if she were about to deposit it on his head.

Wendell threw a glance at Roy and got back a grin of solidarity. What do you do with one like her?

Now Janie studied her drink pensively. Then she studied the people who were leaning on the piano. Wendell waited.

"What are you smiling about?" she snapped. She threw back her head and closed her eyes. Wendell was grateful that this had happened a time or two before, so he would know what to expect. He took the chance and grinned again at Roy, adding a shrug. Roy made a small she's-cuckoo circle in the air. It gladdened Wendell's heart, filled him with energy and verve.

He leaned forward and murmured to Janie.

"What's the trouble, Janie?" He could hear the laughter in his voice and so could she. She cut her eyes at him.

"My father says he wonders if you have the right stuff," she said.

Wendell was taken aback, as if she and her father had been conversing at the table and he hadn't heard them.

"Meaning?"

She shrugged.

"I work for your father. I have a job. A good job. Prospects. What does he mean? What does it have to do with us?"

"He says he doesn't want me dating a person who isn't a serious person. Someone with prospects and the right stuff." She shrugged again.

"We're still pretty young," Wendell said. He heard a small plea in his voice, and hated it. "Why are we supposed to be so serious?"

"I'm not supposed to be," she said. "You are."

She hummed dreamily with the piano.

"How old was your mother when she had you?" she said abruptly. A typical Janie move, out of the blue.

Wendell felt a stone in the pit of his stomach. Her father was poisoning her against him. Because of his mother. Why couldn't they just let him and Janie be young together? That was the thought that flew across his mind. Why did it always come down to who's trash and who isn't? Who is worthy to have some blitheness in life, and who isn't.

"Old enough," Wendell said curtly.

"What happened to your father?"

Wendell felt his face heating, the tips of his ears growing fiery.

"He was killed in an accident, if you must know," he said.

"When I was a baby. And my mother's parents were dead too, and so there we were"—he tried to reclaim a certain lightness, knowing it wouldn't work—"up a crick without a paddle."

"What kind of accident?"

"In the line of duty." It was coming to him fast now. He used to say simply that his father had gone away when he was a baby and died in an accident. Even as a child he had tried, on the rare times he was asked about the man, to convey some glamour and danger so intense it defied articulation. With Janie, he knew he had to be specific. She navigated by specifics, even if they were lies.

"He was a detective in California, tailing counterfeiters and booze runners. He and his partner tracked down some big operation, and the operators went on the run and they took off after them. They got special permission to cross state lines. I think they had some kind of informal arrangement with the feds. Anyway. They got to the Twin Cities and there was a shootout in an alley, and he took three bullets. Couldn't get out of it. They found his body with three bullets in it."

He was trying to see it better. "It was raining hard," he said. "He was alone. The partner said he'd come up the alley from the other end. Well, it turned out he'd told the bad boys what to expect. For money. Got caught later and sang his little rat heart out about all of it. That's how my mother knew the story. A few months after the murder, I was born."

He turned to Janie to see how he'd done. "Wonder if he smelled a rat," she mused, lighting a cigarette with the candle that flickered in a red glass globe. "Don't they usually smell?"

Wendell shrugged. He was thinking of a young man who looked like him, stopping in an alley caught in a flash of guns. Knowing in an instant his friend had betrayed him. Hitting the deck. Too late.

Roy across the room had leaned forward to whisper something into his girl's ear. She was a round brunette, with a sharp, hard little face. He brushed back her hair—something, Wendell realized, that never would have occurred to him to do—and spoke into her ear. She sat with her back ramrod straight. Whatever he said put a catlike smile on her face, then she tipped back her head and laughed wildly and at length. You could hear her through the piano and the crowd.

On their way out, he and Janie stopped to say good night to Aidan Tierney, the assistant county attorney who had helped prosecute the murder of the submarine man, the recluse Calvin Rydell. With Tierney was a man his age, a big squared-off, clean-collared type. Tierney introduced him as Roland Taliaferro. Said they'd been FBI together and Taliaferro still worked for the Bureau in Butte.

Tierney seemed unusually talkative. He was ill with some long-term disease, pale and quiet a lot of the time. They chatted about the trial for a few minutes while Janie took herself off to the powder room.

Taliaferro wore a black onyx ring, square and heavy, which Wendell admired. He noticed it because the man had a way of punctuating a statement by chopping the air with his hand. It was a restrained but extravagant gesture, the kind Wendell wanted for himself. There was personality and decision in it.

Opal Mix's statement about the bear got another working over, and they all laughed, and then Taliaferro chopped the air and said Mrs. Mix might be in for some unpleasantness in the next little while. A man who had worked as a teenager for her and her husband—sort of a johnny-jump-up at the mortuary, as Taliaferro put it—was threatening to sue her for some sort of reparations connected to the husband's "misuse" of him, he said. The man claimed Porter Mix was not so good at keeping it to himself.

"Not that it will go anywhere," Tierney said. "She may be batty, but she's a pillar of the community, as they say. Husband was too. The guy who's coming forth with all of this has got a pack of debts and some credibility problems connected to his tendency to beat up his wives and lie about it. Not to mention the statute of limitations."

"Not to mention Mix isn't in the best position to defend himself," said Taliaferrro. "Being as he's been a stiff for seven years, I believe it is."

The conversation was making Wendell uneasy. He felt the

older men were looking at him expectantly, as if he had information to contribute about Porter Mix.

"All I know," he said lightly, "is that Mrs. Mix plays not with a
full deck." Janie was back and looking bored. "Opal Mix is my
neighbor," Wendell said, palms up. "Known her for years. Borrow
a cup of sugar when I run low."

"For his cupcake recipe," Janie chimed in coquettishly. The
men looked at her alertly, but she didn't have a next thing to say.

Snow blew in light curtains across the tall windows of the hotel
lobby. Above the huge fireplace, which was flanked by all-white
pines, a single reindeer pulled a sleigh in a drawing that struck
Wendell as very sleek and of the moment. Wendell liked the lobby.
As they left, he thought briefly that he and Janie should just sit
themselves down in one of the wing chairs or on the divan before
the fireplace and have a conversation like adults, like comrades.

There, that woman over there reading. She had the neat con-
tainment, the absorption in another's story, that might be possible
in Janie, might be an aspect of her, if they both gave it a chance. It
would certainly be a version he could live with better than he could
with this inchoate, flittering, upset presence beside him. Perhaps if
he just sat down, she would think it a good idea too and they would
have taken the first small step toward a new stage in their relationship.

He sat down. She looked down on him, surprised, still pulling
her gloves on.

"What's wrong?" she demanded.

"Not a thing," he said.

"Are you sick? What are you sitting there for?"

He looked around the room, hoping she would too, and that
she would catch sight of the contained young woman and her
book. But Janie just put her hands on her hips and watched him.
She was something of a drawing herself in her stylized slimness.
Her wild mop of hair, a cute nipped waist, and neat ankles and
feet. Eyes too small but very avid, very awake. You got the impres-
sion she blinked twice as often as anyone else. A hummingbird

heart in her. A heart-shaped face—sweetly shaped, really—with a droopy little mouth that she made very red with lipstick. The pencil thinness.

He leaned back, mildly engrossed in his small act of resistance, and studied the deer and the sleigh. The tiny-hoofed deer with long legs like cigarette holders, like Janie, vamping through the snow with the delicate sleigh behind it, piled with wrapped presents. Studying the drawing, he felt as he sometimes did as a child when he looked at one of his picture books, engulfed in a yearning that wasn't simple. It wasn't a need to go to the places pictured and described in his books, because he went there in his mind. What he wanted was to be there more completely. That was always the feeling he got, especially with his favorite, *Green Mansions*. When one of his mother's men friends informed him that it was a sissy boy who read *Green Mansions*, he put the book away with some other treasures under his bed and left it there, unread, which made it all the more alive in his head.

He closed his eyes upon the indignant Janie. He let the sleigh be pulled, himself in it, the little tock tock of the deer hooves on the icy snow as Janie marched across the glassy linoleum floor to flick her cigarette in the fireplace.

"Okay, my lady," he said, stretching to let her know how little her impatience affected him. "Let's get you home to your worried daddy."

She lobbed the cigarette over the screen into the low-burning logs.

"He is not worried," she said, standing by his chair again. "He is concerned."

"Since when has his concern ever been your concern?" Wendell said. He felt good, as if he'd accidentally discovered in the lobby chair the locus of hidden restorative powers. Also, he was about to be rid of Janie for the night. There was always a certain relief in that.

They walked home. Now she was in a slump and so, suddenly, was he. He felt as if they were between acts, wandering around behind the curtains waiting for the stage manager to give them the

high sign. A thin, watery quality was entering into their relationship. He could feel it. She was growing bored. She barely said good
night. It was just before one.

He walked back through the snowy night, restless; back to the
hotel lobby where he took the same chair he'd had earlier. He pretended he was passing through town. He smoked. He wanted this
room instead of his own little box of a house with his ailing mother
snoring in a resigned sort of way. Home was low ceilings, a floor at
a slant, a stupid lamp his mother liked—the translucent shade was
painted with two mallards in cattails—and which she left on for
him when he was out late.

He saw Taliaferro, the FBI man, leave the dining room—burly,
shooting his sleeves, walking a shade too purposefully. Ten minutes
later Aidan Tierney entered the lobby. He had a look of such pale
and utter loneliness that Wendell turned his eyes away. But Tierney
had caught sight of him.

"What happened to your girl?" Tierney asked him.

"She called it a night. I'm a night owl. Newspaper hours. Midnight, one o'clock—that's when I'm going full throttle."

Tierney nodded. He tapped Wendell lightly on the shoulder.

"*Hasta la vista,*" Tierney said. "Talk to you after the holidays."

Wendell tipped his hat. *Just go.* What he didn't need at this
moment was a wraith like Aidan Tierney, bravely off alone to his
bachelor apartment to try to sleep, or failing that, to fill the time
with something undespairing. Wendell felt he knew exactly what
the night would be for Aidan Tierney, and he hated the fact that he
recognized that aloneness. He wanted no kinship with that.

The woman in the suit still held her eyes on her book, but
Wendell now realized that she wasn't turning the pages. She
wasn't sleeping either—she touched her hand to her face from
time to time; she adjusted her hem and recrossed her legs—but she
did not turn the pages of her book. The book was a sham. Something else was going on. Was she waiting for a man who never
showed? Had she had an argument and didn't want to return to
the room?

Suddenly she, too, carried too many problems with her and she infused the lobby with them and Wendell was reminded of how much he hated the holidays, how they seemed designed to refuse or diminish daily sadnesses, and thus amplified them.

He walked back out onto the street. Snow fell. The traffic, what there was, moved very slowly and left tracks. The world was wrapped up and quiet and mysterious now. He turned up his collar. Maybe he'd stick his head into the newspaper and see if they needed help putting it to bed. Maybe he'd stop in at the Elks for a nightcap.

He was calm again. It would work out with Janie or not. Probably not. She was so far from the kind of woman he'd envisioned for himself: someone strong, quiet, receptive in a dignified and undemanding sort of way. Someone who offered absolute understanding and support; who had a mind of her own but didn't use it to undermine and rattle him, the way Janie so often seemed to do.

Roy Wellington's car pulled up to the curb as Wendell walked toward home. It was the car Roy had inherited from a brother who'd been killed on Iwo Jima. Roy called to him to quit prowling the streets like a bum. The night woke up; the street woke up. The snow still fell, but there was a window in it now, and Roy's laughing face was in the glass. Wendell's first, quick reaction was fear, a cellular fear that stemmed from the ancient playground beating and carried with it the smell of a hobo camp. There it was, despite all the intervening ameliorations. Then he reminded himself that he was Janie Quist's boyfriend and he and Roy were allies in the battle against female insanity, and he went over to the car.

Roy sat in the winter dark breathing out white puffs of air and cigarette smoke. Wendell rested a bare hand casually on the edge of the frosted roof—he'd forgotten his fancy new gloves and his hand burned, but he left it there—and he bent over and chatted with Roy about something. Something came out of his mouth. He had no idea what.

He got in. The heater was revved up. It made a little whine. Roy smelled pleasantly of cigarettes and booze and some kind of aftershave.

Wendell realized as he lit a cigarette and laughed at something Roy said that this seat, here, was where he felt absolutely right and at home. It was the antidote to the woman in the lobby not reading her book. A horsehair seat and the lurid Christmas lights outside and snow falling like scarves of chiffon and the night still ahead. It was a weekend, for Pete's sake. Who went home to his mother?

"Our ladies have gone off to their beauty rests, it appears," Roy said dryly.

"Miss Jane and I weren't seeing eye to eye this evening," Wendell said.

"I had to deposit Miss Des Rosier on her porch," Roy said. "She called me a brute, and callous, and, um, let's see, what was the other one?"

"I'm sure it fit," Wendell said.

Roy drooped his mouth in such a clownish little-kid way that Wendell laughed and he sounded to himself like a boy.

"The ladies, Wendell," Roy intoned. "They'll be the death of us, the ladies."

They were stopped at a light. A cop with nothing to do, walking the beat and covered with snow, sauntered over to them and shone his flashlight at the frosty window. It was a guy they'd gone to high school with and they waved him off, him and his cop costume, which is how it seemed to them.

He kept the light another moment or two on the windshield and it lit up the edges of Roy's profile. The combination of frost and the white flashlight and the dimness of the car made Roy look like something in a painting. Wendell was instantly embarrassed by the thought, but couldn't banish it. Roy *did* look as if his name should be Tyrone or Atticus—something that went beyond this little town and these times. There was something in the way he looked—that profile, that full mouth, the set of his shoulders— that was sculpted and timeless, like something you could touch, just lightly, and it would make you something more than what you were.

And then the cop's light was gone and they were moving slowly down the white night. Roy wanted to drive to a roadhouse ten or so miles east of town. The place was lively on the weekends before Christmas. Terrible weather, but so what. Was Wendell game?

He thought about his mother at home. How had she sounded when he'd called good night to her on his way out with Janie? Ill. Definitely ill, but sick the way you sound with the grippe or a bad cold. She would have fixed up a poultice and left the duck light on, and though she was probably sleeping lightly because of her congestion and fever, she wasn't going to sleep any less lightly just because he was home in his bed. He was game.

They headed east, out of town. Roy's windshield wipers worked away busily, but the snow was at the exact point of wetness that it froze when it hit the windshield and made an opaque scrim, so they had to stop every mile or so and try to scrape it off with their gloved hands. Wendell found a stick on the shoulder of the road, which he broke in two so they could scrape with that. There was no question of turning back, though. They were in the highest of spirits, off on this adventure in the winter dark, holding in their minds' eyes the low glowing lights of the Pines.

They worked out a scraping system, top to bottom, each with exactly half the windshield, and they finished each time with a swordsman's click of the sticks, and then they jumped in and Roy revved the car and off they went at a creep.

A half hour down the road, Wendell stole a look at the gas gauge, and then he calmly asked Roy if it was working. Roy bent forward to squint at it and slapped his hand hard on the dash, as if that would make it register true.

He swore cheerfully. "I forgot," he said. "Someone at the Pines will have to give us a ride back into town. Damn. Can you believe it?"

"Where are we?" Wendell said, trying to see through the snow, trying to find a shape or a light out there. The highway was empty. Somewhere out here the boy in the jail had built his campfire on the highway.

"Past the point of no return," Roy said. "We're closer to the Pines than we are to town. I'm pretty sure of that. Keep a lookout, though. If there's a farm or something, we better pull in."

The next time they stopped to scrape the windshield, Wendell had to hold a hand against the side of his face that the wind was hitting. It had grown stronger and much colder, with a quick sting that turned in a matter of moments to a tingling numbness. They got back in. Sat for a moment.

"Decision time," Roy said. His voice was still light, still larky. "We run out of gas, we lose our heat."

"Check," Wendell said.

"We're about out of gas."

"Check."

"We think the Pines is pretty close, but we're not sure."

"Check."

"What would the stupid person in a panic do?"

"Drive until all the gas is gone," Wendell said, "then get out and walk and freeze."

"Or stay in, wait for help, run out of gas, and freeze, but slower," Roy said.

He pulled the car onto the shoulder as far as he could and turned off the motor. Then he turned it on again to confirm that it would start. It did, quite easily.

"What do you think?" he asked Wendell. "Every fifteen minutes or so? A blast of the old heat?"

"Yes," Wendell said. "I think so. Someone will come along if they haven't closed the road."

It was very quiet in the car. Wendell thought of his mother, and how worried she'd be if she woke and didn't find him, but he didn't care. Not really. Everything was out of his hands. There was absolutely nothing he could do to make himself or Roy safer or get them home.

The driver who took them back to Missoula, an hour later, dropped Wendell off, and he waved a casual good-bye to the samaritan and Roy, who'd go back in the morning with a can of gas. The snow was coming down steadily and thick. It made the town very quiet. It softened his house, his and Edna's, and made it, in the light of the streetlight, seem cozy and out of time, its gauntness erased. Edna had left the porch light on. He let himself in quietly, left his shoes at the door.

He turned on the duck lamp. Edna had forgotten, for the first time, to leave it on for him, and his feeling was one of relief. She is learning, he thought. She is accepting that I am an adult with my own hours.

He went straight to bed. He was exhausted. He felt like weeping, and then he did weep. He lay on his back in the muffled night and let the tears fall down the sides of his face.

He seemed to hear Edna's steady breathing, but then he thought perhaps it was his own breath alone. He consciously steadied it. He thought about the next day, the next week. He was going to start to put together something on Opal Mix for the newspaper. She was so incompetent as to be dangerous. She was a fraud, an idiot, a liar. It was time—past time—for her to stop being the person who told the world how people had died, or hadn't.

Two weeks later, elapsed time that he would never be able to recall in much detail, Wendell returned to his job on the police beat. Templeton had been his fill-in and had handled the story and obituary about Aidan Tiernay, about how and where his body was found, about Opal Mix's saying the shot was through the mouth. He had also written the brief story about Opal Mix's resignation as coroner and her decision to return to the Midwest, where she had grown up.

She had estimated the time of Tierney's death as Saturday, December 16, the day after Wendell and Janie had seen him at the Flame with Roland Taliaferro, the agent from Butte. The body hadn't been found for a week.

"Did you check it out?" Wendell asked Templeton. He knew that, whatever Templeton said, he should contact Opal Mix himself and review the circumstances of the death. But the mere thought of it exhausted him.

"Oh, sure," Templeton said. "The guy was pretty sick. Friends weren't surprised."

"Did you check her records?" Wendell asked. "The death certificate? The coroner's report? She's famous for, to put it politely, discrepancies and mistakes."

"Sure I did," Templeton said, so easily that Wendell knew he was lying. But he couldn't, for the first time in the job, make himself care.

"They had me working fifteen-hour days for a while there," Templeton offered.

On Saturday, December 16, Templeton had taken the call from the doctor who said that Wendell Whitcomb would not be coming to work for the next week or so. Mrs. Edna Whitcomb, he said, had succumbed to the effects of an untreated toxemia in the early morning hours, and her son was severely distraught.

Wendell felt, still, so insubstantial, so hollowed out, that the sensible-sounding sentences coming out of his mouth surprised him. Templeton watched him warily.

"You take it easy, kid," Templeton said. "The Tierney story is over and done. You take it easy for a while."

SEVENTEEN

1946
Missoula

ROLAND TALIAFERRO ZIPPED UP AND LEANED forward to study his face in the bathroom mirror. He ran his hand under the faucet, patted his thick hair and combed it smooth. He didn't look as tired as he should have, given the nature of the day.

He practiced a few expressions: furrowed-brow concern; the wide canny smile: the adamant chop of his big hand to make the important point; the slow, evaluative nod. He could have stayed in the bathroom longer. He could have stayed forever. But he needed to go back to Aidan's office and carry on this old-pal farce.

The man frightened him. He admitted it now. He'd heard the stories; he'd imagined frailty, diminishment. But what he hadn't expected, when he shook Aidan's hand after all these years, was the shock of feeling the bones in that hand. It made Aidan chinalike and removed. Roland had to scramble to recall the old version, so beefy almost, so rosy and hearty and present.

He also hadn't expected the terrible tightness in his throat when he shook that hand. The wave of tenderness. The urge he'd had to throw this sad-eyed man out of the path of some dangerous mowing-down thing. Throw him heroically and competently out of the path, and somehow, in that act, saving them both.

He began a list. Things to talk about. Things to talk about first.

So there he was this morning in Butte, in Hennessy's, buying a pair of socks because he'd had, let's call it, a falling out with Marcella and she'd told him to buy his own socks and keep them washed too and hang them to dry where she and Charlie, the baby, wouldn't have to see them and be reminded of his reprehensible giant-footed presence. Big indulgent laugh at this point. Shake of the head.

And there he was at the sock counter when who should look up and offer her assistance, not registering who he was for a moment or two, but Lenora Wing. Home in Butte since 1940, living with her mother, the toughest invalid in town. Fine. She looked fine. A little older, something wary and careful he hadn't remembered in her, but fine. Good, in fact. Unmarried, as Aidan undoubtedly knew. Major surprise to see her. You can lose track fast.

He'd stop there; let Aidan add to the story if he knew more.

Actually, she'd looked forty if she'd looked a day. Everything coppery and shiny about her seemed to have tarnished. Her skin color wasn't good. She had moved in a contained, almost careful, way, and he remembered how she'd sometimes complained of bouts of fierce bone pain, all over, and the urge to do nothing for a few days but sleep. Maybe something had settled in, become chronic. The truth was, he really didn't much care. As soon as he'd told her he was still with the FBI and worked out of Butte now— recent transfer from Indianapolis, organizational shakeup, doing a stint in the old hometown—her face had clicked off and she had turned wintry and quiet, ringing up the socks with nothing further but the rote salesperson exchange and a crisp good-bye and good luck, then her back to him as she helped another customer.

Versions of that snub had happened with a few others he'd known from earlier days. He wasn't surprised, exactly, but his sense of disorientation increased a little with each episode. Everything about Butte and his place in it now felt like the margin between sleep and waking, the leaving inextricable from the arriving.

He would summarize it that briefly for Aidan: strange. It felt strange. A little disorienting. And then, he hoped, they would move on. Maybe to Petey, the kid sister.

Petey had moved back to the family home, where she devoted herself to mourning the dead young soldier, her husband of a few months, who was already a figment. That was the word she used with Roland. She didn't know what else to do yet, or who exactly she should be, in the war's aftermath. Especially with their mother now dying, too, a process that had turned Petey pale and grim.

Roland didn't like to stop by the house, so he found reasons not to. An easy one was the presence in his life of the new wife and baby, Marcella and Charlie. Marcella, the German grocer's daughter who'd changed her name from Birgit. Marcella didn't hit it off with Petey, and Charlie was a crier, a noisy one who clearly set Petey's nerves on edge, so Roland had a ready excuse for staying away.

He'd been sent to Butte to investigate the presence of Communists or sympathizers among the unions. As Aidan well knew. Had Aidan been well enough to stay in the Bureau, had he been sent to Butte, that's exactly what he would have been doing too.

Communist influences, and the expertise a hometown boy could bring to the identification of them—that was the stated reason for the transfer. The unstated reason, all the more obvious to Roland for being so, was that he was undergoing a test. This, he wouldn't share with Aidan. The Bureau wanted to know how far Roland's loyalty and alertness reached. Four years ago he'd been transferred from headquarters to Indianapolis because a submarine in the Bureau had snitched about his drinking on the job, and he'd been warned twice, in Indianapolis, that he walked thin ice and was close to getting fired. Butte, the hometown, was Roland's last chance.

He straightened his tie as he chewed on a few Sen-Sens. He gathered himself, blinked hard to clear his thoughts, and headed back to Aidan's office.

Opal Mix, the coroner, was still there. He could hear the two of them talking. And then it was only the sound of his own amiable saunter across the shiny floor. Aidan and the coroner stood silently at the office door. Aidan appeared to be ushering her out. His movements were tight and his face had closed down. She had fingers at the hollow of her throat, as if she was trying to catch her breath.

"Good evening," Roland said, in his butler voice. She swept past him, down the dim hall and down the stairs.

"What?" Roland said to Aidan. "What's the problem with that one?"

"She's got a screw or two loose," Aidan said lightly.

"Which screws, exactly?" Roland said in his inquiring-doctor voice.

"The ones that are supposed to keep her from making a fool of herself," Aidan said. He shook his head. His expression was coming back to life.

"She wants me to be her dinner date. At her house. On a daily basis." He raised his dark brows. "I think she's got designs on my person, Roland," he said solemnly.

Roland had a vision of the jowled harpie wearing a frilly apron, and he belted out a huge laugh. Aidan shook his head again and smiled. Roland laughed harder, for the relief of it.

They walked through lightly falling snow to the Flame, the snow dusting their hats and the shoulders of their heavy overcoats. The next order of business: a drink or a few. Roland badly needed a drink and, maybe later, a beefsteak.

Aidan would not be eating. He had already had dinner at the hospital, where the nuns made him and a few others their strict meals. But he handed his overcoat to the check girl with a certain panache, a certain expansiveness, that suggested the prospect of a pleasurable evening ahead. Roland suspected he now employed his charm simply in order to save energy. Keep routine human interactions smooth and amiable and you produce nothing unforeseen in the other person, nothing to chafe or delay.

The soft plink of the piano on the far side of the room rode a wave of laughter from a party gathered around the pianist. Candles fluttered in red glass lamps. There was a lazy haze of cigarette smoke and filtering through it the smell of charred and salty beef, and winter too: damp wool, the stray sneak of frigid air across the feet.

Aidan immediately excused himself and moved off in the direction of the restroom. He had to be forty, fifty pounds lighter than he was the last time Roland had seen him, just before he left for Argentina. Thin Man, he called himself.

He had been large, solid. And now he looked to be in retreat from his suit. It hung on him, the sleeves an inch too long, the cuffs too floppy, his neck reaching out of his collar, knobbled. His good leather belt had been pulled in, past the groove of the old waist.

Nothing had changed about Aidan's resonant voice, however. And nothing had changed about his gestures: the way he cocked his head slightly to listen, the way he lit his cigarette with a farmer's match struck off his fingernail. But there was about him an automatic quality. Roland had expected a gleam of craziness, not this mechanical watchfulness, though he'd seen versions of the same affect in others back from the war. You felt they had a bird's-eye view on their civilian selves and watched the normal day-to-day movements of those selves with controlled amazement.

In Aidan, the cool remove was shocking. He had always before seemed so invested in the moments of his life, so of a piece with them. He had had, once, the gift of utter engagement. And if you were his friend, that quality rubbed off on you and conferred a slow-burning sense of hope in your own prospects.

Now Aidan walked away briskly and slightly bent, as if he protected something with the curve of his torso. Roland finished his drink and waited. Aidan returned to the table contained and furious.

"Señor Lobo," he said, tipping his head in mock obeisance to something that might have been standing on the edges of the room. "Señor Lobo likes to tear my guts out, Roland." He wore a thin smile now. "Whenever the señor senses the opportunity is his." He flicked the broad white napkin and smoothed it over his lap.

What do you say to a statement like that? Roland had no idea. How do you handle a condition that keeps you hopping up every

twenty, thirty minutes to find the nearest place to shit burning
bloody water? You must feel the presence of a tyrant—exacting and
ravenous, as they all are—and you give him a name to tame him.
The lean shriek of him gets a name.

Well, he had in Aidan an adversary. Roland had no doubt
about that. "You will not win, señor," he could hear Aidan say. "I
will put on my diaper and press my suit pants and go into the
world. I'll leap when you bite, but I'll sit down again at the desk,
the bridge table, the dinner table—here, for instance, with my old
friend Roland. I'll wipe my forehead, have a laugh, have a smoke,
wait you out."

And what happens to your mind when you know your body to
be in the throes of its own disinformation? Roland wondered. This
is what the doctors had told Aidan. No parasites were involved. His
body, in response to certain precipitating conditions and inade-
quate treatment in the early stages, was attacking itself, was its own
saboteur.

"You won't guess who I ran into this morning at the sock
counter in Hennessy's," Roland said.

"I suspect it was Lenora Wing," Aidan said. "We've kept in
some kind of touch over the years. A note now and then is about
what it amounts to."

"Just that?" Roland said.

"Lenora and I remain friends," Aidan said stolidly. "It wasn't
going to work. For a number of reasons, it wasn't going to work."
The tone of his voice shut the subject away.

"Well, then," Roland pressed on buoyantly, "I've got you ear-
marked for the kid sister."

"Petey," Aidan said absently.

"Still in her version of widow's weeds, still living with my
mother. She seems to be, temporarily at least, a devotional sort. She
can't seem to deny herself enough. Next thing, she'll take the veil.
I'm hoping it's a phase."

He allowed himself a brief vision of his sister and mother at
the table in the dingy, high-ceilinged kitchen, the gray-faced father

long buried but his chair still there. Would there ever be a table for any of them without that empty chair?

At the next booth, invisible to them, a woman laughed delightedly at something her date murmured to her. They waited for her to stop.

"I showed Petey some of the letters you sent me from Argentina," Roland said. "Those were great letters. The ones you wrote before you got sick. Petey said those letters made her feel she was breathing in South America through her pores."

Aidan had offered detail upon detail about the look and smell and feel of the place; about the women and the church bells and the cacophony of languages and cultures; about the big stinking yellow river and the low life along its wharves, about a trip he took up north, to the mountain country, to spend a weekend at a rich man's *estancia*. About peddlers on burros carrying cages of red birds, and a country inn where he was served eggs-on-horseback.

He said nothing about his work, of course, and made only a cursory mention of his cover, the meatpacking plant where he, the up-and-coming young businessman, plied his commercial skills.

The letters with all their bright details framed something at the middle of the easel that was the secret work. Roland had sometimes felt he could almost make it out, see its shape, and he was surprised at how frightened it had made him feel.

In the last of the Argentina letters, Aidan had signed himself "Quixote."

The letters stopped coming after the one in which he'd told Roland he was grappling with some condition that seemed to have twisted his intestines into knots, that the winter was damp and bone chilling and he was expecting the meat packer to send him packing soon, home to the States for better medical care.

Then there was, for a long while, silence. Roland asked around and learned that Aidan was still in Argentina two, four, seven months after that last letter. No one seemed to have specifics about his health, though the special agent in charge in Indianapolis knew that Aidan was still very ill. "I wouldn't want to be down there," the agent had said. "Bugs, bad food, bad water, bad cops, god knows what all. You can get your body burned up. I wouldn't want my body burned up, would you?"

No, Roland told him, he wouldn't want his body burned up.

And then Aidan was back, posted at the Houston office. But no letters to Roland. They only started coming again after Aidan resigned from the Bureau, and they seemed, then, to be written by someone entirely new.

They came to Roland at his apartment in Indianapolis—four letters over a period of a year.

Aidan told Roland that he ought to know, for his own good, that Hoover was a laughingstock among the State Department men in Buenos Aires, and the embassy men, the Brits, the American business community. That all of them thought he was a detail-driven fool; a naïf; a thick-necked cop who couldn't begin to imagine the silvery, snaky quality of all the wartime alliances in the southern hemisphere and who thought his earnest bright boys were gathering information on foreign corporations for black-listing purposes when they were really, finally, scouts for American business interests. He said he had tried to bring this to the attention of his superiors, who punished him by refusing to send him back to the States for the medical care that might have spared him his ongoing illness.

We were corporate spies, thinking all the while that we were getting the good on the Reich. The Brits knew it the whole time; knew it was about postwar fortunes to be made. They complained about it all the time. They're nobody's fools, the Brits.

Roland was so shocked that he numbly reread the signature to make sure it was Aidan's. Then he burned the letter. Then he thought: You're way in where you shouldn't be, old buddy. The Old Man wanted his men methodical, obedient, presentable, and loyal. He detested so-called independent thinkers. Wouldn't abide them. Knew how to isolate and discredit and destroy them. Aidan had to know that.

You know how you can listen to a song on the radio and not make out the words, until suddenly you do? You hear this word and that word, but they don't string along right, until the signal clears and then you have it, plain and simple?

Early in 1943, Aidan, ostensibly a young executive-in-training at the huge American meatpacking plant, had attended a banquet in Buenos Aires, keynoted by the president of the American Chamber of Commerce. The banquet hall was full of American and German businessmen talking happily to each other. As he took in the scene, he began to apprehend what the speaker was saying.

He was talking about postwar investment opportunities. The postwar scenario.

He listened to the man, watched the audience nod and smile, and thought about his brother Neil back in the United States, training to fly bombers. *I thought: They're already divvying up the spoils. They're charting, unapologetically and openly, their postwar fortunes. And everything I do, until such time as the war is done, will be in the service of those fortunes. Everything.*

Roland burned that one too.

In another letter, Aidan asked Roland to consider the disparate entities in Argentina who, in 1943, considered Communists the enemy. There was the new president, General Ramirez, and his up-and-coming labor minister, Perón. There were the U.S. industrialists operating in the country, *including, of course, my meat packer, whose employees are particularly union smitten. And why not? Those workers live like farmyard animals.* There were the Nazis in Argentina who were smuggling out war supplies, spying, receiving looted and laundered currency, but who also shared with important and powerful Americans, and the Argentinian government, an abiding hatred for Communists.

There was the Church and its vehement opposition to Communism. *And finally there is the Old Man and us, his minions. If there is something the Old Man does not hate more than a Communist, I don't what know it is.*

So there we have a stew. If the FBI, the Nazis, the Church, the

Argentinian despot, and the American industrialist agree on a common enemy—well then, we might have some problems. If they agree that the Communist is the worst enemy, then we might have a nightmare of hidden collaborations. Do you see this?

Oh, the bedfellows, Roland. That's where it can get very strange, very disconcerting, for your American gumshoe in foreign lands.

He asked Roland to think about global pharmaceutical alliances in a time of war; about insurance companies that do business worldwide, and what role they might play in what gets bombed and what doesn't get bombed. *Throw in Fritz Mandl, the arms manufacturer playing both sides, who gives a million pesos to the Red Cross because it is the darling of the American ambassador and he hopes the ambassador will see to it that Mandl's American operations are not blacklisted. Throw in . . .*

Roland burned that letter before he got to the end.

From across the dance floor of the Flame came a young guy and a stiletto-legged girl with a mop of curly hair under a French beret.

Aidan called them to the table and introduced Roland to Wendell Whitcomb, the newspaper's police reporter. Wendell introduced them to his girlfriend, Janie Quist, daughter of the paper's editor. Roland made a mental note of the editor's name. He hadn't had a chance, yet, to familiarize himself with the local movers and shakers he'd need as contacts.

The girl nattered on about something inexplicable, and Wendell shook Roland's hand gravely.

"Our Mrs. Mix," Aidan said to Roland. "Mr. Whitcomb here had a sharp eye out when the lady coroner was conducting her recent investigation. The case of the bogus bear was only her most blatant mistake. Mr. Whitcomb here does not let much escape his attention. He's got Mrs. Mix in his crosshairs."

The kid looked embarrassed and pleased. He offered his opinion of Mrs. Mix's mental faculties and they all laughed. She was a good topic of conversation, Roland thought. He would have been happy to talk about Mrs. Mix all night.

He threw Wendell, the reporter, a bone. There was some new

business involving alleged perfidies on the part of Opal Mix's long-dead husband. Might come to nothing, might not. Wendell nodded and thanked him for the tip, and then he and the skinny girl were on their way.

Roland and Aidan didn't look at each other.

"You know, Roland," Aidan said conversationally. "I'm quite sure I'm being followed. There is a man in town, the right age, right complexion, who might be following me. I first saw his face in Buenos Aires, during those months they left me there, so sick, in order to chastise me for my intemperate observations and theories."

Roland didn't know what to say, so he said nothing.

"Sometimes I tried to hobble a few blocks to Mass, and there he would be, across the street, this pale, red-haired fellow with a mustache who walks as if he's leaning into a stiff wind. Turned out the priest was a Nazi drop, so I stopped making that particular effort on behalf of my immortal soul. But I'd see the guy in front of my building sometimes, doing not much of anything, though he had a knack for looking busy." He shrugged.

"Then Houston. A block ahead in that rippling wet heat, there he was. And now here. Just yesterday I think I saw him cross the intersection and get into a car. Same walk. Same pale face but without the mustache."

Roland listened with a faint sense of relief. He wanted the presence of paranoia in his old friend so that he could discount him. The idea of a half-mad Aidan fortified him.

"You wrote those letters to me in order to let off steam, I take it," he said, plunging in. "Venting is good, so the head doctors say. I burned them, Aidan. All but the one I've got with me now. I don't need those letters hanging around and neither do you."

Aidan lit a cigarette with a farmer's match. Then he put it out and leaned toward Roland.

"The place was crawling with Nazis," he said. "And I wanted a chance to get something on them. I wanted to do real work, Roland. Why do you think I signed up for hazardous duty in the first place?

"When I told them I thought I was being used for commercial

purposes, shall we say, they sent me out of the city to check an old chicken farm that was the likeliest radio transmitting site for Becker, the big man. They sent me alone. No backup. 'You want Nazis? Go get your Nazis.' Bingo. There they were, transmitting away. Terrible conditions. I was soaked to the bone and half sick, snaking around in the mud, and Becker's men caught me. They put me in that cell." He patted his midsection lightly. "That's what set off all this, you know. What happened in that cell."

Roland vehemently didn't want the details.

"And the Old Man got you rescued, didn't he?" he snapped.

"And you're pretty lit, my friend," Aidan said mildly.

"Don't call me that. Don't keep calling me that. It's patronizing as hell."

"I mean it, though. You're my friend," Aidan shrugged. "That's why I say it."

Roland retrieved a letter from his vest pocket and set in on the table between them. The envelope was addressed to him. He slid out the letter, a carbon-paper copy, which was addressed to Hoover and dated a month earlier. He placed his fingertips on it and slid it toward Aidan.

Aidan gazed at it with something like fondness.

"Think hard about this letter, Aidan," Roland said.

"Oh, I have," Aidan said. "I certainly have."

Dear Sir,

Five months ago I wrote to you to inquire about the possibility of receiving disability compensation for a medical condition acquired while I was on undercover duty in Argentina. You responded that you would inquire into the matter for me. Having heard nothing further, I eventually wrote to the United States Employees' Compensation Commission to ask if the Bureau had presented my case to them. They responded in the negative, saying that the Bureau must make a formal presentation of the case before they could take action. The Bureau, they said, had made informal contact but had declined, on grounds of national security, to present the details which they needed in order to proceed.

When I was in Argentina and very ill, I requested your assistance in obtaining the drug penicillin, which my physician there felt might prove effective in treating my condition and which he had not been able to obtain. You responded that the units of penicillin were not available to noncombatants except in cases of dire emergency, and took no further action.

This, then, is my dilemma: Due to the secret nature of my wartime assignment, I do not seem to "exist" as a war combatant who might rightfully and justly have obtained medical relief when it could do some good, or financial relief, later, for a disabling condition acquired in the service of my country.

Sir, I have been grievously wounded, perhaps permanently wounded. I acquired my illness under extremely unfavorable conditions in the line of duty. I cannot work more than three or four hours a day due to extreme fatigue, and even this amount of time is subject to constant interruption to attend to my physical needs.

When I first became ill and requested a transfer to the United States, you sat on the request. Not for one month. Not for two. But for seven months. While I became more and more ill.

I had requested a transfer to a stateside bureau where the climate and conditions might enhance the energy I had for my work, and you ignored the request for months, and finally placed me in Houston, Texas, where the heat and humidity are the most formidable of any station in the United States. Because of the internment camps housing German nationals from Latin America, Texas was also a location that presented certain risks for those of us who had done service in Latin America, as you well know. After two months in Houston, you requested my resignation on grounds of my ill health.

I am an attorney, sir. I know when an organization is protecting itself from liability incurred by its own questionable practices.

That is not the worst, however. Permit me to say, sir, that I was a sap. And perhaps you were, as well. Did you know what we were doing in Argentina? I wonder. And perhaps, in a backward way, that is to your credit. With all due respect, I believe you to be an innocent and a chump. You do not know how to imagine a world in which *morals are irrelevant. You do not know how to imagine real cleverness, real greed.*

You put on your blinders and sent your men forth, and did some of us in. Perhaps now you will do one more thing. Perhaps you will acknowledge to the appropriate people that I acquired my ruined life in the service of my country and am entitled to the same recompense—no more, no less—that any former member of the armed forces would get. My entire livelihood is directly affected by my medical condition.

I have no wish to embarrass the Bureau in any fashion, but I must do what I can to mitigate my circumstances, and I trust you to understand your role in that process.

Sincerely,

Aidan Tierney

"You don't seem to fully appreciate what you're saying here," Roland said, tapping the carbon.

"Oh, I do. I absolutely do." Aidan bent to retie a shoe. His back was so thin you could see the wings working. He gave Roland an appraising look.

"It's all true, you know," he said. "It all adds up, Roland." He drank the last of his drink and excused himself. The waiter returned with a double for Roland, and he drank half of it fast. Then he drank the rest. He tried to decide what to do. He could try to undermine Aidan's sense of his own stability. He could confess that the Butte office had sent him over to ascertain Aidan's intentions. He could warn him, flat out, that he was under the most intense kind of scrutiny.

What a fool he is, Roland thought. What an arrogant, treacherous, naive fool.

Aidan seethed. Aidan was prepared to undermine. There had always been in him a renegade quality, and here was its culmination. He was prepared to be a questioner, a blackmailer, a certain sort of traitor just when the Bureau most needed the loyalty of its men. The Old Man had his work cut out for him in the current political climate, all his old enemies ready to dredge up his methods during the fast-and-loose Palmer days. He needed all the reinforcements he could get, from the ranks and from without. Aidan had to know this.

The woman in the booth was laughing again. Roland clenched his eyes.

He decided on kindness, on friendship. When Aidan took his seat again, he said, "Look. You're scaring me some. You seem to think you can just crash around. You know the kind of damage you could do by spreading theories about whom the Bureau's been in bed with, wittingly or not? I mean, what's the plan, Aidan? What's the plan to embarrass the Old Man?"

Aidan folded his hands on the tablecloth. Then he took off his glasses and cleaned them with a napkin. He looked so exhausted suddenly, so drained of every kind of fight, that Roland felt as if he'd hit him. When Aidan spoke, his voice was flat.

"You seem to think, Roland, that you have some kind of real ally in them. Look, though, how they will twist you and turn you. Why do you think they brought you back to Butte? Why do you think they set you to hunting for Communists among your old buddies in the mines?"

"No one likes a Communist," Roland said lightly.

"You went to grade school with those men. You've seen the mines eat up their fathers' lungs and now their own. You've seen their mothers crying. You've heard the whistles and watched the stretchers. You've seen the cost close-up.

"And now they've sent you in there to rat on them, my old friend. Not that they are actually going to talk to you anymore. They know what you are. But there will be some among them who will pass on certain bits of information to a third party—a bartender, a priest—if they have been convinced by that third party that it might rebound to an advantage for themselves or their families. Money. Another job. Who knows? That's how it works, isn't it?

"And you're setting it up. For some so-called higher cause. Well let me tell you, the higher cause is riddled and bogus. And you, my friend, are mostly a form of entertainment."

Roland took three long breaths and consciously relaxed his

clenched hands. His mind began to walk away from the conversation. But first, the question again.

"Why are you telling me all this?"

"Because," Aidan said in a very low voice, "it's time the scales fell from your eyes. I realize you think the guy walks on water, old buddy. But maybe it's time you got yourself a new dad."

Roland got up then and left. Buttoned up his coat, nodded curtly, and walked out the door. He left Aidan sitting there, hands folded, and went on to make a night of it. He didn't remember much after the first bar, though an old college friend referred later to a long conversation they'd had that night about a couple of girls they'd both dated. Roland had no memory of running into the guy. Not a shred.

When he woke the next morning, the yellowed shade tapping the dirty window of his hotel room, he put in a call to F. X. Travers, Butte's longtime special agent in charge, and was told to stay in Missoula a few more days. Travers wanted his assessment of the conversation.

"He's furious," Roland said bluntly. "He feels wronged. The guy's sick as hell."

Travers wanted to know if Aidan was blowing smoke.

"That I couldn't say," Roland said. "That I couldn't say."

Travers told him the Old Man himself wanted a full report from Roland about Aidan Tierney's state of mind and whether or not Tierney intended to follow through on certain threats he'd made to cast the Bureau in an unfavorable light.

"I don't have enough information to say what he will, in fact, do," Roland said. "He likes to think for himself, and act for himself."

"Well that really isn't good enough, Agent Taliaferro," Travers told him, becoming official all of a sudden. "Meet with him again. Spend a day with him if you can. Go do something. Shoot some ducks. Go bowling. Something. Get some sense of what he's got in mind, exactly. The press? Some sort of screed in the newspaper? Loose talk with the lawyers? What the hell is he up to?"

Roland felt a long weariness fill him. He wanted this ended.

He didn't have the energy or the heart for it. But no one wanted the Old Man's wrath. No one wanted to be the object of the protracted, almost ceremonial, degradation he was known to exercise if he felt one of his men, one of his troops, one of his golden sons, had badly let him down.

EIGHTEEN

1946
Missoula

IT WAS A CERTAIN SORT OF bachelor's residence: dark, cramped, neat, with a nod here and there to a young man's idea of a gentleman's club. A big easy chair and a leather hassock seemed to take up most of the room. The chair faced the fireplace and was flanked by an iron floor lamp with a faded pink shade and the kind of waist-high ash receptacle you saw in hotels. The carpet was earth colored and dense as boiled wool. The walls had been painted many times, and were a thick beige enamel.

There was a print of Man o' War on one wall. On a small table next to the closeted Murphy bed, a *maté* gourd with a silver straw rested on a priest's breviary written in Spanish. They were the only obvious tokens of Aidan's time in Argentina.

A rag rug at the door. A sink and a hot plate and an ice box. A tiny bathroom the color of Pepto-Bismol. A small desk with cigarette burns on the edges.

It was a basement apartment with its own entrance and two casement windows. Watery light stopped in wan pools below the casements. Curved iron bars protected the windows, and the shadows of the bars fell across the pools. Through the bars you saw feet go past sometimes. A dog's nose and paws.

Aidan had the lamp on. Outside, it was bright and crisp, with only a skiff of snow on the ground. There had been a break in the weather, and in just a day, the arrival of the false spring that surfaced a few times every winter.

"Why don't you finish your lecture as we drive," Aidan said. "I need a signature on a deposition, and I need to drop this shotgun off at Mallette's house. You can keep me company." Jim Mallette was an old law-school friend. He looked at his watch. "I borrowed it thinking I might shoot some grouse if I got feeling better, then never did. Told him I'd get it back to him before I left for the holidays."

"My lecture is very short," Roland said. He pretended to examine the *maté* gourd. "I lost my temper, but I'm not angry now and I want to be clear. You don't want to make a fool of yourself, Aidan. Is that your intention? To press ahead and make a fool of yourself?"

Roland felt he had somehow lost the capacity to gauge Aidan's temperament, the way he had been able to when they were first friends. In law school, feeling ragged with the pressure of studies, night jobs, no money, no women or not the right ones, they'd give each other a look, on a Saturday morning, say, and meet a few minutes later in Roland's old jalopy in their woolens and caps and boots. They had known, without ever having to say it, that they needed to pay attention for a while to something outside the dailinesses.

And then for a few hours, a morning, occasionally most of a day, they drove up to Ninepipes Reservoir and they tromped around, and they shot ducks. It had a way, that focus on something discrete and outside their daily lives, of recasting frustration— making a sort of play out of it—so that it got articulated and was allowed to drift away. At one point they thought about going in together on a water dog—they'd have to keep him at a friend's because their boardinghouse didn't allow pets—and although they quickly abandoned the idea, they pretended they hadn't.

They named their ghost dog Rowdy and whistled him into the

car whenever they set out. He smelled bad and shook water on them, but he was good company and he paddled like a king.

"Here's an idea; let's load up Rowdy and shoot ourselves a Christmas duck," Roland said now. "There's that marsh on the west side of Frenchtown, and you've got this nice old 12-gauge."

"And the old boy who needs to sign the deposition lives on the way, and that won't take more than five minutes," Aidan said.

"Are you up to it?" Roland said.

"I think so, yes," Aidan said easily. "I've got a jacket for you and some boots. Get out of that undertaker's suit, for God's sake. We'll go for an hour, maybe two. Take turns with Mallette's weapon. Shoot ourselves a Christmas duck or five."

Roland had a brief vision of stepping out of the car into the white-dazzle sun; of listening to the mechanical lap of the reservoir, the squeaky-spring sound of the ducks, the wind rustle of the icy long grass.

He put on the heavy wool jacket Aidan got for him, yellow plaid and frayed at the wrists, some boots, and a stocking cap. Aidan told him they'd meet outside in Roland's car. He'd change his clothes, use the facilities.

It was a lengthy sort of business, whatever Aidan was obliged to do, and Roland finally got out of the car to walk briskly up and down the block. He remembered that later—how he seemed to know that he had to stay limber and moving, even that early on what would become a day without an end.

The sun lit up the frost that coated the fence posts and the fields, and they moved almost blindly through the dazzle, hands shielding their eyes. Aidan directed Roland down a rutted road near the tracks, and they found the deposee, a train brakeman who lived in a splintery leaning shack that belched smoke through a piece of corrugated pipe. Roland stayed behind the wheel while Aidan went in. His head pounded from the night before.

He found his aspirin in the glove compartment and washed down a few with the Four Roses he kept under the seat. He held the bottle up to the light, incredulous, then polished it off. It had been full when he left the Flame, and he thought he'd done all his drinking in the bars. *Thieves in the night, hair of the dog, thieving dogs.*

He thought about going in to see if he could speed along whatever was happening with the brakeman. Chatting, probably. The endless need of the lonely and alone to chat, adding up to exactly no information of any value to the species. And who finally cared that much about an old boy who had a useless arm because the railroad had put an engineer up front who was untrained, a fill-in who didn't know enough to keep his brakeman's arm from being crushed during a car coupling.

Roland was amazed it had gotten this far. The railroad's New York lawyers weren't inclined to let something get this far. They'd threaten or buy off or settle quietly. Aidan must have pushed it. He would do that. They must be finding him briefly amusing. They must be in the mood to set the kitten after the ball of yarn, for their own momentary amusement.

"Mr. Roses," he asked the bottle, "what shall we do with the noble Aidan?" He felt as if he shared the car with an old, calm friend who liked to contemplate puzzles at some remove, and who, by his very presence, allowed Roland to do the same. It seemed a valuable perspective, and humane in its way. He closed his sun-tired eyes.

The next moment, Aidan was sitting beside him in the car, relaxed, as if he'd been there for a while. He was reading a page of the deposition, as intently as a judge. Roland's heart gave a little lurch, as if a ladder had broken and his foot reached frantically for a rung. And found it. When did the man let himself into the car?

Aidan flipped to the last page and showed Roland the large shaky signature. He folded the paper into an envelope that he tucked in his inside vest pocket. He gave the dashboard an exuberant slap, then quickly, as though someone had called his name, swerved to look at the backseat.

"Down, Rowdy!" he said. "We'll be there soon enough."

They would hunt for a while—Aidan wouldn't last long—and then they would have to talk, Roland realized. He needed something clearer to relay to the Old Man. If Aidan still sounded bullheaded, he'd minimize it. The thing to do, it occurred to him now, the thought gently lapping across the doorsill, was to get the spotlight off both of them. Because it was a bright one, and hot enough to evaporate them both.

The marsh was surrounded by glittering cattails. There was just enough melt on the edges, just enough density to the tall grasses, to conjure the presence of birds. The groundcover was seeded with birds and wearing its bland and secret smile.

Aidan walked with the shotgun broken over his elbow. They drew closer to the water. He loaded the gun.

"You really need to think about what I told you," Roland said. He knew that Aidan hadn't taken it in. In his arrogance and his bravery or his stupidity, he was ignoring Roland's warning, leaving it back there in an earlier part of the day like a cup of cooling coffee. "You really do, Aid," Roland said. "It's going to matter that you do."

"Right over there," Aidan said quietly, pointing to a line of low bushes. "Perfect blind, I bet, if we can get there without them seeing us."

They got to the blind and crouched inside it. It was a little room hollowed out of the tall reeds, clearly used by others before them. They cleared away some mudballs and cigarette papers from the ground around them. Tidied the place a little. Aidan handed the shotgun to Roland. He examined it and admired the way it was put together, so clean and functional and elegant.

Aidan said he would take a little walk, a quiet little walk, and be back soon. Roland could hear Aidan's rustles, and then he couldn't, and the silence brought surprising, deep relief. *Just stay gone. Just keep walking away.*

If Aidan did that, if he would only do that, then a certain order would restore itself to this outing, this day. There would be spaces in it to think. There would be time to look around with a certain leisure and see the world in its frank simplicity. The clean lines of it. The treeless white mountains around the valley's edge, the riffles and ice chunks in the river, the tall steel smokestacks of the mill. That blackbird perched at the very top of the willow below the blue sky and its wafery waning moon. Without this business to attend to, this ferreting out of intent and potential treachery, a person could simply feel the day and watch the weather—that deep-colored shelf on the edges of the sky, bringing back winter and snow—and he could shoot a bird for a Christmas table. Simplicity. Why did that seem so much to ask? His eyes teared briefly with self-sorrow.

The reeds in the blind had a green tinge. They had been fooled into waking up a little. It was a pale yellow-green, running thinly down the edges of the blades. Right now, right at this moment, Roland was unseen and safe in the green hideout. He could almost take a nap. He could stay all day. But self-pity had crawled into the reedy room with him, and he knew there wasn't time for it and so he cocked the gun and leaned forward to peer out.

No sign of Aidan, but he could guess right where he'd be. He would be crouching in the brush, maybe twenty yards away, at Roland's back.

Roland scanned the distance. Something like the old feeling came to him. The grand hush, filled with the smells of grass and weeds and standing water. The sky like a cymbal, flat and shining and waiting to rocket down sound. The fixed gaze in which the frame of your vision is emptied of everything except potential birds.

There was a sudden whir off the edge of the frame, over to Roland's left, much closer than he had expected. Seven or eight ducks lifted just above the reeds and the cattails with the sound of shuffled cards. They flew left, and low. He led with the gun, the movement as instinctive as riding a bike. He stretched his eyes wide open, sighted just ahead of the first.

Something rustled and jumped, ahead in the tall weeds, and the barrel of Roland's gun dropped fast, as if a big hand had pushed it down. And then it was the echo of the boom in his ears, falling off the hard sky, and he was leaping forward.

Later, whenever he reviewed this train of events, he tried to stretch the space between the rustling sound and the echo of the shot to try to see what the space contained. You stretched a muscle as far as it would go, let it stay there, tricked it into thinking it had to go no farther so that it would relax, and then you stretched it another inch, two inches. He tried this with his memory. But the space between the before and the after was negative space, filled with event and information that he could feel, and even know in some sense, but which he could not see.

More than twenty years later, he would read the first descriptions of black holes in space and find that he had a way, for the first time, to think of the moment after he watched his gun barrel drop. Black holes had gravitational fields so strong that light could not escape them; the eye could not articulate them. They were caused by the collapse of a very large star, and collapse was indeed the feel of it. Utter capitulation to the act.

A shot was fired, and what Roland would never know, the rest of his long life, was whether he saw or knew the target before he fired. Or whether he could have stopped himself if he did.

When he parted the curtain of cattails and saw Aidan on the ground, dark blood across his sternum and growing, Roland felt first as though he had come upon a highway accident. Hit and run, the taillights veering red in the far distance. Aidan's glasses hung from one ear. His eyes were open and then they blinked. He was lying on his side, a solicitous hand on his ribs.

He said something Roland couldn't hear, and so he fell to his knees and put his head down to Aidan's. He could smell the blood, like a fresh-gutted deer.

"What?" he begged Aidan. "What did this?" Aidan looked at him then. His eyes were a dark gray-blue and very large without his glasses. He wore a small forbearing smile, with something in it of the victor. Something in it of relief. He closed his eyes, then opened them again as if he'd gathered himself for an explanation that would be difficult to make clear.

"They shot me, Roland," he explained in a low, confiding voice. His hand inched across his ribs, then back to the ground by his side, which he patted as if it were a child's hand. Roland cradled

Aidan's head with one hand, and tried with the other, fingers scrambling, to locate the source of the blood, all the blood. "Aidan," he called, because he could see him receding. He jiggled the head a little.

"I'm shot, Roland," Aidan explained again, now whispering. He held Roland's eyes. "I lie here shot."

Roland called Butte from a pay phone outside a gas station and told Travers there had been an accident. He had trouble for a moment fixing the time of it because he wasn't perfectly sure he was living in the same day that it had happened. It was spitting snow now, and the temperature had dropped fast, though sometimes the sky rearranged itself so that a shaft of weak sun fell through. He was shaking and coatless. His car was parked behind an abandoned warehouse a hundred yards away. In the backseat was Aidan Tierney, under the coat he'd loaned Roland. He appeared to be sleeping it off.

The tone of voice in which the instructions were given to him, after a rather long pause, was empty of interest or emotion. He had never heard such coldness in a human voice. Again, he felt engulfed by self-sorrow and had to mutter his replies because he felt he was about to weep. Before he had rung Travers, he'd had the idea that the call was something of a courtesy, a formality, and the next one would be to the police. Accidents happened all the time, and most of them partook of tragedy, and most tragedies had elements of inattention or bad judgment or poor reflexes in them.

But when Travers asked him where Tierney's body was, Roland knew when he told him that he had lost any claim on the scenario of the simple accident. He had hidden his friend, telling himself he did so only to buy a few moments of peace and remove before the wheels began to turn. But he had hidden him. And he had done so because he had known he had to, and Travers had known it too. Police would not be present until it was time for them to be.

"What you do now," Travers said very slowly and very carefully, "is take your poor friend home. And take him inside and put him in a chair. You know how to manage that.

"In his chair, your friend was examining his shotgun."

"It wasn't his," Roland said. "It was a friend's, and he was about to return it."

"He was examining his friend's shotgun," Travers revised himself, "and he began to get up from the chair and somehow dropped it or bumped it."

The phone line hummed. A wind had come up and Roland turned away from it, trying unsuccessfully to close the broken door of the telephone booth.

"He didn't know, perhaps, that it was loaded," Travers said.

"My fingerprints are all over it," Roland said.

"Well, you're the fingerprint expert," Travers reminded him.

"It was an accident," Roland said, his voice breaking.

"No one is saying it wasn't an accident," Travers said. "It wasn't your accident, or the Bureau's accident, however."

Roland closed his eyes. "I'll call you in a while," he said.

"No need," Travers said, his voice lighter. "No need, Taliaferro. You'll do fine. You handle this right, and your competence will speak for itself. So I'll see you tomorrow morning in Butte, after the details of this day, and we'll talk then." As Roland hung up the phone, a tiny last voice came from it.

"Will we not?" it said.

It was afternoon now, and would be dusk soon. It was winter and it was Montana and so the day would be dark in some little while. Roland told himself these things as he drove down a gravel road that ran along the highway. He would stay on the edges of people until it was safe not to. He could feel Aidan's bulk, his deep quiet, in the seat behind him. He drove slowly but not too slowly. The shotgun lay on the floor.

While he waited and drove, Roland went undercover with himself. That is, his sick and frantic self was joined by someone cooler, with access to rationality and an agenda. The cool one laid it out. In through the basement door, talking a little, laughing a little—but all very quiet—a friend discreetly bringing a passed-out buddy home.

The body in the chair. The gun wiped clean and reprinted with Aidan's hands.

And what of the noise? Wouldn't someone in the apartment building have heard it and checked? And what about the shot itself? Under any real scrutiny, would it seem accidentally self-inflicted?

As the cool one reviewed all of this, and Roland drove until dusk, the necessary intimation became clear to him. The man had killed himself. He had been very ill. His frank and sometimes cheerful demeanor had masked a degree of despair that not even his closest friends had gauged.

The coroner, Opal Mix, would investigate, but the Bureau would make sure she offered the ambiguous explanation they wanted her to. Gunshot wound. Probable accident. However, the victim had been in poor health, she would be sure to add when she talked to the newspaper. No evidence of foul play.

If she demurred on any point, well, her record as coroner and the shenanigans of her dead husband made her persuadable.

The Old Man would write the family with the details that made a freak accident plausible. Because suicides were a blot. Family members who were devastated over a suicide might choose to see the Bureau as the cause of the despair, and make trouble. A freak accident, the Old Man would reassure them. Thorough investigation. Terrible tragedy. Terrible loss of a young and honorable ex-agent.

But would they buy it? Aidan was a sharpshooter. Aidan had been handling shotguns since he was nine years old. Carelessness was antithetical to everything about him.

So the suggestion of suicide would remain. Enough vagueness that the family could deny the possibility, but enough power in the very word, even unspoken, that they wouldn't dare pursue the facts. A terror of further knowledge would have to be instilled in them. And it would be very easy.

By late evening of the endless day, Roland had negotiated the last of a freezing-ice highway and pulled into Butte. He'd been driving for three hours. The temperature was just below freezing but beginning to drop rapidly. Dirty-looking snow fell in a desultory fashion, and the streetlights burned more orange than usual. He made the basic list in his head, the cool one still awake, still alert, though filled now with disdain for the Roland who felt like a quivering piece of fish. Stunned and cold. Flayed.

It was a short list. Aidan's coat and the plaid coat Roland had covered him with were buried beneath brush near the river. He'd tried to burn them but his hands were shaking too much to get an adequate fire going. And he didn't want to call attention to himself.

The backseat had been cleaned of blood, though a small patch remained that wouldn't scrub out entirely. The key to Aidan's apartment was back on its hidden nail. The body and the gun were arranged, the best Roland could manage. But everything about the setup looked fraudulent to him.

He had not been seen. He was quite sure of that. He did hear the landlady in the apartment overhead shouting loudly into the phone, then slamming it down. Clearly, and fortunately, she was quite deaf.

There was the newspaper reporter, Wendell Whitcomb, to worry about. His reputation for delving, for getting beneath the bland and arranged surfaces, was perhaps going to be a problem. Especially since Whitcomb seemed to have a bead on Coroner Mix.

He'd let Travers worry about that, Roland thought as he pulled to the curb and shut off the car. All he wanted was a few drinks and oblivion. Marcella would be asleep. She no longer bothered herself about his comings and goings, and the baby, Charlie, slept most nights as if he couldn't go deep enough into his dreams.

Their house, a three-room on the side of a hill, had an uneven floor and bats in the attic. The kitchen window looked out on the poison-filled flats below, the lights blurred through the smoke and the lazy snow. Roland pulled a straight-backed chair up to the kitchen table and retrieved a bottle and a short clear glass. He held the bottle in one hand, the glass in the other, and he simply watched them for a while.

Then he set them down and went to the sink and washed his hands. Gazing out the window, into the murk and its muffled lights and the snow that was now getting serious and covering the filthy little city, he washed his hands. With a toothpick, he cleaned his nails. He let his fingers feel his cold face.

All he could see, at that moment, was a tipped head. A young man's full-haired head tipped a little forward as he sat in his reading chair by the grate.

There were a few early strands of silver in the hair. Just a few. He had a meditative gaze, the young man. He seemed to be listening, the way Aidan Tierney had listened so many times to his friend Roland Taliaferro, and he seemed also to be thinking very hard about everything he had seen, and learned, and about all that remained to be known.

NINETEEN

2003
Missoula

ROLAND TALIAFERRO SAT IN HIS WHEELCHAIR staring ahead. He had extracted the packet of yellow letters he kept in his shoe box of memorabilia—the early, innocent letters—and the sheets of paper lay loose on his lap. After all these many years, the dam had burst and a crystalline wall of water rushed toward him as fast as a train, making no noise. He clutched the arms of the chair and watched it. It was a dazzle of mirrors, each of them containing a face, a room, a voice, a moment. He saw them all, now, with terrifying clarity.

He heard Aidan's calm, deep voice behind the sentences on the page, telling him stories about Argentina. There was the voice, and there was also the look and sound of the stories, separate from the voice.

A Pan Am airliner flies very low over an immense estuary the color of tea. Shacks and tankers and packinghouses line the water. Lorries move along the banks, pulled by huge platter-hoofed Belgians. All of it is clangorous and fetid in the dead-bolt November heat. Raw sewage spews into the river. The sky is yellow.

Aidan gets out of the plane and into a long car that moves among tin houses and shacks and tenements. Little boys pee on the sidewalk, aiming at passing chickens. An old man has no arms.

There, at the green front end of the adventure, he has a certain real excitement. He feels like a soldier sliding into enemy territory. Hazardous duty. He requested it, and now he has it.

Away from the river there are massive old buildings with carved pillars, latticed Moorish windows, biscuit colored and hip roofed, contained and extravagant. The new apartment buildings among them look like fresh-painted bureaus with the drawers pulled out. So American in their cheap, frank hope. One is twenty-seven stories tall, towering over the rest, air-conditioned to the top. There is a British clock tower. Basque milkmen, Bulgarian beef slaughterers, real gauchos driving cattle to the stockyards at dawn, fake gauchos performing skits outside the cafes, residents driving American cars, smoking British pipes, wearing Swiss watches, carrying German cameras, going to American movies, and English tearooms and Viennese coffee shops, and German saloons, Parisian cabarets, and Syrian groceries. Crammed narrow streets with trolleys and horse-pulled lorries and unbudging doormen and coffee drinkers, and shouts in five languages and the Big Ben tolling of the British clock.

That night Aidan sits on the iron-grilled balcony of his apartment and studies the city map they have given him. East is on the bottom and north at the right. In the wide avenue below the balcony, cars move along the wrong side of the road. And the sky is wrong too. All the nights he spent under the stars in Montana, there was always the Big Dipper, and the North Star, and now it is all wiped out and he is among different constellations entirely.

The water goes down the drain backward. He has never felt so alone.

At the receptionist's desk, Charlie Taliaferro flirted with Freda, the girl at the computer. She had just shared with him a long tale involving problems with her ex-boyfriend and the unreasonable demands her mother was making on her time, particularly when it came to the upkeep of the mother's yard. Charlie wanted to keep her talking, if only to hear again the charming way she said "foliage."

Flower sellers mill around the gate of the Recoleta Cemetery, doing a brisk business. Aidan buys a bouquet so he will not seem the gawking outsider, and he walks slowly but, he hopes, with an aspect of solemn purpose along the paths of the stone city. Cypresses line the lanes. The grounds are impeccable.

Charlie tried to think of a way to contribute some familial drama of his own. He told her about the way his father, Roland—right over there in his chair—had resigned precipitously from the FBI, not long after the war, and moved the family to California. Something had happened. Someone was dead. Quite likely, Roland was moved for his own protection. If the dead person was a target, then he was too.

This colored his own entire childhood, Charlie said, deciding as he said it that it might be true. It made his father preoccupied and, at times, uncertain of himself. Perhaps there was never a time when his father hadn't felt hunted.

"That must have been hard for you," Freda said, because that's what she would have liked him to say to her.

Charlie thought for a moment. He saw his father trudging out to the truck that he drove around sweltering Bakersfield with its delivery load of freezers, refrigerators, and later, air conditioners. He seemed to shimmer in the impossible heat, even in the mind's eye.

He saw him with a drink in his hand, rocking slightly as he stood at the edge of a neighbor's pool, yelling at Charlie and his friends to dive for coins he threw into the vivid water. Like dogs, they did it. He was big and adamant and not to be crossed.

Down the silver coin fluttered, through the stinging water, gorgeous and free of them all, to land and tip and land on the seamed concrete bottom. All the bubbling children pushed themselves down to it, their hair slicked back, eyes bulging, and the one who retrieved it, who came gasping to the surface, to the feet of the towering loud man, didn't even get to keep it. They tossed it back to him, and he leaned back too slowly, and threw it again.

On the edge of the Recoleta Cemetery, the cathedral pokes into the sky, its alabaster windows giving it the look of a blind queen. The graves in the cemetery are stacked. Children upon parents, upon grandparents. And inside the church with the alabaster windows there is the familiar smell of incense and old rocks.

Aidan prays. Aidan would have prayed. To do his work with fearlessness and imagination. To do well what he has come to do for his country. And if he is killed, he prays that his family will be told how it happened. They have such ways, the enemy, of making a death look like an accident, a suicide. But the Old Man will give them the right version should it come to that. He has no doubt of that.

He prays for his family. For his brother training for the air war. For his fellow low-voiced, business-suited soldiers and the success of their muffled troop movements.

For his true friend, Roland, who is fingerprinting criminals back in the States.

"Well," said the pretty Freda to Charlie. "Do you think your father has issues with his past? Does he become angry like my ex-boyfriend does, and lash out about something that happened, like, years ago?"

"Not really," Charlie said. "He's just really old." He heard the kindness in his voice, which surprised him a little. "Really quite old."

"That's what my ex-boyfriend does," Freda said. "He just lashes out, and then I go, 'Why are you directing this at me? These are your own personal issues and you need to get professional help because of these anger management issues. And also, if you just explode, but don't tell me what the real problem is, how am I supposed to know?'" She glared at Charlie.

"It's just, with my dad, I think he had what I'd call a failure of will, somewhere along the way," Charlie said. "A failure of belief in himself somehow, is what I think. You wonder what would cause a thing like that." He hoped he conveyed how far beyond his ken the idea of absent self-confidence was.

Freda scanned the room in a professional sort of way and stopped at Roland.

"He's crying," she said.

Roland was bent over in his chair, his face in his hands. His big head of silver hair jerked softly. His feet in the big slippers tipped up slowly, as if they were feeling for something in the air. Charlie looked back at her, aghast.

She put a cool hand on his forearm. "They do that," she said. "They do that all the time."

PART 5

TWENTY

2003
Missoula

THE TALL, SOUTH-FACING WINDOWS OF THE common room shook
with the spangled light of the gold-leaved willow on its other side.
Roland watched the glass tremble and felt the mathematical repetition through the tops of his hands. He counted off the intervals.
Beyond the willow and the road and a fence, the golf course ran
languidly toward charcoal mountains in the far distance. The sky
was partly the precise darkness of the mountains and partly a
young blue.

He pushed himself to his feet, pausing halfway to summon the
second half of the effort. He balanced himself on the upright piano to get his bearings and his breath. For a week they'd been getting him upright a few times a day, and he had walked, once, the
full length of the hallway outside his room. When he stood or
walked, he could feel his leg muscles conferring with each other,
balking, urging each other on.

The piano glowed with polish, and the sheet music on it was
old and well used. "Carry Me Back to Old Virginny" was open and
ready to be played. It was a tune Roland probably could recall if he
thought about it for a while. He thought about it, and he heard a

player piano spooling out the tune. He'd always loved player pi-
anos, the way they conjured an invisible human at the keyboard,
the way they never made a mistake.

It was full autumn now—had just turned that last notch into
full autumn—and the weighted sun caught all the components of
the air. Roland could see lazy golden motes and a strand of a spider-
web stretching out blindly. He watched the motes and the web, and
then some sun wriggles on the floor.

"Look how the gold leaves jump out from those dark clouds,"
said an elderly woman to an elderly man.

They had just come into the room. Craig, the attendant, told
them to wait while he checked with the receptionist about something they wanted to know. They parked themselves in a love seat
near Roland and nodded at him politely. A strand of the woman's
white hair had come loose from her knot, making her look a little
wild. She was very pretty, with a tall, elegant forehead and wide
dark eyes and frank, bright lipstick. The man with her was angular
and straight backed. He wore a tweed driving cap and gazed around
the room with pale blue eyes beneath tufted eyebrows. One of the
eyes looked sore, as if it were infected or had been struck.

Despite their handsomeness, there was something exhausted
and wary about both of them. They had the look of both grief and
anticipated grief, Roland thought. The anticipated grief was by far
the stronger presence. He wondered who they were visiting in Rehabilitation and what the prospects were for the person they feared for.

The man removed his tweed cap and stared out at the golf
course. He covered one eye with an old hand, then covered the
other.

"Stop that," his wife said.

"I can't believe what I can see," he said, directing his gaze now
to the coffee table. "The whiteness of that paper there, for instance." He moved his hand to the other eye and shook his head.
"In the old light, it's yellow. Like old newspapers."

"Stop doing that," she said. "You look peculiar."

"I *am* peculiar," he said.

The suggestion of a smile passed between them, as if they

listened to an exasperating, predictable exchange between another couple they knew well.

They looked familiar to Roland, both of them. But many people looked familiar to him. Some members of the staff, young as they were, reminded him of someone from another part of his life. The aide who'd helped him with his slippers when he first arrived—she was a dead ringer for Raquel down in Bakersfield. And there were others too. Wendell Whitcomb, with the stroke, had a voice that was vaguely familiar to him. He felt he had known him slightly, sometime just after the war. Whitcomb said they'd met, and Roland wasn't prepared to doubt it. In Montana it usually took about two minutes of conversation with a stranger to establish some sort of connection. Either you'd previously met the person you spoke to, or the two of you knew people in common. He'd forgotten about this small phenomenon during his many years in California.

He studied the man in the tweed driving cap out of the corner of his eye. If I speak to him, or try to, he will cock his head to the side and listen very intently, Roland thought. He knew this to be true, that the elderly stranger was some kind of known quantity to him.

On the other hand, people he was expected to recognize looked like utter strangers. This tiny woman sitting on the piano bench, for instance. His sister, Petey, hauled over from Butte by Charlie, looked to him like someone from a TV program he'd watched only once. She wore slacks and a big pink ski jacket and a crocheted hat, declining to remove the hat or coat because, she said, she took a chill in public places. Roland looked for something he recognized in her. Maybe the hands, maybe something in the movement of those hands would make her known to him. He located what he was looking for. On her right ring finger she wore the opal that had been their mother's. Roland watched it glide through the air as she turned the pages of a magazine, and he felt his throat swell. The ring looked full of death power, like something from a pharaoh's grave.

"Charlie!" Petey called. Roland's son stood near the front desk, talking again to the pretty receptionist. He looked up impatiently and made some kind of apology to the girl and ambled over to his aunt. How soft and fading he is, Roland thought. He didn't feel tender or pitying or disdainful. He felt detached. He wondered who this middle-aged man really was, and how he bore any relationship at all to himself. *My one child and he could be anyone's. He could be the UPS man.*

He'd had the thought before, but now it opened upon a new one, and he sighted in. *I've been too terrified to let myself love my son.* He tried to examine the idea, but it evaporated because it was too terrified not to.

"That poor girl," Charlie said to Petey, carefully glancing at the receptionist. "She has this ex-boyfriend who should be put away and nobody's doing anything about it. Zilch. He calls her up, seventeen sheets to the wind, and makes threats. He won't take the medications he's supposed to. He comes by at the end of her shift to give her a ride home, with her car sitting right out there in the lot." He pointed to the lot. "She's panicked, actually."

"I wonder if she can tell us anything about Deedee Valentine," said the pretty old woman to her husband.

"Deedee is a young girl from Neva, where we live," she explained to Roland and Petey. "She was injured in an accident and had brain surgery to relieve the pressure, and we've been driving down to see her from time to time." She paused to arrange her thoughts. "My husband arranged to have a cataract removed yesterday, here in Missoula, when we thought Deedee was still in the hospital. We should have checked with her mother about where she was."

Her husband raised the palms of his hands toward the ceiling, looking encouragingly at his wife.

"At the hospital they said she'd been sent for rehabilitation," she said, "and we realized when we got out to the parking lot that we didn't know where this rehabilitation took place. We're worried that she might have taken some kind of turn for the worse that made the rehabilitation necessary."

"And then we saw this place, attached to the hospital, so we came in to check," she said. "Because it says 'Rehabilitation.'"

The effort of the explanation had made her face concentrated and taut.

Wendell Whitcomb walked into the common room slowly, as if he were memorizing his steps. He gave them all a vague salute and sat down at the jigsaw puzzle table, his back to them.

"There's a dragon on his jacket," Petey said. "Look how gorgeous it is. Hand embroidered, I'll bet." She leaned forward to squint at it. "It seems to be wrapped around a globe, devouring its own tail." She got up to get a closer look.

"Petey!" Charlie said. "Give the man some space."

A car backfired loudly in the lot. They all jumped.

Petey introduced herself to Wendell and said she was from Butte.

"You know," Roland said, "when Lindbergh flew into Butte, the company presented him with a set of ashtrays hammered out of copper from the mines." The whole sentence was perfect.

"I bought this jacket at a yard sale," Wendell told Petey. "A long time ago. Eons ago. I don't know if it's hand embroidered, but I suspect not, given that I paid two dollars for it." They pulled part of the back around so they could both peer at the threads.

"I like your hat," he said.

Pleased, she pointed out some puzzle pieces that might work in the lower right hand corner. They did.

Craig, the head attendant, came over to the elderly couple.

"Deedee Valentine isn't here anymore," he said. "She's in very good shape. So good that they sent her home. She might do a little outpatient rehab with someone up in Neva, but she probably doesn't need much. So the doc says."

Sometimes, Roland thought, you can watch faces become dismantled. The parts that link in order to interact with the world come undone, and the real person, the yearning person, comes flooding through.

As it did, this moment, as the couple thanked Craig for the news. The woman had a glisten of tears. Her husband closed his eyes and shook his head hard, and then he threw his old head back and smiled in a way that lit up his whole face.

———

"Tell your father about Lenora Wing and her cruise and her collapse during her slide show," Petey said to Charlie. "I get it mixed up. I told it to you the right way, when you stopped by with that Taylor girlfriend of yours. So tell your father. You keep things straighter than I do."

She turned to the smiling couple in the love seat. "My brother"—she pointed to him and he closed his eyes—"knew a friend of mine very well when they were young people. At the university, before the war. And then she came home to Butte during the war to take care of her mother, and she had some kind of illness herself too. And so she really never left again. And then, recently, she died."

"I'm just trying to update him on various people he knows, or knew," she said. "Not that he seems to care much, from the way he brushes off news about them."

"I brush off nothing," he said, stopping for a long moment to get the last word right.

"Well you could have fooled me," she said briskly. "It's his medications," she explained. "They make him sort of in and out."

"He fell on his head," she added. "Charlie had him in a very nice facility in California and he took a header, and then they moved him to Montana for the cheaper care, and that's why he's in here. He needs to get the highways and byways of his nervous system hooked up right again."

Roland studied her. "Highways and byways?" he said, or thought he did.

"And if he falls again, it could kill him. Couldn't it, Roland?"

He offered her to the couple and silently rehearsed what he was going to say, and then managed to say it. "My sister, the voice of cheer."

She unzipped her ski jacket and tucked a strand of hair back under her hat. "I'm the realist in the Taliaferro family," she confided.

The elderly man in the tweed cap lifted his head and studied Roland intensely. His face looked drained, suddenly, of all color. He got to his feet and extended his hand. It shook a little.

"Neil Tierney," he said very slowly to Roland. "We're the Tierneys, Neil and Rosalind."

Roland lowered himself into his wheelchair. He felt that the room had split open. There was a thunderous sound in his ears, a chanting, a roar.

"How did you get here?" he tried to say. Something else came out that he didn't recognize.

"My father, Roland Taliaferro," Charlie said to the couple.

Tierney blinked his eyes hard. "From the Bureau," he said.

Roland nodded.

"Many, many years ago, he was," Charlie said. "And then he went into another line of work."

Some kind of flutter in the air reached Roland, a whiff of something, a little crackle of danger. He felt the way he had when he'd discovered the intruder, the doper, in his house in Bakersfield. Something acrid and moving was in the air.

It had a sound. It was a man at the receptionist's desk talking too loudly. Roland realized he'd been hearing him for a few seconds and noticed him now because the volume had changed. He stood up. He steadied his big body. He looked around at the others. The Tierneys had walked over to the tall bright windows and were talking intently in low voices. From time to time, Neil turned to stare at Roland. Wendell joined them, his head tipped quizzically. Charlie was bent over his running shoe, relacing it. No one seemed to sense the danger that Roland sensed.

All he could see at the desk was part of the receptionist and the back of a man. He was no taller than she was, very thin, with red hair and a scrawny mustache. He hunched toward her, one hand jammed in his jeans pocket, the other pounding the counter.

Her sharp voice reached them all. "No!" she shouted. And then, "No! I need you to leave! Now!" The man's hand flew out of his pocket and both fists began to pound the counter in a steady, punctuating rhythm. She had moved as far back from him as she could, against some file cabinets.

There were running steps somewhere, a hard urgent sound.

The man at the desk whirled around. He shouted something. Craig rounded the desk corner and grabbed the man's upper arm. The man shook him off and caught him under the chin with his fist. Craig staggered backward and the intruder reeled down the hall. He hit the large print of the canoe on the lake, knocking it shattering to the floor, and then he ran back to the desk.

He grabbed one of the girl's braids. She screamed and twisted and swung an arm that hit him hard on the side of the face. Craig yanked him away. Two other male attendants circled him with their arms low and out, and there were the running sounds of others on their way.

He shouted again. "Bitch! You fraud! You were never who you said you were, never!" She had squatted down behind the desk, and he leaned over the counter to scream at her. His voice had a wild quaver on the edges, an animal sound. He took a huge gulping breath. "You lied and lied and lied," he cried. "You have broken everything. And it will never, ever be fixed."

For a few moments he seemed to collapse in on himself, head bowed. The attendants grabbed each arm. They were muttering and swearing and shuffling the man around on his feet.

In one smooth, wide-armed, fanning move, he reared up out of them, knocking them all off balance. He whirled twice and ran into the common room. He pulled something from his jacket pocket that had a glint.

The sun had fallen enough to fully ignite the leaves of the willow, making it an almost blinding fountain. For Roland, everything slowed down, broke down, arrayed itself for him, moment by moment, frame by frame. He moved to the edges of the room.

Somewhere inside the blinding light, the young man appeared to be hunched against Tierney, his right hand with the weapon jammed against Tierney's ribs. Tierney had a calm, quizzical expression on his face, as if he visualized a complicated game in his head and was trying to predict the next move.

Roland felt entirely competent, though his blood raced. He felt as alert as it is possible for a human to be. Data came to him in shiny streams, and he sorted it expertly. On the edge of the room that abutted the hallway and receptionist's desk, some kind of emergency response team had assembled. They were big, strong-looking men, but they had the look of amateurs. Their faces were too open and young. They clearly had not dealt with this sort of thing before.

The captor shrieked something indecipherable to them.

Time was rushing in on all of them, and Roland saw that it was all going to break loose in the next few moments. He moved backward a step, grabbed a large chess piece from a card table, and threw it as hard as he could at the window behind the man with the gun. It hit with a sound like a shot.

The man whirled, and Roland's big body began to move. He ran hard, as fast as he could remember ever running, and threw himself at Tierney, his body Tierney's shield. His face smashed into Tierney's scratchy wool overcoat. They tipped forward together, as shouts and feet ran past them. There was a sharp smack and a new rain of sound that had small sirens in it.

Roland lay atop Tierney, who was safe. Roland could feel him breathing steadily. He could hear him say something in a reasonable voice. The noises of all the others were receding, leaving the room. All that was left now were a few voices that sounded like birdcalls or the mournful, automatic squeak of a child's swing.

Tierney's hands were under Roland's head. Someone else was dabbing at his forehead very carefully. "His head," he heard a woman cry softly. "His poor head." There were busy institutional sounds all around, some of them urgent—sharp commands, running feet—and some of them the aquarium gurgles and chirps of the intercom and the larger apparatus of the place.

"Okay, he's out," someone said briskly. Were they referring to him? He opened his eyes quite wide to let them know they were wrong.

He heard another woman crying softly. The receptionist? A sympathetic onlooker? Perhaps his mother, late at night, after the old man was finally asleep.

A young person in a lab jacket tried gently to move Tierney

away, to help him to his feet, but he didn't move. Roland let his head rest in Tierney's hands, and he studied the sagging and canny face, the pale eyes.

Very clearly, speaking very slowly so there could be no mistake, no misunderstanding, he talked to that listening face. He talked for quite a long time, it seemed. Everything came out right. He paused now and then to think about how to phrase the next sentence, and then he launched into it, and it was perfect. He watched the man understand him. He watched him nod. He added one last part of the explanation, and then there were doctors, and he was alone with them, and he was finished speaking.

TWENTY-ONE

2003
Missoula

PETEY SAT ON AN UPHOLSTERED BENCH near the entrance to the rehabilitation center, studying a strange piece of artwork in order to try to calm down.

It was two pictures, actually, or rather two frames for a single landscape. Why would you do that—frame the left half and frame the right half and hang the frames a scant inch apart? It was some style she'd never seen before.

The landscape was a marshy area with lots of cattails and ducks flying over it. In the distance were mountains with some snow on them, autumn snow, and deep piles of clouds in the sky. There were no humans that she could see. She got up to examine it. It was exactly the kind of scene where you would expect to see a bird hunter on the edge, his red dog roving ahead. But there was nothing animate except the ducks, and even they looked pasted to the sky.

Maybe the artist knew it—knew he had a painting with no life in it—and separated the halves so that anyone looking at it would have to imagine, at least, the movement of the two halves joining. Or she. Though there were not so many lady painters who took as their subject ducks.

Petey waited for Charlie to pull up to the door in his car and take her to see Roland. The staff people had taken her brother to the hospital next door and Charlie had gone to confer with the doctors about what happened next. There wasn't much question in Petey's mind. As far as Roland's head went, he was probably back to square one after knocking it so hard on the floor. Or further. He might be dying.

The thought gave her a little body pang, and she realized she should probably be over at the hospital, too, in case Roland wanted to say good-bye to her, or at least signal it. There were signs and corridors that led to the hospital, but they looked very confusing. She set off down one, and saw how far it stretched, and decided she'd go into the place that said CHAPEL first. Maybe she'd do the most good by stopping off there and saying a brief prayer for her brother.

It was a chapel with no evidence of religion in it, except a small table like an altar that had, instead of Jesus or even sun rays, a painted glass depiction of a mountain with a cap of snow. A very serene mountain, a perfect cone, which gave anyone in there something to fix an eye on and maybe become serene. Though Petey was dubious.

She had the room to herself. She sat in one of the folding chairs and noticed that the dim lighting had such a greenish tinge that she felt as if she were underwater. It made her a little nervous, that feeling—she had never been comfortable in deep water—and the mountain wasn't doing much in terms of directing her thoughts or prompting a prayer. She got up to walk around. A table in the corner had a box of tissues on it and a guest book. In the book, she saw to her surprise, people had written notes to God. Here was one that was embellished with big floppy flowers. The hand was loopy and extravagant. A young girl's, she guessed. She stooped closer to make out the message. *Lord help everyone here who suffers!!!!*

Petey stepped back from it. She felt she could almost hear the young, aggrieved voice. Oh, honey, she thought, you've got so many years ahead of you.

Back near the main door, she zipped her ski jacket all the way up and waited. If Charlie had swung by while she was in the chapel, he'd be back. But there should be no further wandering on her part, she realized.

She was exhausted. That scene in there with Roland and all those people—how could she, in her wildest apprehensions, have pictured something like that happening? She'd felt in her bones that she was far too old for the two-hour trip to visit him, and she should have listened to herself, because she'd been right. Leave home, and you stepped into this new world in which all the circuits were tripping, and the most amazing and terrible surprises erupted right and left, above and below.

She saw Roland on the floor, his thick silver hair. Poor Roland. May he not suffer, she thought.

A determined, strong-jawed woman in an electric handicapped-person scooter whirred past. She had a big American flag flying from the scooter's canopy and a SUPPORT OUR TROOPS sticker on the bumper. In the basket in front of her lap, she had everything she might need for the next little while: hand lotion, a notebook, a newspaper, a thermos. She was maybe the most organized-looking person Petey had ever seen.

It felt good to make plans, to feel organized. Especially on a day like this.

A few feet away from the separated duck-pond picture, there was a folder hanging from a spike that said, on its cover, Emergency—Immediate Response Guide. There were many sections: Fire, Respiratory or Cardiac Arrest, Bomb Threat or Suspicious Device, Internal Disasters, External Disasters, Infant/Child Abductions, Hazardous Material Spill, Blood/Body Fluid Exposure. They had various codes.

Well, she thought. I just lived through an official Emergency. That's how she'd put it when she told the story.

She dug into the pocket of her jacket and retrieved her little notebook and Eversharp. When she made plans, she liked to look at them.

What would it involve to bring Roland home to Butte if that turned out to be possible? Home, perhaps, to live with her in the house where they'd both been children. If she had suggested that in the first place, Roland wouldn't be in the hospital now. She opened her notebook and wrote his name at the top of the page and underlined it twice. She gazed at the ducks and the water and the mountains, and she thought.

If he could do even a few things for himself, they might manage. There were all these people who came to your home these days to help you do things. Charlie could figure out the details before he went back to California. She wrote Charlie's name down and underlined it twice.

Roland could sit in the big chair that Romey liked to curl up on when she was too busy to let him lounge and purr on her lap. She'd make Romey another bed, maybe inside the fireplace she hadn't used for forty years. It was cleaned out and the chimney plugged, and cats liked to feel tucked back and sheltered, so it just might work. She wrote down *Romey* and, underneath it, *Fireplace.*

And what would they talk about, she and her brother? Well, maybe he wouldn't be saying much at all, which she certainly didn't wish on him, but it would simplify matters. At least until they'd become familiar with each other's company. He might be speaking pretty well by the time they felt they knew each other again. Meanwhile, she could show him photos and old newspapers and catch him up on what had happened to everyone they'd known so long ago.

She started to write down *Memorabilia,* but the spelling didn't look right to her so she erased it and put her notebook and pencil away and folded her hands.

A slam startled her awake. She frantically tried to establish where she was, but nothing seemed real until the man at her elbow murmured her name. It was Charlie. He helped her to her feet. They stood there for a minute while she attained her balance. She tried to prolong the moments until she would have to look at him.

When she did, she saw a man in middle age with a pale, puzzled face. He cleared his throat. The car waited outside the door.

"And the news?" she said, her voice sounding strong to herself. He cleared his throat again.

She nodded and took his arm, and they started, she hoped, for home.

TWENTY-TWO

2003
Missoula

WENDELL WAS TO BE DISCHARGED FROM the rehabilitation center in a few days. Though his left side certainly had a way to go, it was expressing interest in cooperating with the rest of his body. That was a development he wouldn't have predicted a few weeks before. He was just off the phone with Flannery. After his discharge, she'd bring him in three times a week for an hour of outpatient treatment.

He'd tried to describe to her yesterday's ruckus with Roland and the yelling redheaded man, but it had sounded so contextless and cheaply dramatic—like an episode on a bad cop show—that he had let the subject drop. Who knew what had prompted the old boy to insert himself so pathetically into the incident? First he was over on the edges of things, and then he was wobbling across the room to smack straight into the midst of them. As he'd tumbled to the floor, he'd hit his head so hard that Wendell knew, as if it had been announced, that Roland Taliaferro had placed himself very near to his earthly end.

When they took him away on the stretcher, Wendell had wanted badly to do something formal for his jigsaw partner, to bestow upon him an amulet, a charm, a blessing. "Take care of him," he'd said instead to the preoccupied attendants, who seemed to hear no voices but each other's. And so Wendell had walked Roland's wonderful little witch of a sister to the main door, where they'd said their good-byes and good lucks.

He strolled to the room where Janie Quist, his brief girlfriend from far back in the previous century, lay in her white cocoon. Her tiny, wizened body, small as a child's, slept inside the tube of netting. Her snores were surprisingly loud. He pulled up a chair and sat by the bed. One of the doctors poked his head inside the door and Wendell made a shushing gesture and the man left.

He thought about telling Janie she looked like something about to hatch, about to be unleashed upon the unsuspecting world. The thought made him smile. He rested his left hand on the edge of the mattress where the netting met a big zippered seam. He sent directions to the fingers and watched them move like a dreamy piano player's. He heard the stiletto ticks of her fast heels on a shiny lobby floor.

"It's time for me to go, Mrs. Wellington," he said in a low, matter-of-fact voice. She stopped snoring, then started again.

A new aide, a young East Indian woman, walked slowly past the door with an old man on a walker. She sent quiet urgings to the man in a voice that sounded like chimes. Wendell closed his eyes to hear her better. "Almost there," she said. "Almost there, almost there."

Back in the common room, Russell Pretty On Top joined Wendell near the aquarium. They watched the fish. Russell leaned his helmeted head against the glass and pointed out the black dwarf, the angelfish. They swam between extravagant columns of bubbles, among silver and green ferns. Russell had watched them so much, he'd given them names.

"Hey, Freaky-Lee," he said in a ghost voice to the big angelfish, which swam over and bumped its nose lightly on the glass.

Wendell thought about telling Russell how strange, even amazing, it had been to see shadows of his long-ago life swim toward and among each other yesterday: Roland Taliaferro, and the old man who turned out to be the brother of Aidan Tierney, and Janie in the background, wrapped in her cocoon, and Wendell himself. All of them parts of a story still to be finished.

In his storage room at home, he had saved his notes on every substantial piece he'd written during all those years on the newspaper. It wasn't just "packratness," as Flannery liked to describe it. It was his sense—his knowledge, really—that the notes were sketches of situations so complicated and interwoven and extreme that they resisted, absolutely, any quick summation. And if he discarded the sketches, he'd somehow lose access to certain important realities that had yet to reveal themselves. It wasn't something he could easily explain.

A surveillance camera above the aquarium watched him and Russell. Wendell stared up at it, then did a little bow, as if he'd been introduced to a packed auditorium. He read to the camera a leaflet that an attendant had urged on him a few moments earlier. It was the announcement of a guest speaker for the upcoming meeting of the Stroke Support Group. She was going to talk about "Relaxation Techniques for Wellness."

The woman in the scooter with the flag tore past Wendell and Russell, and Wendell called out to her. She spun around and zoomed up to them. Her broad face wore a sheen of sweat. He handed her the leaflet with no explanation. She scowled at it and stuck it in the basket with her notebooks and other items, and then she was off.

TWENTY-THREE

2003
North of Neva

NEIL TIERNEY AND TROY GROVE, THE man from the environmental group, rumbled along a rutted track that wound through the Sweet Grass Hills. Grove's Expedition charged up and down the hills and gullies as if it was finally doing the work it was born for, and he looked pleased and almost happy.

He was in his forties, maybe early fifties, and had the fit, evenly tanned look of the rigorously unencumbered. His eyes were a strange cat color, a pale hazel that was almost gold, but the rest of him was so undisturbed by anomaly that it was hard to remember him visually when he wasn't present in the flesh.

It was two months to the day after Neil, trying to catch Grove in his Expedition, had hit Deedee Valentine and her skateboard. A lifetime, he thought. Ending in immense reprieve.

They were making the drive because Grove wanted to visit the Hills up close and take an inventory of the native plants. He also wanted to examine the sites of a couple of old gold mines. Neil knew where everything was, so he'd volunteered to be the guide.

So much looked different to him, with his cataracts removed, that he had begun to mistrust much of what he thought he'd been seeing before. He realized he had been filling in imaginatively. Instead of an actual intersection of two streets, he'd seen stopped cars. Instead of a particular look on her face as his wife talked to him from across a room, he'd heard the nuances in Rosalind's voice and manufactured an expression for them.

Now, some mornings, Neil stayed in his big chair for an hour or more, gazing at the intricacies of the given world: the etched rooflines; the crisp, twirling leaves on the cottonwood tree; the nervy little squirrels running along the branches; the way the magpies could fly straight into a tangled treetop and out the other side, untouched. It was an intricate navigational maneuver, that headlong dash through the thicket, and he had begun to think about it at some length. From a pilot's perspective. How, exactly, did the birds accomplish it?

Everything that was white—the sides of houses, the clouds, the borders of his magazine pages—made him remember the dazzling cape of Fuji, the sheets on his mother's clothesline, snapping in the white wind. The Hills today looked multigrassed and gullied and iconic. Everything he saw, he saw in a new light.

It was a tawny day, warm in the middle and cool on the edges. They'd passed only two pickups on the gravel road, then no one at all, once they were off the gravel and onto the dirt track. When they stopped periodically for Grove to get out and examine a weed or wildflower, all Neil heard was the faint crunch of his footsteps and, now and then, the sounds of hidden birds. Grove made his notations in a small, neat script and pursed his lips like an old man as he wrote. Neil had the urge to put a calm hand on his forearm, to tell him nothing was as dire as he seemed to think it was.

Grove was flying to Taos the next day. His sister had a gallery there, and a woman he was interested in was showing horses in it that she made out of blown glass. So far, he'd told Neil, they'd only met by e-mail, but there was something about her that felt totally in sync.

The road got rougher and narrower and Neil pushed himself back against the seat for stability. He was having a little trouble getting his breath because of the change in altitude. Any deviation from the norm could feel mildly assaultive to an old body. He'd known that for a while.

He'd noticed it this morning when Rhea Valentine stopped by with her daughter, Deedee. He and Rosalind had been looking one last time for the diamond she'd lost from her ring those many weeks ago. Probably it had gone out with the trash somehow, or fallen down a radiator to lie at the bottom of the furnace; a speck of glitter in the blackness and the soot. One last look, and they'd give it up for gone.

Suddenly Rhea and the girl were at the door. Seeing them with no warning like that had given Neil a sharp pang in his chest.

Their visit turned out to be a generous act on Rhea's part, a formal gesture of forgiveness and getting-on-with-it. Deedee was bashful and neutral and bright eyed. In a note, sent before the visit, Rhea had told them that the girl had occasional episodes of dizziness and spaciness, but they were expected to go away in time. With luck, she would be 100 percent in a year. She thanked them, very much, for their personal and monetary support.

Hair of an ordinary color was growing in over the shaved area, and Deedee had cut the rest of it off and put goop on it, so it stuck out like something wild and terrified. Rosalind complimented her on the style, and clearly meant it. Her own washing relief extended to practically everything these days.

"I spent the night out here alone when I was, let's see, nine years old," Neil told Grove. "Farther out on the plains, actually, the Tower to my back."

Grove gazed out on the broad table of land. "You're joking," he said. "Who would let you do that?"

It was too complicated a story.

"Oh, everyone did," Neil said. "We ran wild."

"That's terrible," Grove said, sounding genuinely upset. "Anything could have happened to you."

He pulled onto a grassy flat spot by the wide of the road, and they sat on the tailgate and ate a lunch Rosalind had packed for them. Grove messed around with his Global Positioning System. He had another one in the dashboard. On the way up, it had talked to them in a soothing man's voice, though it sounded unsure when it was time for them to leave the highway, and then it had stopped talking altogether.

"What do you want to know?" Grove asked, hunched over his toy. "How far it is to Great Falls as the crow flies?"

Neil didn't care. He didn't want to know anything that the GPS could tell him. Grove tinkered, adjusted, squinted at the numbers. He explained something about bouncing signals off satellites—he pointed to nothing in the sky—and how fast the data gets transmitted and translated.

"One of these, and it's virtually impossible to get lost," he said. "You always know exactly where you are."

I know exactly where I am, Neil thought. He thought a little harder, remembering. *I am very near the place where the branch hit me off my horse, very near the place where I began that night out here alone.*

Where, Aidan, are you?

The long weeks of wondering about the hurt girl, of not knowing how it would all turn out, had felt to him at times like that endless night on the prairie with his breathing horse. And like the long later night over the Pacific in a battered silver bomber, his navigator siting by the stars, the fuel needle shaking near empty.

Where will I be when this night is over? he'd thought both times. Will I be found?

He saw the big dawn and his brother's silhouette on horseback. Señor Sombra. Mister Shadow. He saw himself jamming the right rudder and tipping the left wing so the long bomber would sideslip down the sky. Onto the tiny island, just in time. *I kept my head and I made it.*

After their lunch, Grove said he would walk around for a while to make more notes on the plants. Neil said he was an old man and needed an old man's brief nap in the cab of the truck. As he watched Grove in his bright, lonely windbreaker disappear over a shallow hill, he rolled the window all the way down and breathed in the sagey air.

He tried to recall the details of the conversation he'd had, after his brother's funeral, with Roland Taliaferro, sent by the Bureau to explain. He would never have recognized him at the rehab center if he hadn't heard the name. All that was left of the younger man was a suggestion of previous bulk and a head of thick hair.

He bore down on his memory, but all he could recall of that long-ago conversation was that a promise had been made. Taliaferro had made the promise of a larger, more complicated, more tolerable story than the one they'd been handed by the monstrous coroner, Opal Mix. A name Neil had never forgotten, though he'd tried to.

He attempted some long deep breaths, but they came shallowly and quick. He put his hand on his chest to calm it down, and tried to think of something else.

He had something he wanted to tell Rosalind when he got home today. He wanted to tell her that he knew he had manufactured the story about Deedee's father, Ronny Valentine, being up in the Sweet Grass Hills, asking about his daughter. He could see the man in his mind's eye—he had built a campfire and was roasting a bird on a spit—but he knew that he had conjured him. In a time of extreme stress—that terrified drive with Rosalind to see if the girl would live—he had conjured him.

He imagined Rosalind's relief when he calmly explained this fact to her. His mind might be going, but perhaps not as fast as either of them feared.

The bird Ronny Valentine was cooking smelled wonderful, but it wasn't a real one.

He wanted to go home. Home to Rosalind who had buoyed and enlivened him through so many years. And he, her. He knew this too. Home to his younger brother, Mike, who didn't leave his bed now.

"Where's the letter?" Mike had screamed at him once, those

years and years ago. "Doesn't it tell you something that Hoover didn't send the letter that the agent promised he would? The agent, that Taliaferro, was feeding you a line. Hoover had nothing to say about any accident. As much as we wanted him to."

Neil had hit him then. Knocked him to the ground. And the subject had never come up again between them, even when Mike's son, the second Aidan, was killed by friendly fire in Vietnam. The sunniest boy in the world.

At the beginning of today's drive, he'd thought about telling Grove about the scene at the rehabilitation center. For mildly perverse reasons, he'd wanted to shake the man up, remind him that violent surprise can't be organized or purchased away. But the story had too many layers.

How could he tell him what it had felt like to watch that frantic boy come running into the room, screaming betrayal? Or how old Roland Taliaferro had seemed to watch the boy in a trance, then snap awake when the kid pulled out a cell phone to call God-knows-who. Or what a shock it had been when Taliaferro came lurching at Neil to push him to the floor?

Taliaferro had looked almost dead afterward, white faced and on his back. The aides helped Neil to his feet. But Taliaferro opened his eyes, and Neil saw that the man wanted desperately to speak. He saw, too, that he must try to help him do it. So he got shakily down to his knees and bent to listen to him. He had a brief, frightening vision of his mother bending down, after her cataract surgery, and coming up blind. But he bent farther, in order to hear.

In a raspy, halting voice, Taliaferro said, "Aidan." He closed his eyes tightly, then opened them again. He licked his lips, and groaned.

"Suddenly, I did," he said. "Hunting ducks." He closed his eyes. "Ducks," he said, sounding disgusted.

He rolled his big head from side to side.

"In trouble, and we needed to talk." He said something then

that Neil couldn't make out. "Moved him," it might have been. Neil nodded and touched two fingers to Taliaferro's lined forehead.

"He was a good man," Neil said. "We've missed him, you and I."

Neil and Troy Grove started back for Neva. Neither of them wanted to talk, so they didn't. Grove had the grace not to consult the GPS voice or play the pygmy music he'd cranked up at the outset of their trip.

Neil took some breaths. His chest felt tight, his left arm sore. His feet were cold. He closed his eyes and thought about making a campfire to warm them. High on the Tower, at night, near the starry vault. He drew his knife slowly down a twig to make kindling. He criss-crossed it with slim branches and reached in his saddlebag for a match. The night breeze lifted the hair off his forehead. Above him were the lights of the bear, the compass, the dipper, the winged horse. The fire caught and he studied the shapes and faces inside it. He knew them all.

He opened his eyes, turned to Grove, and found he could not speak. He summoned Rosalind and his faraway daughters, his house and the magpies shooting through the branches of the trees. He summoned Taliaferro and Aidan, and heard the sound of a big piece of machinery, a gear maybe, clicking softly into place.

"They got us," Taliaferro had muttered. Or "the goddess." He'd taken a long breath that had a squeak on its edges. "Sorcery," he'd said then. Or "so sorry." And they had lifted him up and away.

ACKNOWLEDGMENTS

My DEEP THANKS TO THE FOLLOWING, who, in their fine and particular ways, so generously helped this book on its way: Bryan Di Salvatore, Megan McNamer, and Jacqueline Carey; Ian Frazier, Sarah Chalfant, and Paul Slovak; Daryl Gadbow, Kate Gadbow, Hugh McNamer, and Patricia McNamer; Pat Strachan; Steve Rinella, Daniel Berry, M.D., and the MacDowell Colony. A number of diaries were helpful to me in re-creating B-29 bombing missions off the island of Saipan, particularly my father's and that of John Ciardi, published as *Saipan: The War Diary of John Ciardi* (Fayetteville: University of Arkansas Press, 1988).